Acknowledgments

As always, I have to give it up to the Creator, for without God, Allah, Jehovah, by whatever name you want to call Him, I wouldn't be able to do what I do and make the pen do what it do. I wanna thank Him for my little King Zion Uhuru, and I wanna thank Him for all of you who are reading my words.

First I want to give a very special thanks to the person that helped most in making Riding Rhythm the book that it is, Queen Martha Weber. You are off the chain, and I can't wait until we do it all over again.

Next I'd like to thank my publisher Carl Weber. Thanks for all the insight on point-of-view and character development. Oh and I have to thank one of my closest friends for way too much to list, Queen Reshonda Tate Billingsley. My boy, Thomas Long, I didn't forget about you, man. Thanks for just being the fool that you are.

And I can't forget the perfect couple, Jameel and Shunda of Booking Matters magazine. Thank you for always looking out, and supporting me and other Black authors. J.O.W. Book Club representing the ATL, thanks for your support and treating a brotha so well. Thanks, Debra Burton, and Turning Pages book club in Oakland. Thanks, Candace, and RAW SISTAZ book club, and the many book clubs that have invited me into your book club families. And Debra Little of Jean Ministries, thank you so much for your insight.

Special, special thanks to the HATERS. Keep on doing what you do; you're helping to get my name and the message out there. It's okay that you won't buy my book because my name is Jihad, but it's not okay that you won't even look the word up and find out that, although it is a Holy War, it means striving and struggling to bring others into the awareness of the oneness of God.

As always, shout-outs to the Bruhs and Sistas on lockdown. Been there, done that; that's why I'm gon' change that. We got to stop the madness and fight the system of ignorance and oppression, instead of each other.

To leave comments or to learn more about Jihad, *Riding Rhythm, Gigolos Get Lonely Too, BabyGirl,* and *Street Life,* go to www.jihadwrites.com and please tell the readers what you think of Riding Rhythm, Babygirl and Street Life by posting a review on www.amazon.com

Love and Life

Jihad

Dedications

I dedicate this book to my mother, Arthine Frazier, my sister, La-Shl Frazier, Pamela Hunter, my friends and teachers, Victoria Christopher Murray, Lolita Files, and Reshonda Tate. All of these Queens have played a very special role in my life, and I just want to acknowledge them.

Queen

Like Lazarus I was dead
until I picked up a book and read
The history of you, Queen
what you did
what you said,
how you lead
And spoonfed
knowledge to me
answering my pleas,
even when I couldn't see,
the forest for the sea of trees and leaves,
knockin' me to my knees.
Without blinkin'
or thinkin',
brokedown and stinkin'
you picked me up,
saved me
from my own demise,
helped me rise,
made me realize
and recognize
all the lies,
that I couldn't see with mine own eyes
as they were focused on the wrong prize.
So no longer out in the fold of the cold,
a lost soul,
to mold with no goals,
BEHOLD
a man
Your warrior, true
revised and made new
chocolate
through and through

all for you
BLACK MAN.
In front of you
I stand,
command,
demand
everything on dry land,
the seven seas
and even the breeze
to freeeeeeeeeeeeeeeeezzzzzzzzzzzzzeeeeeeeeee.
And seize a still scene
long enough to bow down
to the Black Queen.

RIDING RHYTHM

To all my folks out there bangin', slangin', or just hangin', it gotsta stop. Peep this piece I done laid out. Yo', this may be fiction to some, but it's reality to so many. Read and feel these pages, 'cause I'm keepin' it real, and I'm bringin' the funk. So check the Rhythm, 'cause that's what I'm writing.

Love and Life
Jihad

Riding Rhythm

ACT 1
Growing Up Black
Moses

Growing up, my momma gave new meaning to the phrase "Jesus lives." According to her, He lived right there with us in our small two-bedroom apartment with the paper-thin walls and floors that felt like they were about to cave in.

I used to always wonder why I never saw Him, 'cause Lord knows, my momma called Him every chance she got. Every sentence began or ended with "Jesus Lord" or "Lord Jesus." After awhile, I started thinking maybe Jesus was my real name and Moses was my nickname or something, because every time Momma called me, she usually said something like, "Lord Jesus, boy, you working my nerves."

I guess my brother Solomon was tired of seeing me jump and run whenever Momma spoke. He broke the news to me when I was four. I still remember it like it happened today. We were in the front room lying on the floor one Saturday morning, watching Road Runner blow up Wile E. Coyote for the hundred millionth time. Momma went to callin' Jesus' name like he was in the next room, and as usual I jumped up and started toward the kitchen.

"Where you goin'?" Solomon asked.

"Momma callin' me."

"How you know?"

I held up four fingers. "She done said 'Lord Jesus' four times now."

Solomon rolled over onto the plastic runner, laughing his butt off.

I turned my head sideways and looked at my nine-year-old brother, before turning to the TV. A "yuk-mouth-'cause-you-don't-brush" commercial was on. We had seen that a million times, so I knew that couldn't be what he was laughing at. I shrugged. I didn't see what was so funny, but it must have been something, if he was laughing so hard. I fell on the floor, cracking up too.

"You must think your name is Lord Jesus," Solomon finally said.

"No, dummy." I sat up and faced him as he sat on the old couch. "I'm Moses Lord Jesus King," I said with authority.

"No, your name is Moses Toussant King; there is no Lord Jesus in that."

"So, why do Momma be callin' us 'Lord Jesus,' when that ain't our names?" I asked, still confused.

"Well, she does that so she won't . . . I mean she doesn't really call us . . . Moses, it's hard to explain; you too young to un'erstand."

I was always "too young to understand," when he didn't know the answer to a question. Still, my brother was my "superman," always showing and teaching me what was "groovy-cool" and what wasn't.

It wasn't just Solomon. I asked everybody stuff, when I didn't understand. Up until I was around eleven or twelve, "Why?", "How?", and "Why not?" were the first words outta my mouth. This became a big problem as I got older.

By the time I was in fifth-grade history class, the teachers started ignoring me. That didn't faze me none; my hand still never went down. And don't let Ms. Thompson act like she didn't see me; that's when I went to waving and "ooh, ooh, oohing."

History just didn't seem right. I mean, we was here and had been for a long time, and the Indians were here even longer than white people, but we never talked about them, unless it was in a bad way. And the only black person we talked about was Frederick Douglass, and I still didn't know nothin' 'bout him, except that he was a slave and had a newspaper.

Half the time I just repeated questions my uncle always seemed to ask when some white man made him mad at work, or while he watched TV. I didn't mean to get the teachers so upset and flustered. I just wanted to know the answers to Uncle Buck's questions too. So, in the third grade, I started repeating Uncle Buck's questions, like, "Why did black folks light firecrackers and sparklers on the Fourth of July, when we still was slaves."

Every Sunday when my Uncle Buck came over after church for dinner he would be talking to the TV, saying things like, "Independence didn't have nothing to do with us or the Indians. Why didn't we do the fireworks and barbe-cue thing on September 22nd?—That's when the Emancipation Proclam-ation was signed."

After I finished quoting Uncle Buck, Ms. Jablonski would usually turn red then say something my brother Solomon used to say all the time, "When you get older you'd under-stand." Seems to me, she just didn't know the answer . . . and they was supposed to be teachers and know everything.

History was my worst class for "understanding," but I still loved it just the same. Heck, my favorite subject in school was school; I just liked knowing stuff, even if it wasn't groovy-cool.

I enjoyed my reign as the class question-asker, until the fourth grade. That's when I met Tharellious Hunt or, as I liked to call him, Captain Cave Nose.

Tharellious Hunt was this big-nosed, mouth-all-mighty, know-it-all kid who had his hand in the air even more than I did, when the teacher asked a question. I ain't never liked him, since he told my favorite teacher, Ms. Terry, to suck his thing, but when he asked Tammy Thomas to be his girlfriend in fourth-grade math class, it was on. Everybody knew Tammy was my girlfriend.

We fought after school for three days straight. We would have fought on the fourth, if we hadn't seen Tammy walking home, hugged up with a sixth-grader. We decided that she wasn't worth it, so we left her alone, after we beat up her sixth-grade scrub new boyfriend.

Ever since then, we were best friends. I started calling him T-Hunt, tired of fighting 'cause someone teased him about his name. Besides, it just took too much time to say Tharellious.

Ms. Tyson's fourth-grade class was where T-Hunt and I first learned about Dr. Martin Luther the King. Everybody talked about him, but I ain't never heard or seen him.

Sweat was fryin' on my forehead, while I was busy hiding the paper from Ms. Tyson. I'd just gotten an 'A' on the test and was now using the paper for an airplane, when she turned on the TV.

I was sitting in a chair that had to be old as my daddy. Names and dates carved on the thing went back twenty years. *These wooden chairs sure make my booty hurt,* I thought, as I leaned up to see the man on the screen.

I'll never forget it. It wasn't even black history week. School had just started. It was August 28, 1963. I was nine years old, when my fourth-grade class watched and listened to the man talkin' on the fuzzy, black-and-white TV.

The cameras started showing more black folks than I thought even existed. It seemed like the whole world of black folks, except for us, were out in the streets of Washington, DC. The man talking even had white folks standing in the streets. I'd never even imagined there was a man that looked like me that could keep so many folks' attention. He had to be the smartest man in the world.

I moved my desk closer to the TV to listen to this man named Dr. Martin Luther the King. He roared into the microphone, "The average Negro is born into want and deprivation. His struggle to escape his circumstances is hindered by color discrimination. He is deprived of normal education. When he seeks opportunity, he is told, in effect, to lift himself by his own bootstraps, advice which does not take into account the fact that he is barefoot."

"Wow," was all I could say. I ain't never heard no black man speak so "hard" and so doggone proud. It didn't matter that I didn't all the way understand what he was saying; it was how he said it. Dr. King talked hard. He wasn't 'fraid of nobody, white or black. From that moment, I knew I was gon' be a hard-talking, proud, 'fraid-of-nobody, suit-wearing black man. I was gon' stand up, when everybody else was sittin' down. I was gon' be the voice for black people everywhere. People were gon' listen to me.

I started telling folks that Dr. Martin Luther the King was my uncle, since we had the same last name and all. It wasn't long after I'd heard him for the first time that I started to listen to others who were "down with the black thing."

I heard a brother named Malcolm X on the radio. That knocked me off my chair. He made the reporter and the questioners sound real stupid. His words had power like I had never imagined. The hardest words I heard Malcolm X say were, "If you are not ready to die for it, then put the word freedom out of your vocabulary."

Heck, I was free, and everyone I knew was free. I didn't understand that statement, until I watched the news one day when I was twelve. I could hardly believe what I was seeing. Some-where in Alabama, police were siccing dogs on black kids while they played around a spurting fire hydrant.

I bet if the fruitcart man, Cornbread Jones, saw what the police had done to those little kids in Alabama, he would've thought twice before answering to the cops the way he did the week before. But then again, Cornbread probably didn't know that he'd done anything wrong; everybody in my hood knew Cornbread was a little "touched in the head."

Me, my boy T-Hunt, and a few others were in front of J.J.'s Pool Hall, when the cops rolled through the hood, four deep, in two cars. Next thing I know, they had the neighborhood winos and a few poor hustlers spread-eagled on the wall outside J.J.'s. While this was going on, Cornbread was standing at his fruit cart, a few feet away from all the action.

"Get on over here, boy. That fruit ain't goin' nowhere," one of the cops said.

With a small water bottle, Cornbread went on spraying down oranges, apples, grapes, and bananas, like he ain't heard nothin'.

"Nigger, you hear me talkin' to you?" The cop approached Cornbread's wooden makeshift broken-down fruit cart.

"Name Cornbread, suh," he said, spraying away.

The cop pointed his nightstick at Cornbread. "Boy, you best get over on this wall with the rest of 'em, now."

"Name Cornbread, suh." He nodded and never looked up; he just kept squeezing the trigger on that little clear water bottle.

The cop, hitting the palm of his hand with the nightstick, turned to the other officers. "Boys, well, looka here—I think we got ourselves an uppity nigga." The cop turned back to face Cornbread. "Boy, you think you ain't gotta jump when we say boo?" The cop, his stick in the air, jumped at Cornbread.

"No, suh. Name Cornbread, suh."

Before I could blink, that nightstick was upside Cornbread's head. As he was falling, he grabbed at the cop for support. Next thing anybody know, all four cops were stomping a mudhole in Cornbread's behind. The winos and hustlers hemmed up on the wall used the distraction to run away. No one stood up. No one came to help. Everyone knew Cornbread was slow in the head, yet no one said anything.

Hours later, everything had returned to normal. The pool hall was packed with hustlers, junkies, and pimps. Across the street from the pool hall, an older woman in a church dress was hollerin', and beating some poor old man with a big, thick brown book. By the way she was using Jesus' name, I think the book she was beating the old wino with was a Bible.

Less than two hours earlier, the cops beat a retarded man within an inch of his life for nothing. But just like then, no one cared. No one was going down to the police station to complain. No one was going to the county hospital to check on Cornbread. It was like nothing ever happened. Everyone had already forgotten. Everyone, but me.

I stared at the Ida B. Wells Help Center down the street, tears running down my cheeks. Right before turning around and heading to the Help Center, I spoke as if Cornbread were right next to me. "On everything I love"—I sniffed as I bit down on my lip—"Cornbread, I promise, I will die, before I just stand by and watch the cops do something like this again."

ACT 2
Am I My Brother's Keeper
Solomon

I was six years old when my little brother, Moses, came outta my momma's womb, raisin' all kinds of baby hell.

From the time Momma's midwife, Miss Aunt Helen, brought baby Moses out of Momma's bedroom, I knew we were in trouble. I looked at Daddy. He looked back at me. We both shrugged. I couldn't understand how something so small could make so much noise. It was like he was mad that Miss Aunt Helen pulled him out of Momma's belly.

As long as I could remember, the harder you pulled was just how hard my little brother pushed. He wasn't a bad kid, just inquisitive and high-strung. Me, I was the exact opposite. I was more laid-back, didn't ask a lot of questions.

Although Momma's final word was law, we were raised in a sort of "democratic-dictatorship-like" home. Daddy was a "whatever, baby" man, you know, non-confrontational. If Momma didn't agree with something he proposed, he would eventually give in, shrugging his shoulders in resignation, saying, "Whatever, baby."

One day (I had to be around nine) I came home from school and found my father sleeping on the living room couch. My first thought was that he must've been really tired to even be able to sleep on that sweaty, hard plastic. I could hear Momma now. I remember thinkin', It's gon' be a whole lot of "Jesus Lawdin'" if Daddy doesn't wake up and clean off that couch before Momma gets home from work.

Daddy knew good and well Momma didn't allow anybody to sit in the living room, much less lay all over her antique, hand-me-down, plastic-covered furniture. It was a wonder Daddy could even rest in the plastic-covered jungle room, surrounded by plastic plants in large gold, metal vases.

I walked on the plastic runner towards him. *He looks so peaceful*, I thought. As I started shaking him, I noticed that he felt hard and cold. I called his name several times, but he didn't move.

I got scared and went next door, and got Miss Aunt Helen. She made me watch my four-year-old brother Moses, while she rushed over to the house without even putting on her gray wig. I followed her with Moses in my arms. I was standing right outside the living room when she said Daddy was dead. I was busy crying, while Miss Aunt Helen rushed home to call Momma at work.

Momma never cried in front of me, but I knew she hurt real bad inside. To this day we still don't know how Daddy died. Back then, Black folk didn't too much have autopsies.

So at the age of nine, I took on the role as "man of the house." I looked after Moses, best I could, but as we grew older I became more involved with the church, while he ran the streets. Him running the streets the way he did sparked many arguments between us.

I was a senior in high school, when Moses and I had our first major blow-up. It was a school night, and I'd not too long ago gotten off work. I was walking home from the bus stop, when I saw Moses holding court across the street.

I hollered, "Moses King, you act like you don't see these street lights."

He ignored me, so I walked across the street to where he was standing on a soapbox, speaking to a small group of kids around his age.

After pushing through the small crowd, I said, "Come on, you know good and well you're not supposed to be hanging out outside of no liquor store; you must've forgot it was a school night."

"I haven't forgotten anything; as a matter of fact, what we're doing here is remembering."

"Remembering what?"

"Remembering a time when we were kings and queens. A time before alcohol was introduced to us by the slave master. Remembering a time before we got so drunk that we sold our own mothers and brothers to 'the Man' so he could enslave and force us to cultivate his stolen land."

I grabbed Moses by the arm. "What you need to remember is that you're only twelve and Momma wants you home before the street lights come on, and I'm gon' make sure you start minding what she say." I waved an arm at the small crowd. "And instead of all you hangin' out outside some liquor store, y'all should've been at Wednesday night Bible Study at Second Baptist or First Corinthians."

Moses jerked away from my grasp and looked me up and down. "We ain't like you, big brotha, waitin' for white Jesus to come out of the sky to rescue us."

Where is he getting this stuff from?

"We gon' rescue our people right now. That's why I'm here. That's why we here. If our uncles and fathers weren't so busy trying to get drunk and high, the cops would've never been able to beat Cornbread half to death the other day."

"Don't bring Cornbread or Jesus in this. You don't know anything about Jesus. Matter of fact, Jesus is who you need." I waved my arm around again. "That's who all you need. Now, come on . . . let's go."

"I ain't coming on anywhere until we're finished. Don't try to make me like you. I love you, Solomon, but you've been brainwashed. I hate to say it, but you're one of them church-going, watered-down, milquetoast, choirboy, we-shall-overcome, come-along-to-get-along negroes."

I had a mind to snatch his little "come–along-to-get-along" behind up in front of all his friends, but I thought better of it. It was too many of them and only one of me, so I walked on home. Moses had good intentions, but he went about everything the wrong way. He didn't understand that he was just one man, and standing on a soapbox wasn't going to change anything.

If he would only put half the passion in studying the Word that he did in studying Negro and African history, he'd be okay. It was because of Moses' short attention span when it came to God that I tried all type of things to get him to be more interested in the church.

I wanted everybody, especially my little, hardheaded brother to feel the joy that I felt when I read the Word, heard the Word, or was simply just in His house. I tried to bring the Word to Moses, using street slang. I tried to show him how the Word was relative to everything he did. The more I failed, the harder I tried. And Moses bucked me at every opportunity, but that just made me try harder.

ACT 3
Be All You Can Never Be
Moses

The pouring rain outside was a welcome reprieve from what was sure to be another hell-hot Chicago summer. I was sitting at the kitchen table, reading some essays by Black Panther party leader Huey P. Newton. Momma was cleaning collard greens in the kitchen sink.

Solomon walked in the door. He'd just graduated high school the day before. "Mom, can you come over to the table? I have something to tell you."

I stood up to stretch.

Solomon saluted and blurted out, "I just enlisted in the Army."

"Man, what the hell you thinkin'?" I asked.

Momma snapped. "Boy, mind your manners. You want me to wash yo' mouth out with soap?"

"I'm sorry, Ma, but Solomon done messed up big time."

"Look, little brotha, I know we've butted heads in the past, but I love you and I am doing what I think is best for me, you, and Momma.

"Since Daddy died I've had to assume the position as man of the house. I'm not complaining, not one bit, but it's been difficult working my way through high school. Now I have the chance to make sure God stays in the minds of the troops in Vietnam, and I can send money back home to help you and Momma out. And when I complete my tour of duty, I'll have money for college."

I looked at Solomon like he'd lost his mind. "So, me and Momma are more important than the millions of oppressed black people in America?"

"Moses, you don't appreciate nothin'. All the sacrifices that your brother has made for this family and you treat him like a Judas."

"But, Momma, he is."

Momma pointed a finger in my face. "Say another word, boy, and as God is my witness, I'll slap the taste out your mouth."

Solomon turned to Momma. "That's okay, Momma. I understand how Moses feels." Then he turned to me. "Moses, I'm sorry, but I have to do this. You know how bad I want to minister to the people. Our brothers and sisters are dying seven thousand miles from home on foreign soil, and there's no telling if they've accepted Jesus as their Lord and Savior. If I can just save the soul of one man, then I will have made a difference."

"Man, don't you understand that our fight isn't with no Vietnamese. Ain't one of them ever called me or you nigger. Ain't one of them ever lynched or raped our people. Our fight is here."

POP!

I tasted blood after Momma slapped me.

"I warned you, boy, Lord Jesus!"—Momma threw her arms in the air—"Jesus Lord, help my child," Momma cried.

Although I hated that he'd voluntarily gone off to war, not a day went by that I didn't worry about Solomon. I loved him and looked up to him; I just didn't agree with that one decision that he'd made.

Over the next few years Solomon sent money home. Momma continued cleaning homes on the North Side of Chicago, and I was policing my hood on the South Side with my crew.

I was always teased about my name being Moses, so me and my small group of friends started calling ourselves "the Disciples."

As we grew, we started calling ourselves "the Disciple Nation." We began having meetings to come up with ideas to make money and protect our folks from the sporadic beatings and cross-burnings that the Klan and the dirty cops inflicted. We were determined to change the world.

ACT 4
Heart and Soul
Moses

It was the first day of school my junior year at Washington High, when I met Pablo Picasso Nkrumah. The school bell had just rung and everyone raced to get out of the building.

Me and my best friend T-Hunt were on our way to tutor math and teach the Black history class at the Ida B. Wells Community Help Center, like we had been doing for a little over a year, when we noticed a crowd gathering around Dino Banks and his boys in the condemned grocery store parking lot across the street from the school.

"Gimme a kiss, you long-haired, pretty muthafucka," Dino said.

"Fuck you, punk-ass nigga," Pablo replied.

"Who you callin' nigga, spic bitch?"

"Ya momma."

I looked on as Pablo, a new kid in school (he looked about fourteen or fifteen, not more than five-four, and a buck twenty) was about to catch a serious beat-down.

Dino was over six feet and nearly as wide as the new kid was tall. Nineteen and still in the twelfth grade, he looked like he could have played the entire offensive line for the Chicago Bears.

All alone and the only Spanish kid at Washington High, the new kid talked bold, but I knew he had to be scared. All of a sudden the new kid sucker-punched Dino in the mouth. He got off two punches before Dino could throw the first blow. I could hardly believe what I was seeing. This kid was lightning, but not quick enough to dodge Dino's boys from grabbing him.

"Let him go," I said. I jumped between Dino and the kid.

"This gon' be a one-on-one. Ain't gon' be no gang-banging today."

"Moses, this ain't for us. I know you ain't sidin' wit' no spic," Dino said.

"Nah, I ain't sidin' with no one, but damn, big man, you twice his size." I shook my head. "You ain't gotta gang up on him; it's bad enough you jumpin' on a kid."

"A kid with a smart-ass mouth," Dino said.

"That may be so, but it ain't like he picked the fight. I saw the whole thing."

"Oh, it's like that, huh?"

Before I could say anything, T-Hunt was all up in Dino's face. "Yeah, it's like that and gon' stay like that." T-Hunt looked Dino up and down. "Now what?"

The cheering crowd swung to our side. They were egging us on to fight. In high school, don't nobody care who fights, as long as there is one they can watch and talk about.

"Fuck that! Let's go. This shit ain't worth it. Yo, I'll see you later, pretty Pablo," Dino spat, puckering up and making a kissing sound at the kid.

T-Hunt and I turned around and were about to walk away. Just then I saw something shiny in Dino's hand, out the corner of my eye. Without thinking, I turned around, jumped in front of the kid, and tackled him.

Sirens blared in the wind. Everybody scattered.

I rolled to one side of the concrete.

Pablo got up with a broken-handled kitchen knife in hand. Dino tried to sidestep the Zorro-like slashing Pablo carved on his chest.

I was rubbing my behind after I got to my feet; I felt like I broke a bone in my butt.

The sirens got closer.

Dino dropped to his knees and fell face-forward in the street.

The kid looked back, and our eyes connected. He whispered the words, "I'll never forget."

All of a sudden a sharp pain shot up my spine.

The sirens got louder.

There was no time for me to see what the cause of the pain was, so I ran like everyone else. Well, everyone but Dino, who was on his knees, struggling to get to his feet.

This was the longest six blocks I'd ever run. I thought we'd never make it to the protective cover of the Ida B. Wells projects. I bent over, out of breath, as T-Hunt and I stood in front of some wino sleeping on the first-floor stairs of the project.

"Moses, hold up. Man, you bleedin'," T-Hunt said.

"Where?"

"Your back—take off your jacket."

I took off my jacket and saw blood all over the side and back of it.

"That nigga Dino cut you."

"That's the sharp pain I felt, when I got up off the ground."

"Huh?"

The wino said, "Y'all go on now—a nigga try'na sleep, damn!"

"Go suck on a bottle, old man," T-Hunt told him.

"Y'all young niggas dese days ain't got no respect."

I turned toward the stairs, where the old man was laying across. "Yo, I'm sorry, pops. We don't mean no disrespect, but I'm hurt."

"Well, just hurry up and get about yo' business. Oh, and least ya could do is let me borrow a dollar."

I ignored the old man. "T-Hunt, we gotta find that kid."

"Yeah, I know."

"Okay, how 'bout loaning me fifty cents?" the wino begged.

"If we don't find him before Dino, his momma gon' be buryin' a son," I said.

"What about your side?" T-Hunt asked.

"I know you niggas hear me. I ain't ast fo' nothin' but fifty gotdamn cents."

I waved T-Hunt off. "Ah, it ain't nothin' but a flesh wound. A little peroxide and a band-aid and I'll be cool. I'll just run home and fix myself up. In the meantime, I need you to go find the kid and bring him down to the old railroad yard."

"Ah, fuck both ya li'l niggas. Hope both ya li'l faggots get ran over by a gotdamn bus."

"Dino kept calling him Pablo. How hard could it be to find a Spanish kid on the South Side of Chicago named Pablo?" T-Hunt asked.

Before we left the stairwell, T-Hunt and I pulled out a few dollars, balled them up, and threw them down at the old wino.

A couple hours later, me and some of my fellas were down at the railroad yard with T-Hunt and the kid. We found out his whole name was Pablo Nkrumah. His mother was Cuban, and his father was Senegalese.

"Pablo Nkrumah," I said, nodding. "That's tight."

"Thanks. God, I ain't ever gon' forget what you did for me," he said.

"You got heart; I like that. I need brothas like you, Pablo."
I put my arm around his shoulders.

"Back home in Brooklyn, my cats call me Picasso," Pablo
said.

"Oh yeah?"

"Yeah, I turn a pencil, pen, brush, or can of paint into a
magic wand."

"And a knife too," I said.

"You know," he shrugged, "it's a jungle out here. A nigga
gotta do whatever to survive."

"So where'd you get Picasso from?"

"Ah, my moms started calling me Picasso when I won a
third-grade art contest for painting a picture of one of my
half-sisters, when I was in kindergarten, and I guess it just
stuck, ya dig?"

"Oh, I can dig it, Zorro. Speaking of knives, I appreciate
what you did outside the schoolyard in the old Marsh parking lot."

My boys were just hangin' around, talking amongst themselves, messing around rusty, old, junked, abandoned railroad cars, as Picasso and I rapped.

"I'm real, god. You had my back, so I had yours—that's
the way I roll, that's the way I was raised. My moms taught
me that."

"So you live with your moms?"

"Naw, she in Rikers."

"What she do, kill a brotha?" I jokingly asked.

He nodded. "Yeah, she shot my pops."

"Damn! I'm sorry, man."

"Don't be? She ain't did nothin' that didn't need doin'.
She was tired of the nigga puttin' his foot up her and my ass.
Hell, I woulda offed that big crazy mu'fucka my damn self
eventually. Even his family, the ones here in the States, understood. They knew my pops was shot the fuck out."

"What'd your pops do that was so bad?"

"You mean, what didn't he do. The last few years of his life he'd gotten into that Santería voodoo shit. He'd speedball, shoot up heroin and cocaine, before going out and finding a stray dog or cat, bring 'em back home, and light candles all through the house and shit. Then he'd start mumblin' some 'Oogoo-boo-goo-goo' shit, before cutting the animals up." He shook his head. "Moses, that was some helluva sick shit."

"That is jacked up."

"And every time my moms put his ass out or had him locked up, when he got out, he'd come right back and kick our asses worse than ever."

"You right, your pops was gon'—he deserved to be dead."

"True dat. His sister had long ago told my moms to get away from his psycho, doped-out ass."

"She shoulda listened."

"Tell me about it. My Aunt Jean, his sister, is who sent for me. I wanted to move in with my sisters and they moms and stepdad in Queens, but my moms wanted me as far away from New York as possible, you know—the old influences and shit.

"Damn, that's some heavy baggage to carry for a kid," I said.

"God, I ain't never been no kid. Ain't had time."

"Damn!"

"My dad was married to my sister's mom when he brought my mom to the States from Cuba when she was fifteen," he said.

"Your mom didn't know he was married?"

"Hell, naw. Not until she was in New York."

"How'd she find out?"

"I'll tell you like my moms told me. One night, this tall, coffee-brown, afro'd out, church-dressed, pregnant lady kicked in the door to the apartment where my moms and pops stayed. My moms told me the woman had the smallest shotgun she'd ever seen pointed at my pop's head.

"The chick told my pops that if he ever tried to come back home she'd paint the sidewalk with his blood. Then my moms told me the funniest thing happened afterward."

"What was that?"

"The woman asked my moms if she wanted to come with her. After my moms looked at my pops, she shook her head, and the chick gave her a piece of paper with her name and number on it and told her that, if she ever changed her mind, she had somewhere to go. After the woman left, my pops snatched the paper out my mom's hand, but not before she memorized the lady's name and address.

"A couple years later, after I was born, my moms looked the lady up. By then, the lady had a new husband and was pregnant with another child. The lady introduced my mom to my two-year-old twin sisters. My moms and my sister's moms were in awe of how much my sisters and I looked alike.

"As long as I could remember, me and one of the twins had been close as twins. We even called each other twin. Outside of my sis and my mom, I don't care much about no one or no thing. "You feel me, god?"

"Right here," I pointed to my heart. "So you ever see your sister?"

"Naw, big sis handlin' her business. She in the books, god. She say she gon' get a degree and move me in with her. Her twin and me are cool, but she into a lot o' other shit. We ain't close at all."

"Damn, your mother is on lockdown, your dad is dead, and you in a new city and already you got a target on your ass. You done been through it, li'l bruh." I knew I just met this cat, but I had no doubt he was gon' be all right.

"All my life, baby—I get it from both ends." Pablo shrugged. "But you know, that's life in the real world, right?"

"That it is, li'l bruh . . . that it is."

"Sometimes, god, I don't know what's worse, Black folks

or white." Pablo looked like he'd been looking for some-body to open up to. "My skin is truly my sin—And I'm tired of answering for it—Crackas hate me 'cause I'm a nigga, and niggas hate me 'cause they don't know what the hell I am."

"Li'l bruh, you black. It's the silly-ass, ignorant niggas that hate on you. There's black niggas and white niggas; igno-rance has no color."

"Yo, that's what I be tellin' everyone, god. Maybe not so poetic and shit, but still, that's what I be sayin'." He sighed.

"One question for you?"

"Yo."

"How the hell you learned to work a blade like that?"

"My sister. Her mom is serious—that's why my pops never put his hands on her. But I'll tell you this—it's all in the wrist. People make the mistake of 'straight-arming' "—Picasso demonstrated—"But once you barely touch the flesh, you flick the wrist—And just like that, people get the message not to ever fuck with you again."

ACT 5
Changing Direction
Moses

Picasso and I developed a big brother-little brother sort of relationship. No one was as proficient with a blade as he was, but eventually he taught most of us the basics.

As the Disciples became more organized, our numbers and our reputation grew. Pretty soon, word got around that a group of young boys wearing black ski masks were robbing white folks that ventured into our hoods. It wasn't something I took pride in doing, but I saw it as a necessary evil.

Before I knew it, it seemed like every kid wanted to be a Disciple. Half the stories that floated around about us were just that—stories. We walked around booted and suited, lookin' like soldiers on business. Black or blue suits with black combat boots were the uniforms of the Disciples.

I came up with the idea of suits from Malcolm and Martin. Every time I saw them on TV, they were wearing suits. But they weren't ready for war. So I figured my army would look good and be ready for war at the same time.

Eventually, I figured since neither I nor any of my people got forty acres, a mule, or were paid for slavery, we'd take our reparations from big business. That's why the Disciples moved from nickel-and-dime robbery to hijacking trucks.

With the proceeds, we purchased cultural awareness books, bought swings, seesaws, and new sliding boards for community parks. We tutored adults that wanted to go back and get their high-school diplomas. We even helped fund and start the free breakfast program in the public school system with the Black Panther Party's Fred Hampton.

The heavier our pockets got, the more we did for the community. Our members were constantly harassed by the police. The local media portrayed us as "villains in disguise." If only they knew. All the publicity was what attracted so many young cats to the Disciples. And like any growing Robin Hood-like movement, weak-minded people infiltrated our organization.

Pretty soon, the police broke up our meetings before they even got started good. Disciples started to get arrested at the scene of hijackings. It became evident that we had traitors amongst us. Some of our members had either made deals with the pigs, or some just ran their mouths to friends and family who were some way connected to the cops.

Sun Tzu's book, *The Art of War*, gave me the idea to split the Disciples into twelve groups, with twelve leaders. This way I figured we could narrow the traitors down, find them, and deal with them accordingly.

I even developed a special set of qualities that every disciple had to exhibit. I called them the L-I-G-H-T—Loyalty, Integrity, God, Honor, and Trust. Once someone earned his LIGHT, he was initiated as a Disciple for life. Until then, he was a scribe.

Every week for the last four years we'd read anything and everything that had something to do with consciousness and African and African-American culture. At our weekly meetings we gave speeches on what we read. And we held open forums of discussion to the community in hopes of coming together to solve problems that plagued the African-American community.

Over the last, I'd say, two years, the police harassment, the negative press, the backstabbing, along with being a gang leader, slowly became too much for me to bear.

I started to feel that what I was trying to do was in vain. The hijackings and robberies eventually started turning violent. Innocent truck drivers wanting to be heroes started getting hurt. Now, most of them carried guns.

When a young Disciple under Picasso's kingdom was killed in a hijacking gone wrong, I had to re-evaluate a lot of things. I knew that in any revolution there would be casualties of war, but I couldn't help but close my eyes and see one of the kids I tutored at the Help Center laying on the ground bleeding. What could I tell the mother of her son?—That he died for the cause?—That he died for freedom? You can't tell this to someone who doesn't even know that they aren't free.

Although I pledged allegiance for life to the Disciples, I resigned at twenty, seven years after I had formed the gang. T-Hunt was elected King of kings, which left a sour taste in Picasso's mouth, but the kings understood and respected my decision to recommend T-Hunt. Picasso was like my little brother, but T-Hunt was like my twin. I just felt that T-Hunt was the more levelheaded, and he'd been with me since the beginning. T-Hunt deserved the chance to lead the Disciples.

I just felt that I could do more out in the open, where I could speak to anyone about anything, without being harassed or looked down on. Don't get me wrong, in my heart and soul, I was a Disciple and would always be. I was just inactive. But the way T-Hunt and Picasso consulted with me, you wouldn't think I was out.

Actually, I spent more time keeping T-Hunt and Picasso

from butting heads than anything else. Picasso wanted the Disciples to venture off into selling drugs to finance free educational daycare, and programs to help sistahs get off welfare.

T-Hunt liked Picasso's ideas, but he wanted to move the Disciples in the direction of investing the hijacking proceeds into stock, and real estate, so the Disciples could legitimately do the things that Picasso suggested.

It was a constant tug-of-war between the two. A tug-of-war that had to end before Picasso left the Disciples and formed his own gang. As it was, the other kings were split between the two, but they respected the hierarchy. T-Hunt had the final decision in all the Disciple affairs, whether the kings or Picasso liked it or not.

Every time I began to question my decision to step down from the Disciples, I thought about my kids at the Ida B.

Six days a week, I worked as a youth counselor across the street from the oldest and largest project housing development in the country. The kids at the Ida B. Wells youth center needed me, just as I needed them. Finally, through the young kids, eight, nine, and ten, I was seeing the difference that I was trying to make. They were actually excited about learning their history and wanting to make sure the negative aspects of it weren't repeated.

I was at the center early one morning, cleaning up after the previous evening's birthday party, when one of my kids walked in. I put the broom up against the wall of the gaming area. "Billy, why aren't you in school?" I asked.

He shrugged his shoulders.

"You don't know?—What do you mean, you don't know?"

He dropped his head.

I knelt down in front of him. "Have you forgotten what and who you are?" I asked the chubby pre-teen standing in front of me.

"No."

I took a finger and lifted his chin. "Well, tell me then, what are you?"

"A proud black man."

"A what? A loud fat man?"

"No, sir. I'm a proud black man," he said, louder this time.

"And who are you?" I barked.

"One of God's finest."

I popped Billy in the chest with my palm. "Well, hold your head up high, look me in the eye, and speak to me with your mouth from now on. I don't understand the language of shrugged shoulders."

"Sorry, Moses." He fidgeted with his hands in his baggy, old jeans pockets. I just want to hang out with you all day, you know, help you out at the center."

I took a seat on the floor against the gray cinderblock wall. "Come here, little man. Cop a squat."

He came to my side and sat next to me.

"I know it's hard out there." I put a hand on his and drew eye contact. "But hard is either going to break you or make you."

"Moses, you don't understand. In school . . ." He sniffed and turned his head. ". . . I'm the fat-ass welfare kid with no real parents. And at home I'm just a paycheck for Ms. Claudette." Tears were freely running down his cheeks. "The Help Center is the only place I feel good. Moses, you make me feel like, you know"—He shook his head—"like I'm somebody."

I had to blink hard to keep my eyes from watering. Unfortunately, there were many kids in the projects that felt just like him. Women just like his foster mother, Miss Claudette, adopted kids so they could get a check from the state and, in turn, get an increase on their food stamps and welfare checks.

I turned his head to face me. "Remember when we read the autobiography of Malcolm X?"

"Yeah."

I closed my eyes. "Everyone thought Malcolm was the coolest, hippest dude ever, right?"

"Yeah."

I opened my eyes back up. "Malcolm became a welfare child, remember?"

"Yeah."

"Remember the book we read a few months ago?"

"Which one?" Billy asked.

"The one about Marcus Garvey and the U.N.I.A."

"Yeah, Marcus Garvey was true to his."

"So, you thought Marcus was hip too?"

"Oh yeah," Billy said with confidence.

"Marcus Garvey was a fat kid just like yo' ugly butt, and a chunky adult. But he was still a bad dude that got respect—you wanna know why?"

He nodded.

"What does that mean?" I imitated him, nodding my head.

"Yes, I wanna know."

"Marcus Garvey was who he was because he held his head up high and demanded no less than excellence from himself first and then anyone that he let into his circle." I extended an arm towards him. "So what am I trying to tell you?"

"Uh . . . that I shouldn't let others make me feel bad."

"No." I put my finger in his chest. "I'm telling you that you shouldn't give anyone's words that type of power.

"It's your words and your actions that should have power over you and others. Before you can become a Malcolm, Martin, or Marcus, you have to become Billy Torrance. You have to get a good education and continue reading, if you want to be the coolest and hippest dude around."

"You forgot one," he said.

"Forgot one what?" I asked.

"One of the famous M men—Moses King—that's who I wanna be like."

I smiled. "You still wanna hang out with me the rest of the day?"

"Can't. I gotta get to school," Billy said, running out the front door.

"Take it easy, little man," I shouted at his back.

After Billy left, I thought back to last year when I decided to fix the Center up. Ever since I could remember, the Center had these gigantic airplane propeller fans circulating heat and dust throughout the place in the summer. It was a shame how the state did the kids on the South Side. Or how they didn't do them.

By June, it was smokin' hot behind the walls of the Help Center. I couldn't understand how the city could fund a program for kids and would not provide air-conditioning.

I'd been volunteering at Ida B. since Cornbread got beat down by the police. Back then T-Hunt and I came in three times a week after school for an hour a day to tutor and teach cultural awareness to the younger kids.

For six years, me and all the kids from the projects across the street had been burning up inside the sweltering walls of the Center. One day I asked Momma Smith how she survived on the budget she was given. All she said was, "God and my two good feet."

Miss Georgia Smith was this short, widowed, Mother Goose-like white woman that started the Help Center. I was fourteen when I first got arrested. Momma Smith had just bailed me out, and we were in her green Ford Pinto.

"Moses King, why did you spit on that officer?" Momma Smith asked.

"I didn't. But now I wish I had, since that's what I was arrested for."

She looked over at me then back at the road.

"I know you don't think I'm lyin'. Momma Smith, I swear all I did was stare the crack—I mean, white man in the face while he was walking the street lookin' for someone to harass."

She nodded.

"Don't gimme that nod. Okay, maybe I shouldn't have stood in the middle of the sidewalk with my arms crossed, blocking the cop's path, but it's a free country. He could've walked by me. He didn't have to stand in front of me, hitting his nightstick against the palm of his hand, while trying to stare me down.

"I ain't no punk. Just 'cause he got a badge and a gun don't make him God."

"Moses, I let you go off on a tangent without saying a word." Momma Smith pulled up in front of the Help Center.

"Moses King, you are a fourteen-year-old very intelligent, young black male. It would be a shame if you let the ignorance of others bring you down to their level, like one did earlier today." She put the car in park and turned to look at me before continuing. "Moses, you have to learn when to pick your battles and who to pick your battles with."

A couple hours later, after locking up the Help Center I walked Momma Smith to her car. After thanking her again for getting me out of lock-up, she asked me what was my motivation for starting the Disciples. I turned around and asked her what was hers for starting a Community Center in the worst black part of town.

She said that she was color-blind, but unfortunately the government wasn't.

That was heavy coming from an older white person.

Since then, we'd been tight. Momma Smith was like a second mother to me and most of the kids that came to the Ida B.

Now, six years after having that conversation I was working at the Ida B. full-time, and finally I understood what she meant when she told me that God and her two feet was how she kept the Center running on the shoestring budget we were on.

When I'd stepped down from the Disciples a year earlier, I used the thirty grand I'd saved for college and began renovating the Ida B. Kids like Billy Torrance made my investment worth more than what any college could ever give me.

I had gathered up about twenty older kids from the Center. "Ladies and fellas, this is our home. I don't like our home, so I am going to fix it up. Now I need a show of hands for everyone who wants to earn two dollars an hour for a lot of hard work and a great learning experience."

As I figured, everyone raised a hand.

After about two months, one of my kids' family members came by the Center, asking questions.

"Excuse me, ma'am, may I help you?" I asked.

"It's hard to believe what you all are doing with this old building." She looked around at the freshly painted orange, red, and blue walls in the game room.

"Thank you, Miss . . ."

"Gina Garan—I'm sorry. My nephew, Sean Carter, can't quit talking about what you all are doing here. He seems to be under the impression that one of your staff members is footing the bill for all of this."

I nodded my head.

"Is Moses King around? He's the savior my nephew speaks so highly of," she joked.

I laid the broom against the wall and extended my hand. "Hi, I'm Moses King, and it's nice to meet you Miss Garan."

"Oh my God." She put her hand to her mouth.

"Can you help me remove my foot from my mouth, please, Mr. King?"

I laughed. "No need. The look on your face says enough. So what can I do for you, Miss Garan?"

"I'm a reporter, and I'd like to do a news story on you and the Center. A little publicity may help bring more money in to help you with the renovations and the fantastic job you're doing with these kids."

Shortly after the story ran on the local news, money started pouring in from all over the state. This was just a local story. I couldn't understand how so many people found out about the Help Center. I guess that really didn't make a difference.

At twenty, I was speaking at high schools and colleges all over Illinois, thanks to Ms. Garan. The sign some of the kids made for the outside wall in the front of the Center became our motto. It read: COME INTO UNITY TO MAKE A POSITVE COMMUNTIY.

Everything was mashed potatoes and gravy, until I started bringing T-Hunt in to speak with me at schools. That's when the all-too-familiar negative press started.

My former gang ties were being revisited so much, that the media started fabricating stories, hinting that I'd never left the Disciples. Just like the Disciples had done in the past, I was using good deeds to cover up the evil that me and the Disciples were known for, one journalist even wrote.

Shortly after these stories began, my whole world came crashing down.

ACT 6
Say It Ain't So
Moses

I had just made it back to my apartment, absolutely exhausted from working eight hours at the Ida B., and another ten trying to get black folks to vote. Being that this was an election year and broke folks, black and white, were very disgruntled about the current city and state administration, I'd decided to embark on a get-out-and-vote campaign.

I'd spent months, weeks, and days educating folks on the importance of the vote. With the help of T-Hunt and some of the other Disciples, we registered and drove people to the polls. My black-and-white NO VOTE NO POWER NO COMPLAINING T-shirts became a big hit all throughout Chicago.

I must have drifted off to sleep because, the next thing I knew, I jumped at a sudden noise. Somebody was standing over my bed. Before I could get out or see who it was, my head exploded, and then everything went black.

"Moses Toussant King?" I heard a voice say.

For some reason, I couldn't open my eyes. I couldn't be dead. I was in too much pain.

"Moses Toussant King?" I heard that same irritating voice.

God, I wish I had a blanket. I was freezing. My head was killing me.

"You hear me, boy?" There it was again. The voice was right above me.

Damn, the air was stale. It smelled like wet dogs and cigarettes.

"Shit. Think we hit him too hard," I heard a different voice say.

"Hell, naw, these niggers are dumb, but they're built for pain. Why you think them boys fight so good? You can take whips, chains, and bats to 'em, and they still come back, like roaches."

Oh no. Must be the pigs.

"Nigger, wake your black ass up . . . before you feel this wood again."

"Ahhhhhhhh!" I winced and arched my back from the pain of being kicked in the side. My eyes fluttered as I slowly opened them. It was dark. I was on some hard, cold surface. I had no idea of where I was, how long I'd been there, nor how I arrived.

"Help me get his ass in the chair, Sam."

"What? Where am I?" I asked as I felt myself being pulled to my feet.

"That ain't important. What is, is that you get outta here, 'fore we run you in for breaking and entering," a pig in a suit said.

"Ha, ha!" I made a feeble attempt to snicker through the pounding in my head.

"Sam, did I say something funny?"

"Nope, not at all, Eddie."

"Boy, what is so friggin' funny?"

Despite the bleeding and the pain I was in, I was now very coherent. "You hit me over the head, kidnapped me, brought me to this house, and now you just gon' let me go. Come on, Tweedly Dee and Tweedly Dum, you two want me to run, so you can shoot me in the back." I struggled to sit up in the chair. "You wanna kill me? You'll have to do it right here, pig," I spat.

"You stupid nigger." One of the cops pulled out a gun and pointed it at my forehead. "If we wanted to kill you, you'd be dead." He looked at his watch. "You've got a ten-minute headstart." He kicked the chair over. "Now git the fuck out!"

After getting up into a crawling position, I looked around in the dark until I saw moonlight from behind a large, cracked-open curtain in the next room. I let my eyes follow the light of that window, until it led me to what seemed like a back door.

I got up slowly, fighting off dizziness, and made my way to the door, without looking back. My ears were keenly listening for any sudden clicking sounds, a gun's chamber, a heel, anything. I heard only silence. My pace quickened, catching up with the beating of my heart.

A few minutes after leaving the house, I heard sirens. I gingerly ran faster through backyards. A jolting pain in my left leg hindered me. My side was still hurting from where the pig kicked me.

I'd made it over a six-foot wooden fence, when someone shouted, "Freeze, asshole!"

I didn't look back. I just kept running straight ahead. Next thing I know, I was on the ground, holding my head, and getting beat with sticks until I lost consciousness.

I was laying on something soft but firm. My arms were spread apart from my body. There was a funny-sounding, rhythmic, beating noise in the background. The air smelled like old people. I heard faint chatter coming from somewhere far away—no, it was close. I opened my eyes to see a guy dressed in a gray sports coat, standing over me.

"Moses Toussant King, you are under arrest. Anything you say—"

"What?—I haven't done anything!"

"Can and will be used against you."

I blocked the rest out. When he finished, I again said, "I haven't done anything.

"Nothing, but murder Congressman Perry Homes and rape and murder his wife Fiona."

ACT 7
Coming Home
Solomon

Over the last year I continued to write and send money home, but for some reason the last three months of my tour I didn't receive any mail from Momma. That was strange. For the last seven and half years I received a letter from Momma once a week.

Not receiving mail from her was a little disturbing, but what mattered most was that it was August 12, 1974. I had completed two full tours of duty in Vietnam and was on my way home to Moses and Momma in one piece, thank God.

On the plane coming back from 'Nam, all I could think of was reconciling with my little brother. I couldn't begin to explain how proud I was of him. In her letters, Momma explained in detail all the good things Moses was doing at the Help Center and around the community.

Moses and I weren't as different as I'd thought. While he raised hell trying to educate and uplift the community on the South Side of Chicago, I was trying to uplift the troops by bringing them the Word of God.

After my first tour of duty, I re-enlisted. I just couldn't leave my troops in Vietnam, not knowing God.

After completing my second tour of duty, I flew into Fort Benning, in Columbus, Georgia to be processed out. The first thing I did after receiving an honorable discharge was call Momma.

"Momma, I'm back in the States," I shouted over the phone. "Momma?"

"Oh, hey, baby. I'm sorry . . ."

"Momma, what's wrong?"

This was the first time I'd heard my mother cry.

"Three months ago your brother was arrested for murder."

No, not Moses. I should have been there to protect him. "I'm on the next flight to Chicago, Mom. I'll be there as soon as I can." So, this is why she didn't write me. She knew I'd be upset and me being thousands of miles away, I couldn't do anything to help.

I don't think I even hung up the pay phone, before darting out into the rain to hail a taxi. My mind raced as the taxi sped towards the airport. I had to get to my baby brother. I had to somehow save him. I just had to. Why didn't I listen to Moses? Why did I leave him and Momma? I could have found work in Chicago.

Almost as soon as I got off of the plane, two men wearing black suits came up to me. After waving FBI badges and IDs in my face, they escorted me to an empty windowless office in Chicago's, O'Hare Airport.

Even before I was forced down into one of the two gray, metal chairs, I saw pictures of my mother on the small, round meeting table. My heart sped up as I looked at my mother sleeping in her bed. In another, she was washing dishes. In another she was in a nightgown on her knees, at the foot of her bed praying.

My mouth hung open. I was speechless. I felt like I'd had the wind knocked out of me.

The short, pointy-nosed agent walked around the table and dropped an envelope filled with a new set of pictures in front of me. "Open it!" he commanded.

Inside the envelope were several pictures of Miss Georgia Smith, the older lady that ran the Ida B. Wells Community Help Center. I continued thumbing through pictures of Miss Smith sleeping in her bed, washing dishes, and working with kids in what seemed like an art class. Once I got to the last few pictures and turned them over, my heart skipped a beat.

"Sweet Jesus, what have you done?" I said, looking up.

Death was no stranger to me. I'd lived with death looming over my head every day for the past eight years, but this was different. Miss Smith was an innocent civilian.

"Why are you showing me these?" I pointed to pictures of Miss Smith being smothered by a pillow, while she fought and struggled in what I guess was her bed.

"Moses Toussant King," the burly-looking agent said.

"Moses? What does my brother have to do with you killing Miss Smith, and spying on my mother?"

Ignoring my question, the short, pointy-nosed agent spoke. "Moses has become a godless cancer in the Negro community." The agent paced the small room.

"What are you talking about?"

He reached inside his jacket pocket and pulled out a picture and dropped it on the table in front of me. "The house your brother is leaving out of was the home of Congressman Perry Homes. If you look closely at Moses' shirt you can see specks of blood on it—the Congressman's and his wife's blood."

"No." I shook my head. "Moses would not have done what you're implying."

"You don't know him. You've been away for a long time, Mr. King. In that time Moses has spread hate throughout the

Negro community, and he's organized a large terrorist gang. He's used the racial tensions in Chicago to facilitate a rash of violent, race-based crimes."

"What does that have to do with me?"

"Nothing . . . as long as you stay away from him. Mr. King, you've served your country well. You've received the Bronze Star and the Medal of Honor, it would look bad for the government if a decorated war hero and good Christian stood by the side of an animal rapist-killer, even if that animal is your brother."

"Rapist-killer?"

The pointy-nosed agent nodded. "I'm afraid so. Moses slit the Congressman's throat and raped his wife before he killed her."

I rose from my seat. There was no way Moses would do something like this. There had to be an explanation for the blood and him being at the house.

"What do you think you're doing?" the big burly agent asked.

"I'm leaving. My brother needs me, and you can't make me believe he'd do something like this. Besides, how'd you manage to take pictures of Moses coming out of what looked like a side or back door?"

The burly agent blocked my way to the door.

I could take him. I know I could, but if I tried, I had no doubt the smaller agent would shoot me.

"We had a surveillance team watching the Congressman. Our intel led us to believe that his life was in danger. The Congressman was also a very popular civil rights leader and Christian minister with a large congrega—"

"That's exactly why I don't believe what you're saying about Moses."

"Before the Congressman was brutally murdered by your brother, he started speaking out against the Disciples and their brand of so-called education."

"I've heard enough. Sir, would you kindly move out of my way," I said to the big burly agent blocking my path.

The agents looked at each other.

"One more minute, and we'll be through here," the smaller agent said. He held a finger in the air. "The Bureau hoped that you would be reasonable, Mr. King, but we prepared ourselves in the event that you were not."

" 'Reasonable'? You force me into a room. You tell me my brother is a rapist and a murderer, after you show me pictures of a woman being smothered with a pillow, and you show me pictures of my mother in her bedclothes."

"Mr. King, these pictures are going to save your's and your mother's life."

"How?"

"Because, you being the rational thinking man that you are, knowing that if we can kill an innocent black woman and make it like she died of natural causes." The pointy-nosed agent walked around the table. Once he stood face-to-face with me, he smiled. "I assure you, Mr. King, if you go anywhere near this trial and if you ever are in contact with Moses King, we will do to your sweet mother what Moses did to the congressman's wife."

"You son of a—"

The agent behind me grabbed my arms.

I closed my eyes. Lord, give me strength.

"And we'll make you watch . . . before we kill you."

The agent let me go and moved out of my way.

"Oh, and if you don't think we will find out, or you think we won't do as we say, feel free to call our bluff."

I didn't know what to say. I didn't know what to do. But, until I figured it out, I had no choice but to do what they said, knowing that as soon as I could figure out a way to help Moses, I would.

ACT 8
The Setup
Moses

The following eight months were crazy. I was moved in and out of eighteen different county jails around the state of Illinois. The city's explanation: it was for my safety, and for riot control. They feared a riot or attempted prison break orchestrated by the Disciples.

The media went crazy on a feeding frenzy. They ran the craziest stories like THE IDA B. WELLS HELP CENTER: A COMMUNITY CENTER OR A GANG RECRUITMENT HEADQUARTERS? Another headline read: BLACK TERRORIST MUSLIM GANG LEADER KILLS FREEDOM-FIGHTING CHRISTIAN CIVIL RIGHTS LEADER.

If I didn't know me, the television news reports and the newspapers would have convinced me that I was a terrorist terrorizing the black and white community too. It was crazy. I wasn't even involved with the Disciples' day-to-day activities, yet I was still linked to them. So, because the Nation of Islam stood behind me, I was a Muslim now. It kind of reminded me of Malcolm X after he broke away from the Nation of Islam. Up until he was murdered the media still portrayed him as an anti-American Black terrorist Muslim that hated all White people.

I had been in solitary confinement for four months now. Solomon had been back for a good month, and he hadn't come to see me or been at Momma's when I called. I know we had some rough times before he joined the Army, but I was still his brother. At least T-Hunt, the Disciples, and my mother had my back.

Surprisingly, my mother was handling my incarceration quite well.

"Mom, how you holdin' up?" I asked one day over the phone. I was sitting in my small cell in solitary confinement.

"I should be asking you that, Moses. Have you been reading your Bible?"

"Yes, ma'am. But, Mom, I called to tell you not to worry about me."

"I'm not worried about you, Moses. I know you didn't kill Reverend Homes or rape his wife. You're a good man. Stubborn as a mule, like your daddy was, but you got a good heart, and the Lord knows this. You just bein' tested by Satan. I always said God had a special plan for you, Moses."

I hope a lengthy prison stay isn't in His plans. "I know, Mom. By the way, how's Solomon?"

"He's fine. Now, I know he has a funny way of showing it, but your brother loves you. He won't tell me why he won't have any contact with you, but he always tells me to send you his love."

I didn't want to hear any excuses. As far as I was concerned, there wasn't a good excuse for the way Solomon was treating me. Instead of harping on the subject, I switched gears.

"Mom, I want you to understand that all the stories you're reading about me are lies. And before it's all over, they'll probably get worse."

"Why do you think this is happening to you, son?"

"Because I've become an empowering voice to the poor and the young Blacks of Chicago. The positive press I've re-

ceived after leaving the Disciples has made me more popular
than ever. Black colleges, universities, and other institutions
have started paying me to come speak to their classes and
student unions."

"If that's the case, why haven't they gone after
Tharellious?" she asked.

"T-Hunt isn't a big enough threat to the system. He still
has the negative persona of being a gang leader, but believe
me, they're after him; they're just not putting nearly as
much energy into him as they are me."

"You keep saying they, and the media. Who is they? And
who is feeding the meee—"

The phone call came to an abrupt end. The fifteen minutes I was allowed to talk on the phone once a day must've
expired.

I was just about to explain that a gang of warrants had
gone out for members and suspected members of the
Disciples after I was arrested. The charges ranged from failing to appear in court on a jaywalking citation, spitting on
the sidewalk, to attempted murder and armed robbery.

History had already prepared T-Hunt and the Disciples
for the police harassment and false charges. After the trial,
everything would be back to normal. I just hoped that T-
Hunt and Picasso could stay off the cops' radar until then.

I could hardly believe the lack of support I received from
the Black community. It seemed as if I was a stranger to my
own Black brothers and sisters. No one seemed to remember my work in the community, the voting drives, the free
turkey dinners for the homeless on Thanksgiving, the adult
high-school equivalency study program, the blood drives,
and my work at the Help Center. The NAACP wouldn't even
entertain my request for them to get involved.

After the Nation of Islam threw their support behind me,
the Black church publicly denounced me, despite my
Christian upbringing. I wasn't even a Black Muslim, but

other than the Disciples, the Nation of Islam was the only organization that fought for me. The Minister spoke passionately on my behalf throughout the whole ordeal. But, not
even he could compete with the television news and what
was being reported in the newspapers across the state and
the nation.

Through the media, I was made to look like a drug-addicted gang leader who preyed on the Black community so I
could enjoy a lavish lifestyle, and help support the addic-
tions of my gang. The media even made Miss Garan's story
on me seem like a front to cover up my criminal activities.
The money I used to begin the renovations was made to
seem like it was my way of laundering drug proceeds, which
didn't make any sense. But I guess it didn't have to.

I guess I couldn't really blame Black people for their lack
of support. After all, I'm talking about the same people that
voluntarily fought on the frontlines of every war and revolution in American history in the name of freedom, when we
didn't even enjoy freedom in our own back yards.

In June, the month after I was arrested, the feds closed
the Ida B. down. A couple weeks later, Momma Smith died
of a heart attack. Now I was mad. Momma Smith hadn't
done anything but help people, and when that was taken
away, she died. Tears of anger ran down my face for days as I
grieved.

Momma Smith was the most caring and giving person I'd
ever met. She taught me to look at people without seeing
color. For that and so much more I would be forever grateful.

My situation reminded me of the time me and everyone
else just looked on as the cops beat up an innocent, retarded
Black man trying to sell fruit from his makeshift cart. Now it
seemed like none of my good deeds mattered enough for
Black folks to stand up. We were still sitting down and letting
the system continue to walk over us.

I couldn't blame my legal team. They did an excellent job. Although they proved the pigs suppressed evidence, coerced the testimony of alleged witnesses, and violated my civil rights, on February 17, 1975, nine months after I was arrested, I was found guilty.

A couple weeks later I was back in court for my sentencing hearing.

"Will the defendant please stand?" the judge said.

As I stood, I turned to look at Momma, who was sitting in the second row.

My eyes were saying, "I'm sorry," and hers seemed to say, "I understand." I just wished Solomon was here. I had so much to say to him.

It was hard to believe that I hadn't spoken to Solomon in nine years. And to this day, my biggest regret in life was turning my back on him when he left for Vietnam. Maybe that's why he turned his back on me.

"Moses King, will you please turn to face the bench?" the judge asked.

I bet if Solomon could've seen what I'd done at the Help Center he would've been proud.

"Moses Toussant King, I hereby sentence you to natural life without any eligibility for parole."

ACT 9
Truth Be Told
Solomon

Lord knows if I could change places with my baby brother, I would in a heartbeat. Eight years I spent in the Army, seven of them in foxholes, woods, and military installations over in Vietnam. Death was my bedmate, and I became accustomed to him chasing me every day. I dodged bullets, land mines, and disease, always one step ahead of death, and now death had me in check, as it held Moses in its grasp.

I didn't know what to do, so I did what I had done every day for the last six months, since threatened by the agents in the dark suits who stopped me at the airport.

"Dear God, forgive and guide me. Show me the way, show Moses the way, shine Your light on him in his moment of darkness, guide him to You," I prayed.

My whole life I'd been the cool head. The one who could and did handle everything. But now, I felt as if I'd let my family down. And it hurt like hell just thinking what Moses thought of me.

I had no idea what I could do for him now that he'd been convicted, but I knew that as a soldier in God's Army, no

man or government could defeat me. But first I had to build
that army. Then Jesus would show me how to knock down
the walls of Babylon that held Moses.

Every day, after my morning prayer, I sat in the small studio apartment I rented and wrote a letter to Moses. And
every day I vowed to one day give him the stamped and
sealed small pieces of my heart and soul.

During Moses' trial, I got accepted into the pastoral studies program at Loyola University.

Before long, I added studying and attending classes to my
daily regimen of reading my bible, speaking to Momma, and
writing Moses.

On weekends, I took the Word of God to the streets and
into the homes of anyone who would listen. I was a Black
Baptist Jehovah Witness, with the Bible as my Watchtower.

Gang hangouts, I didn't care if it was Moses' former gang
the Disciples or their rivals, the Gangster Gods, I was there
with my Bible. Poolhalls, outside of liquor stores, project
playgrounds, hospitals—I went anywhere and everywhere I
thought I could find folks that couldn't find God.

I never asked for money. Prostitutes, drug dealers, gang
members, and even winos just started to give. And I
promised them that every penny would be used to build a
place for them to go and worship.

And that's exactly what I did when I leased out the old
building that used to be the Ida B. Wells Community Help
Center.

In less than six months a miracle was achieved. No one
would've believed it unless they'd actually seen it for themselves. Winos, prostitutes, dealers, and gang members
helped me paint, clean, carpet, bring in pews, and do all the
needed renovations.

Six months later, the city gave us a permit and the nondenominational New Dimensions First Church of God opened its doors to the public in late fall 1976.

Ironically, my biggest benefactor was the leader of the Gangster Gods, a young Hispanic-looking man named Pablo Nkrumah. Accepting donations from the Disciples' enemy didn't bother me one bit. As far as I was concerned, both the Disciples and the Gangster Gods needed Jesus, and I'd be damned if I didn't try to bring Him to them.

At first he started giving me a couple hundred dollars. And over the next couple years, two hundred dollars turned into two thousand and sometimes more each week.

When I asked Pablo why he gave so much, he replied, "I'm just payin' rent to the Man upstairs, for my stay in His world."

I'd only had the opportunity to see and speak to Pablo three or four times, but during those times I noticed a worldly wisdom about him.

Most of the time when I came home from school or woke up in the morning, the money Pablo sent was in an envelope under my door. That confused me. It would have been so much easier for him to bring the money to the church.

I knew the money was dirty; most of the money I received was, but what mattered most was what I was doing with it.

Between school, the church, and my outreach to the streets weekend program, I didn't have time for much else.

In my third year at Loyola, I was given an assignment to do a research paper on the negative effects of the Islamic religion on American culture. At the time, the only thing I knew about Islam was it was a hate religion, and its followers, called Muslims, worshipped a pagan god they called Allah.

This research paper would be a breeze, I thought, and I had the whole semester to complete it. I was always the type, when given an assignment, to do it immediately; I'd never been a procrastinator.

So, the evening after Professor Adderly gave the assignment, I went to the school library and did some research on Islam. I found out the address of a mosque near the school.

The following afternoon, the first thing I noticed after entering this Islamic place of worship was that there were no church benches or chairs inside their worship area. It was just a large carpeted auditorium.

I waited in a hallway outside the worship area, while a barefooted black man went through some kind of prayer ritual on the green-carpeted floor.

Afterwards, we shook hands and made our introductions. Nazir Abdullah Shaheed was the head minister of the Mosque.

"Call me Imam, or Nazir," he instructed as we took a seat inside his small, cluttered office.

On his desk I was shocked to see a leather-bound Bible next to a matching book called a Koran.

I took off my backpack and pulled out my tape recorder, my notebook, and a black pen. "Do you mind if I record us?" I asked.

"By all means, go ahead," he said.

"Thank you." I crossed my legs. "Imam, this God Allah that you worship, can you tell me a little about Him?"

He smiled. "I believe you know Him well."

"No, sir. I've only heard of Him through media stories of Malcolm X and the Nation of Islam."

"Brother Solomon, the word Islam means submission to the will of God or Allah," he said in a soothing tone, "And a Muslim simply means one who submits to the will of one God." He paused and leaned over his desk.

"Okay." I nodded and took notes.

"So, if you have a man and that man believes in the one"— He pointed his index finger up in the air—"singular God, and he gets on his knees, and he prays to this God, and calls Him George, James, or Henry, do you not think that the all-knowing, all-understanding, Alpha and Omega does not recognize when someone's speaking to Him. Do you think God doesn't know whom that individual is addressing?"

"I don't know."

"Sure you do. The Bible speaks on God's knowledge, and His power being infinite. It speaks of God, the Father being all-knowing, all around us, and His influence being in everything. If this is true, then that means God is not relegated to one name. His identity is effervescent in everything and everyone."

An hour later, I walked out of the mosque a different person. The Imam made me re-think a lot of things; so much so that I went out and bought a Koran and read it for myself.

The Imam was right—both the Koran and the Bible were history books that had the same author.

Three months later I turned in my twelve-page research paper. I just knew I'd gotten an A. I put more into that paper than I had put into every paper combined that I'd written thus far.

At first, I was angry when the papers were given back and I'd received an 'F' as well as a half page of negative comments from Professor Adderly, questioning my faith.

After I'd completed my classes for the day, disappointed, upset, angry, and confused, I walked across the college campus towards the theology building.

I was right outside Professor Adderly's office, when something the Imam said popped into my mind.

"Religion is a divisive tool created by man," he said; "spirituality is God-made. For generations we've been trained in the ways of man, and the only way we can truly get back to what was ordained by God is if we unlearn the ways that man has taught us to worship."

I turned around and walked away, wondering if Moses would he have started the Disciples if he had met the Imam. But since it was hip being a member of a street gang like the Disciples or the Gangster Gods, it was up to me to make it hip to be a member of God's gang.

That meant I had to go to Momma's and borrow some of Moses' books on Black history.

ACT 10
Law's Reason
Moses

A week after the marshals transferred me from the county jail to the Atlanta Federal Penitentiary, I sat down in a corner of the prison law library after evening chow to read and begin answering some of my mail.

"Pssst! Pssst!"

I looked up to see this freckle-faced, light-skinned, afro-wearing brother beckoning me to come sit with him on the other side of the small library. Wondering what he wanted, I got up and walked over.

"Cop a squat, Youngblood. Let me bend your ear a minute."

"Lawrence Wahlberg. All the bloods call me Law. I like to refer to myself as Lawrence X."

"Moses King."

After I shook his hand and sat down, he began to tell me his life story. Why, I don't know, but it was sad and interesting to hear.

In 1940, Donovan Wahlberg, an outspoken young, White, Jewish, civil rights attorney was working out of the San

Francisco NAACP headquarters, where he met and fell in love with Evon Adams, a law student interning for the NAACP. A year later they married and had a son, Lawrence Donovan Wahlberg.

At the end of the decade, not long after the NAACP pressured President Truman into signing an executive order banning discrimination by the federal government, W.E.B. Du Bois asked Donovan to go to Montgomery, Alabama and head up a powerful group of legal minds to thwart Governor Wallace's attempts to ignore President Truman's referendum on desegregation.

Donovan was only too happy to have been chosen to harpoon the walrus, the hated Governor Wallace's nickname, in many circles.

In 1950, Donovan Wahlberg moved his beautiful coal-skinned attorney wife and their eight-year-old son from peace and love San Francisco to Jim Crow Montgomery, Alabama, with dreams of slaying the dragons of segregation, and spearheading an era where Colored folks could enjoy the same educational rights as their White counterparts.

Law's father, Donovan, so detested the system of White oppression that, as a juvenile growing up in an orphanage in Brooklyn, New York, he completely disassociated himself with anyone he thought was remotely racist. To him, what Whites were doing to Blacks in this country was akin to what the Germans did to the Jews in World War II. The difference was that the American government was the Black man's Hitler, and they had the ovens burning low and slow.

For the ten years Donovan and his family had been in Montgomery, he'd been the victim of fourteen cross burnings, five attempted kidnappings, seven beatings, and countless profane remarks. And after all this, he still fought the system with the same vigor and passion as when he'd first touched down on Montgomery soil. It was these reasons that the Blacks in Montgomery not only didn't see color when it came to Donovan, but the young Blacks nicknamed him White Daddy Warberg. Warberg instead of Wahlberg, because Donovan always seemed to be fighting for someone or something.

The love and trust from the city's and state's civil rights leaders, Baptist preachers, and Black residents is what kept the Wahlbergs in Alabama so long.

Lawrence was only sixteen, when he started organizing the young Blacks on the west side of Montgomery. At first, Donovan's son, the radical Afro-wearing Black Jewish kid started out to protect his mom and dad from the cross burners, but it grew to fighting anything White that didn't seem right that came on the Black side of town. The young gang of teenage boys called themselves the Warbirds.

In no time, the Warbirds became over a hundred strong, policing the streets, preventing Black blood from being shed. The Klan, The White Citizens Council, and several other White gangs had, at one time or another, felt the bats, bricks, and fists of the Warbirds.

Two years later, Montgomery was in an uproar. The townspeople wanted Black blood. Police harassment and beatings were at an all-time high, as were the beatings the police took in return.

Late one breezy, clear October night in 1960, responding to a tip he'd received earlier in the day, out of fear for his son's life, Donovan and his family packed up and left for Atlanta.

They were pulled over on Highway 85 and ticketed three times over a twenty-mile stretch, before getting off and taking the back roads out of Alabama. They were less than five miles from the Georgia state line, when yet again, flashing lights appeared in the rearview mirror of their ten-year-old Lincoln.

*   *   *

As Law sat in the law library recounting the story to me, it was almost as if I were there. It was as if I was feeling the anger, the pain, the helplessness. Law seemed to remember every single detail, as if it happened yesterday.

Suddenly gunfire erupted.

Law said his father shouted, "Everybody, down in your seats now!"

"Our Father who art in Heaven," his mother began.

"Pop, what are we gon' do?"

Glass was all over and around Law, as the rear window of his father's Lincoln shattered into a million pieces.

"Dear God in Heaven, the police are shooting at us," his mother shouted.

Donovan turned his head and grabbed his wife's hand. "We'll be across the state line in about thirty seconds."

As soon as Donovan focused his eyes back on the road, Law's mom let out a piercing scream, as a tire exploded and the Lincoln started spinning out of control and came to a stop in a wooded area, right off the dark road they were traveling on.

"Is everyone okay?" Donovan turned his head and asked.

Quiet "Yeahs" resounded from the wrecked Lincoln.

"Thank God, we're in Lagrange, Georgia," Donovan said.

A Montgomery patrolman shouted from outside the Lincoln, "Everybody, out the friggin' car. Now!"

"Johnny Boy, they're at least a mile into Georgia," another patrolman shouted.

"So what? You know who we got here!" the pot-bellied patrolman at the passenger-side car door said, his gun drawn.

"Nigger bitch, move!" the patrolman called Johnny Boy screamed, roughly grabbing a handful of Evon's hair and pulling her kicking and screaming body through the open window.

Donovan jumped out the driver's side, ran around the car,

and grabbed the officer, while Law climbed over his mother's shoulder and bit the cop's hand.

"Son of a friggin' gotdamn bitch!" Johnny Boy let go of her hair and fell to the ground, Donovan riding his back.

"POW!"

The sordid smell of gunpowder and blood filled the late-night air.

"Donovan!" Evon screamed in anguish. She crawled the rest of the way out of the window and fell onto the moist, cool, spring-evening ground.

After getting out of the car on the driver's side, Law was ushered to the other side of the car, on his knees, by Johnny Boy's shotgun-wielding partner.

"Boy, I hope your dogs don't have rabies." Johnny Boy circled a bloody Donovan lying on the ground, struggling to get to his knees.

"Please, sir, my husband needs an ambulance," Law's mother cried.

Her pleas seemed to excite Johnny Boy.

"Ahhgg!" Donovan writhed in pain, when Johnny Boy kicked him in the stomach, forcing him back on the ground.

"Yep, he needs an ambulance all right. Whachu think, Bobby?"

His partner shook his head. "Let's just go, Johnny."

"In a minute."

"You cracker racist pig!" Law lunged at Johnny Boy.

For the second time the night exploded with a single gunshot.

Law screamed, as he grabbed his bleeding shoulder.

"You need to keep this one on a leash."

Donovan somehow managed to lurch forward at the patrolman holding the smoking gun.

Johnny Boy stepped forward and slammed the butt of his pistol into Donovan's head.

Feminine screams pierced the air.

"Gotdamn it, Bobby! Shoot that rabid mutt nigger!" Johnny pointed to Lawrence as he lay on the ground still holding his bleeding shoulder.

"No." He shook his head. "I won't do it. I'll do a lot of things, but I won't kill innocent people. Johnny Boy, you can come with me right now, or I'll leave your ass!" Bobby started backing up and seemed about to turn and go.

Evon held her legs to her chest, rocking back and forth in front of the deflated front tire on the passenger's side of the wrecked Lincoln.

Johnny Boy turned and began walking toward his partner. "Innocent people?—They're not people." Johnny Boy pointed back at Law's family. "This here Jew, commie, bastard lawyer and his nigger mutt is the reason the niggers on the Westside, from Broad to Central, done lost their friggin' minds. They're the reason my nephew is sittin' home with twenty-seven friggin' stitches in his head."

"I hear you, Johnny Boy, but we are officers of the law. We can't just go and kill these niggers in cold blood."

Pow! Pow! Pow!

Bobby was dead before he hit the ground in front of Law.

"Friggin' nigger-lovin' loser!" Johnny Boy spat a glob of snuff on his dead partner. Then he snatched Bobby's revolver out of his holster and grabbed the shotgun he'd been wielding.

Donovan was coughing up blood as he struggled to crawl over to his wife. Johnny Boy stepped on his back and unloaded shotgun fire into the back of his head.

"Noooooooo!" Law screamed and reached out.

Law's mother didn't flinch. She just kept rocking to a rhythm that only she could hear.

Next, Johnny Boy stepped towards Lawrence.

"Shoot me, Satan." Law leaned up against the Lincoln, holding his wounded shoulder.

"No, boy," Johnny Boy said. "I got big plans for you."

Law winced in agony as Johnny Boy jerked his arm from his shoulder and slammed a set of cuffs on one wrist, then the other.

Law's mother was still in the same place, rocking to her own rhythm, in her own world, far removed from this one.

Johnny Boy walked over to Evon, bent down, and began to place another set of cuffs on her. She hawked and spat in his face.

He then took out a handkerchief and casually wiped his face. Next, he slowly turned his shotgun so the butt was aimed at her head and violently jack-hammered the gun butt into her face until she lost consciousness.

"Damn, boy! I'm friggin' winded, and this nigger bitch done made my water rise." He unzipped his pants and stood over Law's mother.

Lawrence refused to let a tear escape his head as he sat on his knees, hands cuffed behind his back, and watched his father's murderer urinate on his mother's head.

Law told me, "From then on, everything was a blur, until the trial six months later."

Law's mother was in an asylum, while he stood trial for assault, and the murder of a Montgomery, Alabama police officer.

Not only was the courtroom standing room only, but the streets outside were packed with protesters. Blacks were demanding justice; Whites were demanding blood. The National Guard was trying to contain the mobs on the courtyard steps and in the streets.

During the two weeks the trail lasted, Law's defense team shot a donut shop full of holes in the government's case. Pictures of the fractured skull, cracked ribs, and the multiple bruises Law's mother suffered at the hands of Johnny Boy drew gasps from the crowded courtroom.

When Law's defense team requested a mistrial on the

grounds of the disappearance of key evidence, such as fin-gerprint molds, and the butt of the gun used to beat Law's mother, the judge refused.

And although Johnny Boy had perjured himself more than once on the stand, twelve tobacco-chewin' "Betty Maes and Billy Rays" still found him guilty.

On August 8, 1960 (I was six years old then) Lawrence Donovan Wahlberg was sentenced to life without parole for the murder of Officer Robert 'Bobby' Dupree Shaw.

ACT 11
Understanding the Game
Moses

I nodded my head. "That's some heavy shit."

"Hold on, Youngblood." He stuck his arm out and leaned in. "Peep game—I'm telling you this 'cause we got the same story."

"How you know my story?"

"Come on, your trial was in the papers. Besides, there's a lot of cats in here from Chi-town. If you get convicted on a federal beef in Chi, yo' either go to the pen in Terre Haute, Indiana, Marion, Illinois, or you come here."

"I don't see why I was brought all the way to Atlanta, when there were two penitentiaries closer to home."

"Think about it, Youngblood—You had too much of an influence in Chicago; the feds wanted to get you far away from the city."

"Okay, so what does your life story have to do with me?" I asked.

"I was just showing you that I could relate to what you're going through."

I shook my head. "You don't understand. I'm not active in the Disciples. Yeah, I started the gang, for the same purposes that you started yours, but I was away from that for two years prior to getting jammed up."

"That's a moot point, Youngblood. Bottom-line is—now correct me, if I'm wrong—I didn't kill no cop, and I don't think you killed that congressman. Am I right so far?"

"Yeah."

"You and me are very passionate about civil rights. We both come from the streets, we both led young men into battle, and we both have a life sentence."

"Okay, I agree. So where are you going with all this?"

"It ain't where I'm goin', Youngblood." He pointed a finger at me. "It's where you goin'."

"I'm not followin' you."

"I hope the hell not. You see, my past is your future, if we don't pull together and do something about it."

"You ain't makin' sense, Law."

"If I'm not, it's because you ain't listenin'. Just here me out, Youngblood."

"Go 'head."

"While I been in here, I done got my high-school diploma, and I've earned a doctorate in jurisprudence—I know my shit.

"In the fifteen years I been in this hell I done been paid well for my services. I've gotten twenty, thirty inmate cases overturned. And with much less evidence of corruption than in my case. But when it comes to my case the appeals courts always say the same thing, 'Denied.' "

"Excuse the interruption, but check this." I scooted my chair up. "I got the best legal team outta Chicago working on my appeal, and it looks good, so if you tellin' me all this to solicit my business—"

"Understand this, Youngblood. First, I don't need your bi'ness. Second, I'm try'na pull your young-ass coat to the game." He paused. "These cats make the rules, break the rules, and change the rules, and while they gangsterize the system, you can't do a damn thing, but be a victim to your own ignorance."

"That's what I'm payin'—"

Law waved a hand in front of him. "Ho-ho-hold on, let me finish. Youngblood, I had the whole muthafuckin' freedom-fightin', we-shall-overcome, N double A damn CP, behind me, but when it came down to it, it was about two things—money and power. And no one has more of either than Uncle muthafuckin' Sam. No disrespect, Youngblood, but your attorneys are nothing but high-priced paper-pushers.

"Youngblood, we wasn't sentenced to life for murder. We was sentenced to life 'cause mighty Pharaoh thought we had a good chance of freeing the slaves. See, Youngblood, without an enslaved mind"—He put his hand to his temple—"There can be no slave master."

I nodded.

"What I'm sayin' is, I done wasted fifteen years fighting a hypocritical ghost that doesn't understand nothin' but money and power." He shook his head. "I don't want you to travel the road I have—that's why I'm pullin' your coat to the game."

"Okay, so what do you suggest?"

"Revolution."

"I don't know what kind of revolution we can start from a prison cell."

"Revolution begins with a thought." He put a finger to the side of his head. "And revolution is the only way we will get out of here, and it's the only way our people will stand a chance."

"So what's your play?"

"The Disciples, Youngblood—that's the play."

"Come again?"

"The Disciples," he repeated.

"I told you that I'm not running things anymore."

Law just looked at me.

"And if I were or had any influence over them, what could I do from in here?"

"Nothing without any start-up capital. Every successful revolution is expensive."

I was just about to speak, when he said, "Hold on now, Youngblood, 'fore you say anything. I have a way to turn a little money into enough money to finance an entire revolution."

"I hope you ain't talking 'bout no Nat Turner-like revolution."

"No, Youngblood, that was a rebellion. I ain't talkin' 'bout anything like that; I'm talking 'bout mental emancipation." Law smiled. "That penny-ante shit, like hijackin' and runnin' numbers, is slow money. I have a way that we can make millions in a few years. Millions is what we are going to need to overturn the system that got us in here."

"Count time. Count time in ten minutes. All inmates back to your cells," a voice boomed over the intercom.

As I stood to leave, Law picked up two books from the floor beside him. "Youngblood, if you interested, we'll finish this conversation after you read these."

"I've already read Sun Tzu's *The Art of War.*"

"Read it again, but before you do, I want you to read this one."

"*Pawns in the Game?*"

"Yes, a racist white naval intelligence officer wrote this in the late '50s. It will explain how, why, and what for every major revolution in history was fought. And after you understand this you can read *The Art of War* and get a completely different understanding of it."

Thirty minutes later, back in my cell, I was lying on my bottom bunk, when I heard a guard call out, "Inmate King."

I jumped up and ran out of my cell. I hoped it was another letter from Billy from the Ida B., or one of the other kids I'd mentored. A few of my kids had been writing me since I first got locked up almost a year ago.

"Yes, that's me," I shouted in the guard's direction.

The guard threw a letter my way.

After picking it up, I walked back inside my cell. Rhythm Azure was the name on the front of the letter. I don't know anyone by that name.

Greetings King,

My name is Rhythm Azure. I'm a second-year law student at Howard University. My roommate, Nancy Stevens, from Chicago, told me all about you, the Ida B. Wells Help Center, and what you were doing for the poverty-torn South Side community of Chicago.

After all the positive energy you were bringing to the people in your community, I have trouble processing why a man such as yourself would kill and rape. It just didn't make sense to me, so I did some research and ordered a copy of your case from the Federal building in Chicago.

After receiving and reading your court transcripts, it is evident to me that you should have been found not guilty.

Please, I hope this question doesn't offend you, and I have no way of knowing if you are lying or not—did you do what they say you did?

I am sending you twenty dollars and a stamped envelope. Please write me back.

Rhythm

P.S. And if you're wondering why I went through so much trouble for someone I don't even know, all I can say is, this is who I am.

ACT 12
Letter of the Day
Moses

This woman, Rhythm, was bold. If I had really raped or killed anyone, what makes her think I would admit to it? Maybe someone inside the FBI wrote the letter and wanted to see how I'd respond. It just didn't make sense for her, whoever she was, to write me and send me twenty dollars.

Then again, she could've been one of those lonely, lookin'-for-a-man-anywhere-they-can sistahs, I don't know. What I did know is that she, or whoever wrote the letter, piqued my interest.

I had to stay focused on getting back what was taken away from me. This woman Rhythm may be just what I need to help me move forward.

Ms. Azure,

I hope this letter finds you in good health and spirits. I noticed in your greeting you referred to me as king, instead of Moses King. I don't know if that was an error, but I like it. Anyway, I want to first thank you for the financial gesture, but it wasn't necessary. I am well taken care of. And, no, I did not kill nor rape anyone. I was framed. At first I thought it was the

Chicago PD, but after vibing with a brotha in here, I have come to the conclusion that they were just pawns in the feds' game to rid society of a Black man perceived as a threat to the socio-consciousness of society.

Have you heard of George Jackson? If not, please read Blood in My Eye *and* Soledad Brother. *This brother was killed by the system for no other reason than he was a voice with independent thoughts, and had a plan that did not coincide with capitalistic Amerikkka. And I spell Amerikkka with three K's because we're governed by and ruled by a KKK-like system. In brother George Jackson's own words, "Nothing is more dangerous to a system that depends on misinformation, than a voice that obeys its own dictates and has the courage to speak out."*

His imprisonment and further isolation within the prison system was clearly a function of the state's response to his outspoken opposition to the capitalist structure.

With all that said, I want to know why you are so interested in me and my problems. You know so much about me, but I know nothing of you.

Moses King

P.S. Don't write anything that you don't want others to read. The guards open all prison mail, and I'm sure all of my mail is closely scrutinized.

A week later I received a second letter.

Greetings King,

I start my letters off with King, because kings and queens are where we came from and that's who we are. Unfortunately due to what I call niggerization, not only do we not know this, but a large majority of us in America act like the animals that we are called.

Secondly, King, your unjust incarceration is not just your problem, it's our problem. Anytime a freedom fighter for our people is shot down, it's the responsibility of the people he fights for to restore him back to his original fighting position, or as close to it as possible.

King, I grew up in suburbia, East Elmhurst, Queens, New York, with my twin sister and a younger stepsister. My mother is a history teacher and a theologian. My stepfather works for the New York City Department of Sanitation as a garbageman.

He had me and my sisters reading books at six years old. Every night at dinner we had to give an account of what we were reading. While my sisters read comics and novels, I read my father's books on civil rights, slavery, struggle, and ancient African civilizations.

These books fascinated me so, because I was learning things that were totally opposite of what I was being taught in school. As a matter of fact, most of what I was reading contradicted what the teachers taught.

I was a smart child. I never wanted for anything; my daddy made sure of that, which frustrated my strict disciplinarian mother. My stepdad was, and is, the greatest man to ever live.

On Saturday mornings, instead of watching cartoons, he took me and my sisters into Bed-Stuy, Brooklyn, to a soup kitchen, where we fed and ate with the homeless. Daddy never wanted us to forget who we were and where we came from.

He raised us to look at all Black people as family. And if they were poor and wanting, then we were as well.

At around eleven, I started to rebel in the majority-White school I attended. I was tired of sitting in class and listening to the lies the teachers were teaching. I had to speak out, when the teacher tried teaching that Christopher Columbus discovered America.

Now did that really make sense? I asked. How could a man discover a place where people were already living? Wouldn't one of their ancestors be the ones likely to have discovered America? I mean, if he discovered America, then I'll just go to

England and take credit for discovering England, since I've never been there.

After that particular outburst, the class broke out laughing, and I got suspended from school.

One time, I embarrassed one teacher so bad that she ran out of the classroom in tears.

I raised my hand so much to refute what the teachers were teaching that they started ignoring me. I just refused to sit in a class where the teachers were reading from books that told half-truths, and whole lies. The White kids hated me, thinking I was prejudiced, and the Blacks hated me, thinking that I was a know-it-all.

My mother scolded me time and again, but my father encouraged me to keep learning and keep exploding the myths that the schools were teaching.

Although I grew up in a Christian household, my family sent me away to a private Muslim school after I was expelled from public school in the sixth grade. My father felt it was best to send me somewhere that was dedicated to raising the awareness in our children by focusing on our story instead of history. The Malcolm X School of Arts and Understanding did just that.

As I grew in knowledge and age, I felt that Jim Crow was successful because there wasn't enough of us qualified to force change in the "just-them" judicial system. So I decided to become an attorney to help make the difference that was so needed.

So, you see, that is why I've taken an interest in you. I can't let them keep you away from us. You are in want, which makes me be in want, and I don't need to be in want. And I've never been one to let anything be taken from me without a fight.

When I become an attorney, I am going to see that somehow your case is overturned, if it hasn't already been.

Moses, you are what Black people need—a person for whom

to fight for and fight with. One who genuinely wants and has
tried to make a difference.

My whole name is Aja Rhythm Azure. Aja means high
priestess in Swahili, and Rhythm is poetry in motion. I've been
taught that parents make a big mistake naming their children
something that sounds good or after a relative. Most times
what sounds good only does because of the slave mentality that
we harbor in our minds. And that relative's name most likely
originated from someone who meant for us to be used as not
much more than farm animals. Everyone should have a name
that identifies their individuality. Until next time, keep seek-
ing, keep dreaming, and keep your eyes on the prize and your
head in the clouds.

Rhythm

ACT 13
West African Archie
Picasso

T-Hunt tried his damnedest to discourage me. "Picasso, we need you. Don't leave us now that Moses is gone," he said.

Fuck that! I had to get paid, and that hijackin' shit and running numbers was too dangerous and too slow.

I was down with the Black thing, like the next man, but watching Black folks turn on Moses showed me that the Black thing wasn't down with me, unless I had money to fight the hate that was being spread.

Black, White, whatever, people didn't respect nothin' but money, and if I was gon' get Black folks to hear what I was sayin', I had to have a lot of it.

When I broke away from the Disciples, I had close to thirty G's, and forty soldiers that I brought with me to form the Gangsta Gods. I collected another twenty G's from my soldiers.

With fifty G's and a dream, I went to New York last year in '75. I figured, if I dropped my pop's name in the right circle, I would get a bite. Although he'd been dead for almost ten years, folks always remembered the crazy, flamboyant ones.

Besides standing out in a crowd with his panther-dark complexion, basketball-player height, and the colorful suits he wore, Pops was one of the most ruthless killas for West-African Archie.

West-African Archie wasn't a man, but a strict militaristic organization of heroin dealers. Archie imported China white, the purest form of heroin from off the west coast of Africa. This was the kind of connect I needed to get my money right and make the Gangsta Gods a force to be reckoned with.

It was a smoking-hot Harlem June. There were vendors and thieves trying to sell a little of everything on 125th street. For two days, I walked those streets, going into bars, pool halls, and after-hour spots, dropping my pop's name, trying to make a connect with West-African Archie. I knew the organization was still in business, by some of the "don't-ask" looks I received after inquiring at a couple bars I went into.

It was Friday night. I'd been in town for three days, without any luck. I was just sitting in my hotel room, depressed, when I decided to get jazzed up and hit the Cotton Club.

Smoke was everywhere, and the music was blasting when I walked through the door.

"Say, Red, can I run my fingers through that black silk you got tied in a horsetail?" some rotten-tooth, spaced-out, drug-addicted-looking broad asked.

I smiled. "Nah, sweetie. I'm looking for someone." I took in the whole smoky club scene.

"Shit! Suga', you just found her. For your tall, red ass, I'll even give you a discount." She puffed on a cigarette and rubbed her bright red nails down my arm.

I turned to face her. "Baby, unless you can lead me to West-African Archie, you can't do nothin' for me."

I walked closer to the stage, where this black-ass, skinny negro with long hair was blowin' a horn, be-boppin' his ass off. And this other cat had his cheeks puffed out like a blow-fish. I mean, he was playin' this trumpet like a boss pimp playin' a two-dollar 'ho'.

I pull some cat to the side. "Yo, who dat, god?"

"Miles Davis and Dizzy Gillespie."

I didn't know too much about jazz, but I was feeling it. I didn't drink, and didn't have no bud. I wanted to get mellow, so I ordered a grapefruit juice and gin.

While sipping on my glass, I was checkin' out the squares. The whole crayon box was represented by the colors of the threads folks were kickin'.

As I scoped the place, checkin' out the finest sistahs on this side of heaven, I peeped these two sistahs down at the end of the bar. They was all right—dressed nice, big-ass tit-ties, slim and shit; I'd say they were anywhere from a size six to a size eight.

I grabbed my glass and made my way down to where they sat. "How you ladies this evening?"

"We're fine, thank you," one of the broads politely said, brushing me off.

I was wearin' my "Mr. Sparkle" smile, when I pulled out a fist-thick wad of bills and told the bartender to give the women another of whatever they were drinking.

The brush-off broad's eyes got so big, I thought they was 'bout to drop off in my glass. She was sweatin' my wad just like a trick.

Her friend asked, "You ain't from around here, are you, sweetie?"

"Naw, baby, I'm from Chi-town."

"What you doin' so far from home, baby?"

"Baby doll, wherever I lay my head is home. The world is my playground. I'm just lookin' for some playmates to play with, ya dig."

"Oh really."

"Really, really. You wanna play?" I asked her.

"We're together," the brush-off broad said, caressing the other's shoulder.

"I can dig it."

"I mean . . . we're lovers."

"Double the fun, double the pleasure," I said.

The other asked, "You willin' to pay?"

"I wouldn't have it no other way." I licked my lips and wondered if all the hookers in Harlem hung out at Cotton.

"Three bills and you get to experience pleasure heaven," the brush-off broad said.

Damn, did all the working women use the same heaven line too?

"For three C's I betta go to heaven first-class and get some coochie coupons to boot."

The girls burst out laughin'.

"Rico . . . over here," one of the girls called out to the bartender.

After the bartender walked up, the brush-off broad said, "Give the man two grams of that boss coke."

After I slid the bartender a C-note, we jetted.

When we got back to my suite, it was off and poppin'. The broads were snortin' blow off each other's nipples.

Next thing I know, one broad had the other's legs in the air, while she stood on the side of the bed, still wearing her two-inch heels. I was thinkin' the broad was gon' suffocate if she didn't come up for air soon. She was lippin' and lappin', slurp-slurpin', just suckin' and lickin' away on the other.

The broad on the receiving end had her head tilted back, one hand on the bed one hand on the other broad's head, moanin' like a trapped ghost.

"Fuck this!" I stripped and walked up behind the cat-lickin' broad. Taking both my hands, I grabbed the broad's ass, spread her cheeks, and eased my johnson between them half-moons.

She moaned.

I started pumping slowly at first.

She came up for air from the bush she had her lips and tongue gorged in.

"Fuck me, daddy," she said, between moans.

As I grip-grabbed her cheeks and started wearin' that ass out, the other broad slid from up under her girlfriend, eased up behind me, and started lickin' my balls.

KNOCK! KNOCK! KNOCK!

"Shit!" I jumped up and grabbed my gun from under the mattress.

The girls froze.

"Who?" I shouted at the closed door.

"I tink you lookin' fo' me," some cat said in a baritone foreign accent.

"Gimme a minute."

"Get dressed, ladies—the party's over." I grabbed my pants, reached in a pocket, and peeled off three hundred-dollar bills.

Only a couple minutes went by before I ushered the ladies out of the room and let this Louis Armstrong-looking cat in. He was clean as the board of health, but he was damn near a midget.

He said, "So, you da son of Chaka? I seen you not since you was a little watoto. Whachu' come diggin' up old graves for, boy?"

"I got warrior Senegalese blood flowing through my veins. I can own Chicago. I just need a connect on some H."

"What make you tink I gon' help you, boy? What makes you tink I can?"

"I'm Chaka Nkrumah's son. I got fifty grand, I got an army ready to die for me, and . . . I can make you a boatload of money."

"I'll say dese fo' you. You got confidence like yo' fada. A ca' will pick you up at eleven in da mo'ning. Dere will be a bag in da trunk wit' tree kilos of heroin in it. Da driver will drop you off at Grand Central Station. You will go back to Chicago on da next ting smokin'. I'll give you sixty days to get me tree hundred fitty tousand dollars. If you should not comply, you will die."

"How do I get in touch with you, when I'm ready to re-up?"

"Da driver will tell you before you get out da car," he explained. Then, while leaving the room, he added, "One more ting—give da fifty tousand to da driver. Good luck, son of Chaka."

ACT 14
The Other White Powder
Moses

Inmates were released to chow by dorms, usually on an honor system based on how clean the dorms and cells were during the weekly inspection by the warden or captain.

Meals were served in a gymnasium-sized building set up like a school cafeteria. The only thing that rang true in the movies I used to see about prison, was the way the chow hall was set up.

As I walked through the chow line, I thought about those television movies I'd seen and horror stories I'd read about prison. Most of these were so far from reality; they were fantasy.

Prison was bad. I mean real bad, but convicts had this respect thing going on. You didn't "play the dozens," and you stepped on no one's toes, unless you were ready for war. Prison rapes, yeah, they went on, but not like I'd thought.

It was White cats, especially a group called the Aryan Brotherhood, who were the most brutal in prison. They beat, extorted, and raped the weak White boys, who they called "fresh fish."

They didn't bother the brothas because, unlike on the outside, in prison, brothas ruled. It made sense; we outnumbered everyone else by at least three to one.

Most cons clicked up for protection. The strongest clicks were the religious ones. Among these, the Nation of Islam wielded the most respect and power. These brothers were polished like a chrome chain. You could always tell who was in The Nation by their black-mirror, spit-shined, prison-issue steel toes, their crisply creased prison-issue greens, the shirts buttoned up to "choke level," and their clean-shaven faces.

To say that they were disciplined was an understatement to describe the members of the Nation of Islam. Their teachings were thought-provoking. I could feel where they were coming from, and I could see where they were trying to go. But I had to travel my own yellow brick road to find my own wizard.

And the guards, if it weren't for their uniforms, you wouldn't be able to distinguish them from the inmates. They didn't bother those who paid to be left alone. And anything you could get on the street—coke, H, weed, or a Big Mac—if you were willing to pay the price, there was always a guard who was more than willing to bring it in.

I'd been in a month before I saw the first fight. The same day a young brotha was brought into the pen, he stabbed a rival gang member to death with a filed-down spoon handle.

During that month, I'd also been approached by a few brothas wanting me to either join their gang or start one of my own. And they even seemed to get upset when I turned them down. The leader of the Ball Bangers, Gray "Pork Chop" Jones, wanted to take a run at me, and would have, if Law hadn't stepped in.

It was rumored that Law had cut a man's throat with a sheet of paper and had put a man's eye out with a paper clip a while back.

I never asked him about it; it wasn't my business. What

mattered was what he did today. Yesterday was what it was. I was just trying to make it to tomorrow.

I didn't know what he was like back then, but now Law was a street-preaching, godfather-Black-nationalist, jailhouse lawyer. It was an event, when Law held court on the rec yard. He attracted so many cons that the guards always dispersed the crowd after about fifteen minutes.

We'd be out in front of the library building, on the side of the quarter-mile dirt track that surrounded the prison vegetable garden. Cons, old and young, would be standing around or sitting on the old rusted-out bleachers.

Law would have one leg on the first step of the bleachers, when he began speaking passionately about anything and everything. And everyone listened just as passionately.

It's like Law had the souls of Black folks in his mouth, and when he released words, he released their souls. He spoke of everything, from dirt to destiny. He explained the connection that everything had to everything. He talked of history being the foundation of all our beliefs and how the acts of our past control our future actions.

While he spoke, brothers started to reply in-between his thoughts, saying, "That's law."

A couple months later, Law had his hands clasped behind his back as we walked around the quarter-mile asphalt prison track.

"Sorry it took so long for me to get the books back to you," I said.

"So what did you think?"

"The international banking system, how it was started and how every revolution was financed by the World Bank, and even instigated by bankers was deep."

Law took off his glasses and wiped the lenses off on his T-shirt. "Did you see *The Art of War* a little differently after reading *Pawns in the Game?*"

"Much differently. I mean, the premise that I originally saw was the same, but now I understand that my methods to achieve freedom for my people were futile."

"You didn't need a book to see that; you can just look at how much you thought you were doing in the streets and how suddenly the powers-that-be crushed you like an ant."

"Rhythm and I have discussed that in our letters."

"You've been corresponding with her pretty frequently?"

"Yeah, it's crazy. It's only been six weeks since we've been writing each other, and it's like we've known each other a lifetime. Enough about her—Are you gon' finally tell about this revolution you've been talkin' about?"

We were coming around the track for the sixth time.

"You think you ready?"

"Ready for what?"

"Armageddon. And I'm not talking about the one in the book of Revelations. I'm talking about getting back out there in the trenches with the Disciples and preparing them and yourself for pull-out-all-stops-anything-goes-no-limit-sacrifice-or-die Armageddon."

"If I understood what you were talking about, I might agree, but if you haven't noticed, I'm locked up behind these walls for life."

"That's what I'm talkin' 'bout." He pointed to his temple. "Restructure your thinking, Moses. I keep tellin' you this— no one can lock you up but you, Youngblood. You have to run the Disciple through your buddy—what's his name?" He snapped his fingers.

"T-Hunt?"

"Yeah. You told me he was, what you call it, King of kings, leader of the Disciples. And the other young brother, Picasso . . . from what you've told me about him, it sounds like between him and T-Hunt we can make this thing happen."

"T-Hunt, maybe, but not Picasso. When I got arrested,

around forty Disciples followed Picasso to start up a gang of his own."

"You can't reach this Picasso character through an intermediary?"

"I probably could, but the young brotha is a stick of dynamite waiting to explode. From my understanding, he doesn't wanna have anything to do with me or the Disciples."

"After all you said you've done for him? I don't understand."

"Me neither. He was bitter about not being elected King of kings. He wanted to take the Disciples in a different direction, and T-Hunt wasn't having it."

"That's too bad, Youngblood. But anyway, as I was saying, from inside these walls I'll help you get the Disciples ready for Armageddon of the mind."

"What do you get outta all this?"

"Freedom, Youngblood—that's what my father died trying to obtain. Carrying on his work and succeeding is my revenge, my retribution, so to say, for everything that the 'injustice system' took from me—that's what I get."

"I hear you."

"But do you feel me? Do you really feel the vibe that I'm kicking to you, Youngblood? I'm talkin' about the freedom that understanding, and acting on knowledge gives you."

"That's why I started the Disciples. And that's why I left the Disciples."

"That's exactly what I wanted to hear. Now, the first thing we gon' do is get rid of the identity that the oppressor beat your ancestors into accepting. I'm talkin' 'bout the name, Youngblood—Moses King. Yeah, you a king, baby, but not the king they want you to be."

"You sound like Rhythm," I told him.

"I call myself Lawrence X, because the X represents the unknown, and my identity will remain unknown, until I emancipate my body from these walls. That is when I will legally change my name to Lawrence One Free. I am but one part of a whole, but that one part is free. And I would like everyone in your Disciple family"—He stabbed me in the side with a finger—"including you, to represent the family by taking on the last name One Free.

One Free sounded good, but how realistic was a mass name change?

"A family should share the same name, don't you agree, Youngblood?"

Before I could answer, Law added, "Imagine a million brothers and sisters named One Free—That's one million votes—Now beat that kind of power."

"That's real, and I feel you. But you know as well as I do that we'd be lucky if we could get three Black folks to change their names. I can hear Black folks now, 'My daddy's name was Jackson, and his daddy's name was Jackson. Ain't no White man gon' hire me with a name like One Free.'"

"Shit! You be surprised. Maybe the over-thirty crowd workin' on master's plantation, too scared to risk they retirement, will say that. But you and this T-Hunt, y'all got the ear of the youth, Youngblood. You got the Disciples."

"I don't know."

"C'mon, Youngblood. You don't sound like the same brotha that went broke to renovate a building so kids could have a positive outlet. You don't sound like the same brotha who started cultural book clubs for youth around the city. Remember why you did all that?"

"Yeah, I remember."

"You believed in Black folks. You believed in the concept of freedom. Don't stop believing. The freedom door is locked, and we hold the key. It's up to you and me, Youngblood. I'll play my role. I'll be the Black John the Baptist, and you be the Black Jesus our people been waitin' for."

"I still don't see how we can start this from in here," I said.

"One word, Youngblood—Capitalism with a capital C. To defeat a beast, you have to become a beast."

I shook my head. "I'm confused."

"The beast that big business and the US government represent."

"Say again?"

"Okay, you heard of Willie Lynch, right?"

"Yeah, that's the White dude who came to America during slavery and explained to plantation owners how to control the slaves by dividing them by belief, skin color, size, and so on."

"Exactly."

"Okay. So what does that have to do with our mission?"

"Everything. We become capitalist, with the goal of rising to the top of big business and owning a large market share of the product that we came to this country to develop."

"Land?"

"Yes. We set ourselves up to buy, develop and re-develop land. Because land is a precious commodity that cannot be replicated or duplicated, once it runs out, it's gone."

I nodded in affirmation.

"No one should know our motivation, until we start to move in the direction of revolution," Law explained.

"So how do we begin to raise the type of money to finance something of this magnitude?"

Law smiled. "The Kennedy way."

"Huh?"

"'The Kennedy way.' JFK coulda never become the first Catholic president if it weren't for his daddy and grand-daddy's illegal drug business. The Kennedy fortune was built on running alcohol during prohibition. That money, aligned with political allies, positioned him for the presidency. We'll do the same.

"Only thing is, instead of whiskey, we'll be running H. The

Disciples are large enough to control the drug game in Northern Illinois and Milwaukee. I'm talking about millions, billions of dollars over a ten-, twelve-year grind."

"Heroin? Black man, have you lost your mind?" I turned and was about to walk off the track.

Law grabbed my arm.

Before my reflexes came into action, I saw something in his eyes that saved his nose from being broken.

"Gotdamn, Youngblood! Let me tell you somethin'—if a negro start shootin', snortin', or smokin' H, they weak from the git-go, and we don't need nothin' but soldiers in the revolution.

"You read *The Art of War* and *Pawns in the Game.* You know that dynasties are built on the backs of the ignorant and oppressed. You know that in every war casualties and sacrifices are the means to the end that warriors seek."

Without another word, I turned and walked off the track, upset and confused.

Picasso had tried to present a similar argument before I got popped. Listening to Picasso's argument for getting involved in the drug game, I didn't know if he was a Five-Percenter or a Marxist. But, whatever the case, from what I understood, his gang, the Gangsta Gods, was slowly taking over the drug game in Chicago.

Did that mean Picasso was on his way to freeing the minds of the oppressed, or was he killing the vision of freedom before others could see it?

Would I be doing the same by getting involved with the sale of drugs? Would I be a slave master or an entrepreneur?

ACT 15
Soul-Searching
Moses

I still couldn't believe Law wanted me to flood the Black community with more drugs. I grew up wanting to be Martin Luther King and Malcolm X. I started the Disciples to stop the killing, not perpetuate it. How could Law even think I would even entertain the idea of selling heroin?

The cell house dorm was quiet, except for the snoring sounds from inmates in other cells.

I started thinking about everything Law said earlier that day. And when I thought about it, whether I liked it or not, he was right. Every dynasty was built off the backs of the poor and the weak. Still that didn't make it right.

Over the next several months, Law and I remained cool, but for the most part, we just spoke to each other in passing.

Rhythm and I continued writing, sharing our innermost secrets, dreams, and fears. She knew all about the way I grew up, how my brother had alienated me, and how I resented it. Other than writing and reading her letters, I continued reading everything I could get my hands on about civilizations and culture.

Once a month I was called out to the visiting room, and

each time I silently hoped that it would be Rhythm, although I knew that was virtually impossible.

Rhythm had been arrested and convicted of resisting arrest and assaulting a police officer at a Black Panther freedom rally in New York a few years ago as a senior in high school. She served ninety days for spitting in a cop's face, but the worst part was that for the rest of her life she'd be a convicted felon. That meant she wouldn't be approved by the prison system to come visit me.

But every month, without fail, T-Hunt's girl, Xena, came to see me and kept me abreast of what was going on with T-Hunt and the Disciples. Most times she brought Zion, her and T-Hunt's two-year-old son. Xena was like a little sister to me. That's why I didn't have any problem telling her about Law and what he proposed.

I was surprised, when Xena told me that she agreed with Law's reasoning. T-Hunt was just as confused as I was. This was what led me on a year-long soul-searching journey.

I smiled as I thought of what Law had told me almost a year ago.

"Trust me, Youngblood, you'll begin to understand once you read *The Art of War, Pawns in the Game,* and a few more books I'll pull your coat to. Take your time. No rush. We can discuss them as you go."

Over the last few months we'd slowly started hanging again. I had way too many questions, and since the books I read didn't provide the answers, I reached out to him.

So, every day Law and I met on the rec yard, and in the prison library, discussing the books I was reading and the way I was starting to think. He never once brought up the subject of selling drugs.

Law was right. My appeal had been denied. The funny thing was that I wasn't discouraged in the least. I was too busy reading, growing, and falling in love.

A year had passed, with Law not even once bringing our discussion about getting the Disciples involved with selling drugs. One winter morning, Law was sitting on his bottom bunk, waiting for the work call announcement, and I was sitting at the metal desk in his cell.

"Man, let's do this. I've talked to T-Hunt, through his girl, of course, and uh"—I nodded—"we're ready; I'm ready."

"You say you ready, and I know that you know. But do you understand what you know, and the power that the knowledge you have represents?"

I was used to his play on words now. So used to them that I even understood what he was saying. I no longer wore that quizzical look on my face when he spoke.

I smiled as I nodded. "Yes, I do." I got up and took a few baby steps to and from Law's cell doors back to his bottom bunk where he sat. I could hear a lot of chatter and scrambling as cons were coming back from morning chow, and preparing to go to their prison work details.

"At one time I thought I could take control and help develop the community by organizing soldiers to rob big business, to fund the education of my people. And as I matured, I realized that what I was doing was counterproductive to the aims and goals I had for the community. So I stepped down from the Disciples and began to work within the system on a grassroots level, to implement the mental re-education process of our people.

"After meeting you and reading more and understanding even more, I realize I had missed some critical steps in the process. Those steps are why I'm here today. The Beast, as you say, sat by and watched until I became a fly buzzing so loud, he swatted me into what he thinks is oblivion. But, the Beast also made some errors."

Law nodded. "Uh-huh, I'm listening. Preach on, Youngblood."

I walked over to the barred window overlooking the forty-foot prison wall. Cons and hacks scrambled from one building to the other, trying to get out of the rain.

"You see," I paused in thought. "The Beast let me reproduce, not in the physical, but in the spiritual sense. I helped mould soldiers with the same aims and goals as I had. The Beast made a mistake by letting me live. By sending me to a prison think tank with another Beast, who has helped to mould me into a Beast."

Law smiled. "Amen to that."

"I'm jumping over the stand to understand what reality is. And reality is what the physical eye can't see. Anything and everything I can put my eyes and hands on is a mirage." I shook my head. "It ain't real. Anything that can change or that can be destroyed is a mirage.

"Love is real"—I palmed my chest—"'cause we can't see it. Freedom is real"—I pointed to the small prison cell window—"because we can't touch it." I smiled. "Happiness is real 'cause we can't hold it. Freedom and the pursuit of happiness is real." I hit the wall with both my fists.

"Work call in ten minutes," the intercom boomed.

"So now you see what I'm saying, Youngblood. Drugs are going to be sold in the hood, whether we like it or not. So why not control it and benefit from it until we have enough money to rid all drugs from the community? The Beast will allow us to do this because we will be destroying each other. You just have to convince your friends in the Disciple Nation to change their game and go along with our play."

ACT 16
Making Moves
Moses

I had the nastiest and the easiest job in prison, cleaning toilets and showers. It was a job and every one in prison either worked or they were thrown in a nasty, dark six-by-nine cell called "the hole."

Since I had to use them, I preferred being the one that cleaned them. The prison was dirty enough as it was, without the bathrooms being filthy-nasty.

I was hosing down the shower area, when Law walked into the restroom.

"What's shakin', Youngblood?"

"The trees and the leaves, baby, the trees and the leaves. Meet me on the bleachers next to the track during lunch, and I'll let you know the deal."

"They smile in yo' face, all the time they wanna take your place." I was in my own little world with my transistor radio to my ear, singing along with the O'Jays, when Law interrupted my jam session.

"Youngblood, what you know about them O'Jays?" He walked up to the bleachers.

"Shit! The O'Jays talkin' ta me, whenever they sing 'Backstabbers,' the way I been stabbed in the back."

"I know that's right, Youngblood. You can give me five on that one." He slapped my palm.

I turned my palm over. "On the black side, baby."

Law slid his hand over the back of mine, before sitting beside me on the bleachers.

"We in business."

"You bullshittin'?"

I smiled. "I just got word this morning. I spoke to T-Hunt over the phone."

"No, you didn't, Youngblood. You know the prison got the phones bugged."

"Now, Law . . ." I gave him a "do-you-think-I-don't-know-that" look. "After T-Hunt and I got off the phone the guards that were listening got a twisted education on fashion."

"Huh?" Law asked.

"Code. We spoke in code."

"I still don't trust that, but anyway, how much money we workin' with?"

"A little over a hundred thou," I said.

"Cool. I'm gon' set up a meet with Felicio Guilliano."

"Who?"

"Guilliano. General Felicio Guilliano, the one-time head of the Nicaraguan military. He's been in for three years. He's the father of Mexican mud."

"'Mexican mud'?"

"Mexican mud is a much cheaper form of heroin, not as potent as China white, but you can still stomp on a ki' eight to ten times and it'll still have the dope fiend's eyes rolling in the back of their heads."

"Hold on." I stuck my arm out. "Slow down, let me get this right. You say I can take a kilo of Mexican mud and stomp on it with eight, nine kilos of plain milk sugar and it'll still make the fiends nod?"

"Yes sirrrr. The general was moving an assload of it over the border. His pass got revoked after he decided to quit paying the rapidly increasing high taxes the CIA and government placed on every shipment he moved across the border through California and Texas. After he threatened government players with going to the press if they didn't renegotiate their cut, he was coerced to come across the border, where he was arrested by FBI and stripped of his rank by the government of Nicaragua."

"Damn."

"That ain't the kicker, though. Peep game, Youngblood— the government twisted the story to look like they had no involvement, and the Nicaraguan government sanctioned the general's actions. And instead of the U.S. retaliating with military force, the Nicaraguan government gave away an assload of land so America could set up military bases down there."

"That's jacked up. I knew that the government was responsible for dope on the streets, but I had no idea they were this deep into it."

"Let me tell you something, Youngblood. If the government can prevent a Cuban cigar from getting over the border, don't you think they can stop truckloads full of H and Coke? None of that shit grows here, but to process it, chemicals from this country are exported to South America to produce the end product. Remember when I said the Beast will profit? This is what I meant. In ten, fifteen years the two biggest industries will be prisons and illegal drugs," Law said. "You mark my words."

"So how can Guilliano help us? No, better yet, why would he help us?"

"One—because he owes me. I got three of the four charges he was convicted of overturned. Now he's just waiting for his extradition hearing. He has maybe six, at the most eight, months before he'll be extradited back to Nicaragua.

"Reason number two is money. Money is his god, and he'll do whatever it takes for a price."

ACT 17
Sweet Smell of Jasmine
Moses

A few days later I sat at the metal desk inside my cell, my eyes closed. I held Rhythm's latest letter to my nose. While inhaling the jasmine scent that came from the seven pages I held in my hand, I imagined clear blue water washing ashore, four sets of toes making imprints on the wet, white sand, two hands swinging in the cool breeze, and two sets of eyes watching the sun set over mountains in the near distance.

Without her even knowing, Rhythm helped me cope with the "loss" of my brother, and she helped me clearly understand Law's "One Free" concept.

She said, "A name is an identity badge. It should tell not only who you are, but what type of person you are, and what tribe you're from."

Rhythm was incredibly deep. At first I was frustrated at the fact that she wouldn't send me any pictures. Was she fat? Was she a bugbear? What?

But she made me understand. She felt that people got so caught up in the physical that they had become blinded to the reality of the spiritual and mental. She felt that the physical self could potentially distract the spiritual vibe that we were sharing.

I had never heard anything like this in my life. No woman had ever captivated my mind. It wasn't long before I no longer cared how she looked. I was into her mind, and that type of beauty far overshadowed any physical inadequacies.

Greetings King,

Wow! Can you believe it's been over two years since the first time I wrote you. Well, I can't. But, anyway, I'm doing well. I take the Bar next week. I'm a little nervous, but I think I'm ready. I guess I better be ready, right?

I've been offered a position in the DA's office in the District of Columbia. Of course it's contingent on me passing the bar next week. You're probably thinking that there's no way I'll work for the other side, but you're wrong. I can learn a lot working in the DA's office.

And trust me, King, I've lived in New York City, and the heart of DC, and there are a lot of animals, white and black, that deserve to be in cages. But I also know that the system isn't just, and this is an excellent way to gain experience and learn how to fight injustice from within the system. I guess I'm sounding like I'm trying to convince myself more than trying to convince you, right?

Anyway, I'm working on another angle to get you back in court. I'm not going to tell you what it is quite yet, because I don't want to get our hopes up too high like last time. I still can't believe the appeals court denied our request for a new trial last year.

A law professor here at Howard thought the brief I prepared last year showed conclusive evidence that a right-handed person slit the congressman's throat, and the missing pictures from the FBI surveillance team of you entering the congress-

man's home should have been more than enough to get you back into court.

But that's the past. Anyway, I'm focused and hopeful. I'm staying prayed up, and I hope you are too.

Until I hear from you again, King, keep your head to the sky and your eyes on the prize.

Love and Life
Rhythm

ACT 18
The General
Moses

I was beginning to lose hope. The day Law and I were sup-posed to meet with the general, he was shipped off to Baton Rouge, Louisiana, where immigration and extradition hearings were held.

Two months later, on Christmas Eve 1977, T-Hunt's girl, Xena, died in a car accident, leaving him to raise their three-year-old son, Zion, alone. I was crushed, so I could imagine how T-Hunt felt.

Despite me being gone for almost three years, T-Hunt and I were as close as ever. And I think we grew even closer after Xena passed. Then, he looked to me even more for guid-ance and direction.

I had just hung up the phone with T-Hunt, when I over-heard a couple of Latin brothas talking. It was hard under-standing their broken English, but it sounded like they were talking about the general. The only thing I understood was the part of their conversation about being "denied and hav-ing to stay in prison until after some election."

I wanted to go up to them and ask them what and who

they were talking about, but it wasn't my business. And I doubt if they would have told me anyway.

Law assured me that, no matter what the outcome of the general's hearing, he had to come back to the pen to be processed out.

The general had been gone for a little over six months before he returned. Not wanting to waste any more time, the three of us met on the track the very next day.

"General, this is Moses King." Law introduced the short, tanned, Mr. Magoo look-alike.

"It is an honor to meet another warrior." The general spoke with a strong Latin accent.

"Thank you, sir. It is an honor as well to make your acquaintance. I hope we can be of value to each other."

"I wouldn't be here if I didn't think that were possible," the general said.

The sun was shining bright on this breezy, but seasonably warm February day. Inmates were lifting weights out on the weight pile in the middle of the rec yard. Others were sweating, playing basketball, or chasing a small blue ball on the prison's many racquetball courts, while the three of us walked the quarter-mile penitentiary asphalt track.

Law and I had taken several strides, before we realized the general wasn't with us. I looked back, and he was just standing like a statue in the middle of the track, his arms crossed.

"General, is there a problem?" Law asked.

"Hemorrhoids." He waved us off. "One second; I'll be okay."

We all laughed.

"Please, call me Feli. All my close friends do, and any friend of Law's is a friend of mine. Now let's talk business," the General said as he caught up with us.

We must have walked twenty laps, while we negotiated.

How the general was still so heavily involved getting heroin over the border was beyond me.

Before leaving the track, we agreed on a three-kilo deal at two hundred thousand, half at the point of sale and the other half due in thirty days.

I could hardly believe it. The wholesale price for a kilo of heroin on the streets was double what we were paying, and on consignment, three times what we were getting it for.

The only catch to dealing with Felicio was that we had to have the package picked up off the Gulf of Mexico in Terrebonne, Louisiana.

Even after T-Hunt got the drugs back, he had to contend with Picasso. From what I understood, Picasso's gang was running most of the heroin on the South Side and uptown. I just hoped he understood that there was enough money for everybody, but knowing Picasso, he wouldn't.

ACT 19
I Ain't No Snitch
Picasso

To this day, I wonder if Moses regretted not endorsing me to be King of kings. Pablo Picasso Nkrumah, King of kings, head of the Disciples. Yeah, it sounded good, but that's about it. It was probably best that I wasn't running the Disciples. There was no way I could have gotten away with all the shit I was into now.

Whether Moses knew it or not, I still had mad love for him. I missed him, but I had to do me so I could do him later on down the line.

Because of everything I was into, I couldn't have any contact with him. Besides, the Disciples thought I was a snitch, and that was cool, because that meant they wouldn't try and fuck with what I had going on.

And the Gods . . . hell, we were over three hundred strong and growing. As long as the money was coming in, they didn't give a fuck if I reported to President Carter.

Three years after I'd made my break from the Disciples, I was on top of the world. Young gods were exploding on the scene, all over Illinois. Money was rainin' down. I had it, and everybody wanted it. The Gangsta Gods were takin' over.

It was Valentine's Day 1978. Hustlers, tricks, and squares were out in droves to see the Spinners and the Stylistics perform hits like "You Make Me Feel Brand New" and "Could It Be I'm Falling in Love."

The spot where everything was happenin' was at the largest club in Chicago, The Talk of the Town. The club looked like a players' ball. Blood-red carpet and pink rose petals decorated the floor of the entire building.

I made my grand head-turnin' entrance like royalty. People didn't know if I was performing or playing. So, I glided into the joint, "white polar bear" furred-down. Under my coat I wore this grape silk dumbo-eared collar shirt under a peach-and-coconut, double-breasted, pinstriped suit with matching grape gators on my feet.

My hair was tied back in a ponytail. I was lookin' like Fort Knox in color, with all the gold draped around my neck. And I had two of the finest chocolate honeys in all of Chicago at my side, wearing grape gowns that looked like they were poured on.

After I got the ladies seated, I excused myself. A minute later I was in the john pissin', when two cats came in and locked the door. My momma ain't raised no fool. I knew some shit was 'bout to pop off, but I didn't wanna play my hand. I went on about my business when, out the corner of my eye, I saw this jive-ass nigga easing up to the urinals, cracking his knuckles.

Like Quick Draw McGraw, I went in my pants pocket and whipped around as this dude takes a wild swing at me. By now, I had "old faithful," my mother-of-pearl, pearl-handled knife out, carvin' this turkey—slice, slice, slash, slash and shit.

His partna lunged at me and damn near got gutted. Muthafucka made me get blood all over my peach pinstripe jacket. That really pissed me the fuck off. I had just picked the shit up from my tailor that morning.

A minute later, I came out the bathroom, all cool and shit, my jacket strewn over my arm. I got my girls, and we jetted the scene while the Stylistics were performing "Betcha by Golly Wow!"

The next day, I realized my blade must've dropped out of my jacket pocket while I was in the bathroom at the club. It must've happened when I threw my suit jacket over my arm. It was cool 'cause, I'd wiped it down, before slipping it in my pocket.

Anyway, word on the street went from me carvin' up two cats, to slicin' and dicin' four pigs. That didn't bother me too much 'cause I was paid-up with the racist, Gestapo, redneck police commissioner, Richard James. I was breakin' him off on the regular, to make sure I didn't have no trouble.

A couple days later, I was playing with my baby pit bull, Fluke, when my apartment door came crashin' to the floor. Before I went to carvin', I saw badges and guns. I was confused and shit—Not only did they not handcuff me, they had a crew that came behind them to replace my front door.

I was sandwiched between two suits, one big blonde-headed, bulked-up "Fred Flintstone" and a French fry-skinny, average-looking White cat. They led me from my apartment to the elevator and down through the lobby past the concierge.

The big one pushed me into the back of a black-tinted limo.

"Y'all clowns makin' a big mistake."

Something wasn't right. Federal boys didn't drive around in dark limousines.

"You need to call the Chicago police commissioner. I don't think he would like you clowns kidnapping me."

The little guy busted me upside the head with some hard metal object. "Say another word . . ."

They were the rabbits with the gun, so I remained quiet

for the entire three hours we rode in the car. They may have had badges, but I didn't think they were FBI.

Next thing I know, we pull up to some old steel plant in In-diana. By now, I'm like, What the fuck is the deal? But I didn't say shit.

After we got out of the car, they escorted me through a damp, deserted building, up some stairs, and into a large well-lit office. The room was void of everything but a metal table, three rusty chairs, a two-way mirror, and a black-and-silver photo album.

"Sit the fuck down, Chico," the skinny one said.

Before I could park my ass in one of those gray, metal fold-up chairs, one of the clowns pushed me.

"Look at your life, Taco." Fred Flintstone opened the album and shoved it in my face.

The album was filled with pictures of me exchanging suit-cases with Li'l Daddy in New York, Detroit, and Chicago ho-tels.

"What?—You got pictures of me and my luggage." I slouched down in the chair.

"Luggage with heroin and cash in them." Fred Flintstone said.

"Whatever?"

"Vladamir Petraka, AKA Frank Nitty, Russian mobster—do those names ring any bells?" The little one laid out in front of me some photos of Nitty lying in his own blood.

"Never heard of him."

The little one screamed, spraying spit in my face. "Bullshit! You killed the bastard; we have proof."

He was right. I killed the big Russian mu'fucka. I had no choice. When I first got in the game, the big Russian tried to extort money from me. He had me all messed up in the game. I didn't give a damn who his ass worked for; I wasn't kickin' shit back to no one but the police commissioner.

"I don't know what you're talking about. I ain't ever seen the cat."

"You slit the man's throat. Look, if we wanted you dead or in prison, you would've been long ago. We don't care about what you've got going on with James."

I was not believing this shit. How the hell did they know I took Nitty out? James didn't even know; at least, I thought he didn't. And that was over two years ago. So why were they coming at me now?

"What do you want?" I asked.

The big guy said, "This is the deal—Jafari Iniko, AKA Little Daddy, was our inside man. We were getting closer to the West African heroine clique known as Archie, before Jafari was found on a Central Park bench with his dick cut off and glued to his mouth a couple days ago."

Oh shit! There goes my connection.

The big one stood next to where I sat and placed his hands on the table. "Jafari gave us enough to put you away for ten lifetimes. You want all this to disappear? You wanna stay on the streets and run your heroin network through your Gangster Gods?"

Shit! Shit! Shit! I don' got way too deep in this shit. "What do I gotta do?" I asked.

"Tharellious Hunt, the Disciples, and Archie," the little guy said.

"I split from the Disciples long ago, and Little Daddy was my inside on Archie, you know that."

"Come on, Pablo, you have connects. You're running one of the largest operations in the Midwest. We're not asking you to actually set anyone up; we have others for that. All we want is information."

"How am I—"

"SHHHHHH," the little guy said.

"And if you decide not to play ball with us, the Disciples will start dying, and you'll be blamed for their murders."

These cats had me twisted. I wasn't no rat. Maybe a fox, but not a rat. I'd give them information, all right. I'd feed them Disciple fairytales and West African Archie fantasies, while I figured out who the hell these clowns were really connected to. And when I found out who these cats were and where they laid their heads at night, we'd see about those murders they were talking about.

ACT 20
The Good Times and the Bad
Moses

Time was what it was. It came, it went, but it was always there. More than a few years had gone by since I'd first stepped foot inside the dull, gray Atlanta Penitentiary walls. Five years to be exact. The '70s were a memory, and a new decade was ushered in with the Supreme Court finally agreeing to review Law's case.

I had no doubt that Law was going home; it was just a matter of time before he hit the bricks a free man with money. Yeah, Law was right, we were making money like we were printing it ourselves. The drug business was booming, and I was in love.

My last two writs for appeal were shot down, but I was still optimistic. Rhythm and I were praying that a new law in reference to the suppression of evidence would be passed later this year.

"Moses King, report to the visiting room. Moses King report to the visiting room," a voice boomed over the intercom.

I wasn't expecting anyone. Since T-Hunt's girl, Xena, died

a couple years ago, Momma was the only one that came to visit, and her visits were few and far between.

I could hardly believe my eyes, as I pulled back from his embrace. Something had to be seriously wrong for T-Hunt to risk coming here.

"All that money you got and you ain't got that nose fixed," I said.

"This nose is my trademark; this is a Watusi tribal warrior nose."

"Looks like a Watusi tribal warrior cave to me."

We both laughed.

"Come over here." I led him towards the middle of the visiting room, where we passed a Hispanic brother visiting with his family.

The visiting room was always packed on Saturdays. It took at least two hours for a family member to get through the search process and into the visiting room. Although the room was crowded and brightly lit, inmates still took turns watching out for the guards, while others took their girls behind the out-of-order coke machine on the back wall.

Only two guards worked the visiting room, one at the front door and one next to the restrooms. The large room was filled with rows of orange plastic chairs facing each other, and small wooden brown tables were bolted to the concrete gray floor.

"What are you doing here?" I asked T-Hunt as we took a seat.

"Look, bro, I know the rules, but shit is crazy out there. It ain't like the old days. That shit we pushin' is causing funeral homes to pop up like spring grass." T-Hunt shook his head. "This ain't why we started the Disciples, Moses."

"T, listen to me, bruh—you're wrong. This is why we started the Disciples—to emancipate our people. I agree, selling drugs is the exact opposite of that aim, but we're only in the game temporary. Just long enough for us to have economic power." I leaned in as close as I could. "You my eyes and ears on the streets. We've built an empire, and we're preparing for civil war. C'mon, you know that takes time, money, influence, and most of all, it takes sacrifice."

"'Sacrifice'? What the fuck you mean, 'sacrifice'? I've sacrificed my life and my soul." He put a hand over his face. "If it was just me, I could roll with it but, Moses, I got a son, and I'm all he has."

I nodded.

"A month ago I took Zion to my summer home in Miami for a little father-son vacation. I woke up at six like I have for years, to go for a morning run. I was on my way out the door, when I remembered the Earth, Wind & Fire tape I wanted to listen to while I was in the Porsche.

"So I went to the garage and opened the door to the Porsche, and Herbert's body slid out with a note burned on his chest—"

"What?" I placed my hands over my face. "Noooooooo. No! No!"

"I'm sorry, Moses."

I took a deep breath. "What happened? What did it say?" I asked hesitantly.

T-Hunt closed his eyes. "It read: YOU HAD TWELVE KINGS. NOW YOU HAVE TEN. SOON THERE WILL BE NONE. My first instinct was to run, but I thought a second and realized if whoever did this wanted me dead, I would be."

"Herb had been with us since we were kids," I said.

"I know." T-Hunt nodded. "I know."

A minute passed before either of us spoke.

"Moses, I cried, man. I just slid to the ground next to my ride and cried. Herbert was like family. In my own garage I felt like a trapped animal. I just wanted to kill the world at that moment, but I thought about that little, brown, big-head boy I helped create."

I didn't know what to say.

"I can't tell you how long I sat on that ground in grief. After I regained control, I got up and walked over to the wall phone in the garage, made a few calls back home, and sent an order out for the Kings to fly down to Miami and meet me at the Sheraton in South Beach.

"Moses, you know I ain't got an inch of bitch in me, but I threw up, when I walked over to the Fleetwood parked on the other side of the Porsche. What looked like bloody chitt'lins was strewn across the car's dash. But once I got closer, I saw Big Ben's face. You never met him, he's a—" T-Hunt caught himself. "He was a Disciple under Herbert's kingdom."

"Nah, nah, nah," I whispered. I shook my head in disbelief.

"Moses, the negro disemboweled the . . . Do you understand what I am saying?" T-Hunt cried.

I grabbed him by the shoulders. "What negro?"

"Picasso!"

"No! No!" I shook my head. "I raised Picasso. No, T, he was angry at not becoming King of Kings, but that was back in '71; eight, nine years ago. We were kids, when I stepped down from the Disciples. How do you know it was him?"

"I found his mother-of-pearl, pearl-handled knife on the ground next to the garage door."

"Picasso was too good. He wouldn't have left his blade. It just don't make sense."

"I know that's the only reason he's still breathin', but then again, he might've gotten careless."

"Why you say that?"

"Word is, Picasso's got a few get-out-of-jail-free passes. Everybody know he killed that Russian, Frank Nitty, but he was never charged. And remember last year . . . he walked on the four-kilo heroin beef, while the other cats went down—what does that tell you?"

"If he's talkin', I don't see how his Gangsta Gods still follow him."

"Money and fear. He keeps money in their pockets and fear in their hearts," T-Hunt said.

"Yeah, Picasso ain't afraid to kill, and what probably scares his crew is he ain't afraid to die."

"Well, I am," T-Hunt said. "The other reason I'm here is . . ." T-Hunt sighed. ". . . I'm out. I mean, I'll see this through, but I'm raising a son without a mother. If something happens to me, he'll end up like me, looking for the meaning to life, and I'll never let that happen."

"I understand."

"Thank you." Switching gears, he said, "You may not agree with me, and I know we don't know if he definitely killed the brothas, but the Kings voted unanimously to take Picasso out."

"Listen to me." I looked into T-Hunt's eyes. "You have to go back to the Kings. Now is not the time to hit Picasso. Don't ask me why; just trust me on this. Please, T?"

ACT 21
Rhythm of Life
Moses

Lawrence One Free did the damn thing. It took another two years for the Supreme Court to rule, but he'd finally done it. A week ago on March 17, 1982, after serving twenty-two years, Law walked out of prison, giving me a mountain of hope.

I was in my cell, thinkin' about my queen, a few days after the U.S. Supreme Court overturned Law's case.

"Why you smilin' so wide, Mo?" my new cellmate asked as he walked in the cell.

I sat up and extended my arm. "The letter you got for me in your hand, it's from my queen."

He placed an envelope in my hand. "How'd you know you had mail?"

"For seven years my baby has never once sent me any mail that didn't smell like jasmine."

"I don't smell nothing."

I held the envelope out to him.

He took it and put it to his nose. "Damn, Mo, you got some bloodhound in you." He handed the letter back over to me and left the cell.

I turned and laid on top of the gray, wool prison-issue blanket atop my bottom bunk and attempted to tune out the noise of cons moving around the prison dorm, anxiously waiting for the yard doors to open so they could go to evening chow.

Although it was fried chicken Thursday, food was the furthest thing from my mind, as I lay with the seven sheets of paper to my nose. My fingers tingled, and my heart jumped every time I received a small piece of her heart and soul in ink.

If anyone would have ever told me I would have found true love from behind an electric fence, steel bars, and four feet of concrete, I would have thought they had lost their mind.

I started reading the pages, and before I knew what was happening, two cons ran into my cell and threw a blanket over my head.

Why I thought the letter was from Rhythm, I didn't know. As I read the two pages on government-decree paper, I could hardly believe it. Missing evidence, government witnesses perjuring themselves, and illegal misconduct were the reasons my case had been overturned, and I was granted immediate release. The next thing I knew, I was packed up and heading towards the receiving and distribution department to be processed out.

The aroma of jasmine and myrrh aroused my senses as soon as I stepped outside the prison doors into the sunny, cloudless, humid Atlanta summer day. It was a feeling that defined the greatest of good that was only felt in the rarest, colorful dreams of euphoric bliss.

She was more long than tall. She had this glowing mocha-cream skin. Her lavender headscarf accentuated her pronounced cheekbones, her full lips, and her round African nose. Her pinkish-brown lips and her chocolate moonlike eyes had an expression that made even the sun smile. The slow, soft, one-drop waterfall flowing from her eyes caused my soul to cry out. She was Rhythm in every aspect.

The lavender-and-black, form-fitting summer dress wore on her like butter on hot toast. Her slightly muscularly smooth, long legs and her baby-skinned mocha toes touched the concrete prison stairs like a jazz xylophonist in slow motion. Her hips and arms played the wind like a concert violinist. As she continued her silent dance towards me, I wanted nothing more than to lose myself in her rhythm on a naked beach void of everything but God's windy music and the ocean's waving orchestra.

We held, we loved, we embraced, as the world stood still. After we cried together, we had a knowing, silent conversation with our eyes and our hearts as we rode in back of a dark stretch limo, headed towards the Atlanta airport.

A few hours later, we were in my old neighborhood, heading towards my mother's apartment. I just shook my head as we passed an older bag lady standing on the strip, all dolled up like a cheap hooker. The saddest thing was, I knew this lady from somewhere; I just couldn't put my hand on where.

After Rhythm and I got out of the limo, we walked past a trail of needles and used dope vials, as we made our way to the second-floor apartment. I was confused. What had happened since I was gone? Why hadn't Solomon stopped this or got Momma outta there? The door was cracked when we reached it.

"Hello," I called out. "Mom! Is anyone home?" I timidly pushed the door open.

No answer.

The stale smell of sweaty clothes, mildew, and urine assaulted my nose. I walked into the apartment, where my older brother and I were raised.

No way could my mother still be living here. Why didn't T-Hunt tell me she had moved?

Old magazines, dirty plates, and cups were all over the place. Old, pissy blankets and sheets replaced our living room furniture. My eyes bulged with fear, when I saw Jesus lying on the ground, torn in half, glass scattered on and around him.

As a kid, my brother Solomon painted a tall, dark, dread-locked, bloody Black man hanging on a cross and wearing a white cloak and a golden crown of thorns. This was my mom's only piece of art, and her most prized possession.

I was lost in fear and thought. I heard a grunting sound. "Mom!" I ran towards the noise. I stopped at my mother's bedroom door. I thought I heard another grunt. I tried to turn the knob. Frustrated and scared, I screamed as I rammed the door with my shoulder. It flew open, and I ended up on the mildewed, blood-stained carpet.

After getting to my feet, I looked up and saw the backside of a naked man kneeled over that old, scraggly-looking woman I'd seen on the way home. She had her head down. One end of a belt was hanging from her mouth, and the other end was tied around her arm, while the man pro-ceeded to jab a needle into her arm.

Shock registered in the woman's eyes, once she looked up at me.

"NOOOOOOOO!" A scream escaped from my mouth as I reached out to her.

"Moses!"

"Momma!"

The man turned towards me, his lifeless eyes boring into my soul.

"I told you this shit was destroying our people. See what you made me do," T-Hunt said.

My eyes popped open. I must've been dreaming. I tried to blink back the blinding white light that was burning my eyes.

It took a minute for the burning to subside, and the ceiling to come into focus.

Where was I? Where was my mother? Where was T-Hunt? Where was Rhythm? Where was Solomon?

What was that beeping sound? Why was an IV in my arm? Was that my blood circulating through that machine?

I closed my eyes and prayed that I was still dreaming, but the pain in my stomach and back made it to hard to concentrate. As I became more lucid, everything started coming back to me—Rhythm; the letter; the two cats that had rushed in my cell; the blanket being thrown over my head.

ACT 22
The Soul King
Solomon

O ver the years, not all people believed in what I was saying or doing, but most liked the delivery of the mes-
sages that I was bringing to the church and to the streets.

Kids on the streets had long ago anointed me with the
name the Reverend Soul King, because of the way I danced
in the streets, spreading and teaching God's Word. I believed that, along with making a joyful noise unto the Lord,
a little fancy footwork didn't hurt either. If anything, it
would get the attention of the party people who'd never
danced to God's rhythm.

Two years after I held my first church service at New
Dimensions, we were breaking ground on a new 50,000-
square-foot super church structure.

The same day I graduated from Loyola with a degree in
theology was the same day I received the news from First
National Bank of Chicago that the loan for the construction
of the new super church had been approved. It was truly a
miracle, I thought, as I gave all credit to God.

The year was 1982, the peanut farmer had left the oval office, and the Hollywood actor had taken over. News analysts

couldn't figure out why the nation was on the verge of a recession.

But none of that stopped me and the New Dimensions First Church of God congregation from prospering. The doors of the new church had been open for over two years now, and all three Sunday services stayed packed.

On Saturday night, folks were dancing at the disco, but on Sunday morning I had them jamming to Jesus. We had a drummer, two guitarists, a sax man, a piano woman, a keyboardist, two organists, a sound engineer, and several choirs. My motto was "Ain't nothin' like a party but a 'God party.'" This was what the people wanted, and I aimed to please, especially if it meant bringing folks to the Father.

That ole-time, traditional religion was okay, but I found a way to get the young folks in the church, which had always been my goal. When I spoke, I didn't preach, I taught. I gave pragmatic solutions to everyday problems, using scripture as a guide and a format. At New Dimensions, I and my junior ministers taught our story, our history, and incorporated that with biblical timelines. When you came to New Dimensions, you were going to school, and to worship, at the same time.

We held workshops throughout the week on everything, from making yourself marketable in the work force, to parenting. We had youth leadership studies for aspiring youth ministers. I tried to implement as many programs as I could, to help the development of our youth and our elderly brothers and sisters.

One lesson that stuck with me that I'd learned from the Islamic leader I met a few years back, was to not scare people into believing, but to teach the truth and let people decide which road to take. Only God can make a Christian.

I faced obstacles that, at times, seemed insurmountable. I was criticized more by Christians than anyone else. I was accused of brainwashing. A reporter from the National

Christian Alliance called me "the modern-day Jim Jones without the Kool-Aid."

Early one morning in early spring, the phone rang while I was preparing a sermon I was to give at the National Christian Convention in Philadelphia.

"Hello," I said.

"Solomon, wake up, baby."

"I'm not 'sleep, Momma. I'm up working on a sermon."

"Your brother is at Frazier Memorial Hospital in Atlanta."

"What happened?"

"All I know is, he was attacked and beaten by some inmates."

"Is he going to be okay?"

"They don't know. They took one of my baby's kidneys!" she cried.

"Momma, calm down. I'm on my way." I hung up the phone.

I got on my knees and raised my head and arms to the Heavens. "Father, God, let me bear the burden of my brother's suffering. Father, God, awaken my brother, as you did Lazarus. Father, God, stop the pain. Father, God, give me wisdom; give me strength. Guide me. Let me be my brother's keeper. Tell me what to do. In Jesus' name, I pray. Amen."

A lifetime of worry registered on Momma's face as I walked through her apartment door.

Later that day, I cancelled my trip to Philadelphia and went to Atlanta. I had to go. I could no longer live in fear of what would happen to my mother or me if I defied the orders of the FBI. I was a man of God, not a man of man. And God said, "Fear me and me alone." I lived in fear for over eight years, but my brother needed me more than ever now. More than even I knew.

ACT 23
Queen Meets King
Solomon

Impatiently, I paced the hospital waiting room, waiting for the results. I'd been in Atlanta for three frustrating, nail-biting days. My little brother was laid up in a coma, and the guards outside his room wouldn't even let me see him.

Not only had Moses lost one kidney, his other one was failing. I didn't think twice about offering up one of mine. Heck, I would've given my life if it meant saving his. I just wished snatching one of my kidneys out and putting it in him was that simple. Of course, it wasn't; I had to be a perfect match for his body to accept my kidney. Even if I was a match, his body could still reject the kidney, I was told.

A soft tapping on my shoulder interrupted my pacing. A young woman asked, "Excuse me, sir, are you the Reverend Solomon King?"

"Yes, I am. Do I know you?"

"Reverend King, my name is Rhythm. Rhythm Azure."

Instead of reaching out to shake my hand, she stood in my path, defiant, her arms crossed. "I'm a close friend of your brother's—remember him?"

"I've heard about you. From what I understand, you've been a godsend to Moses."

"Really, now? I don't see how you would've heard about me. From what I understand, you haven't spoken to Moses in forever."

Before I could reply, she burst out, "Moses is a beautiful man. Why haven't you reached out to him, Reverend?"

"I think about Moses every day."

"That's not what I asked." She tapped her heels on the white-and-black-speckled hospital waiting room floor.

Flustered, I threw my arms in the air. This woman was getting under my skin. "Look, I'm tired and stressed. I'm going down to the hospital cafeteria to get some coffee." I turned and started for the elevator. "You can join me, if you like."

Once we were sitting at a table away from everyone else, I stirred my steaming coffee and opened the wrapping over the cinnamon roll I'd bought.

"Rhythm, I don't know if you know him, but Moses' best friend, Tharellious Hunt, gets letters to my mother and keeps her updated on Moses and his well-being, and these updates are relayed to me. So I've been kept abreast of the situation, and that is how I know about you."

She leaned forward. "Mind if I call you Rev?"

"Sure."

"Rev, it's like this—Moses has been a big brother to hundreds, thousands of young kings. He's led them in what he feels is the best way to reach the results he seeks for Blacks everywhere, but he has no man to lead him. Now, Rev, will you just answer my question and tell me why you haven't been there for him."

"I'm here now."

She stood up and looked down on me. "You call yourself a man of God. How can you be a man of God, when you've turned your back on your own flesh and blood?"

I stood up. "I haven't turned my back on him; I will never turn my back on my brother. I did what I felt was best for him and our family. And instead of me organizing and leading a gang of misguided, militant, drug-dealing young men, I've been out in the streets trying to reverse what Moses started." I held a hand out towards her. "I know the Disciples started off with good intentions, but look at 'em now. Look at the Gangsta Gods and the others. God is leading me to organize a new type of gang. A gang of soldiers in His army."

"I've got a close relative in Chicago. He keeps me informed, and when I'm in town I watch Channel 3 on Sunday morning. I listen to the rhetoric that spews from your mouth." She looked me up and down. "I've heard you speak, referring to your parishioners as soldiers in God's Army, but I don't hear you talking about the government and the unjust way your brother has been treated." Rhythm turned to leave.

I grabbed her by the arm.

She looked at me and then down at her arm. "Let go of my arm!" She violently jerked away from my grasp. "You come here after all these years. You say you wish you could speak up for Moses, but you haven't. It's great that you're offering up a kidney"—She put a hand over her heart—"And for that I am truly grateful. But what Moses needs is a big brother."

I was ashamed. I tried to avoid telling her, but I could see that she really loved my brother, and it was time for me to tell someone. After all, if something happened to me or my mother, someone should know.

"If you sit down, I'll explain why I haven't been there for him."

Reluctantly, she sat back down.

I explained the whole FBI scene at the airport—the pictures, them killing Miss Smith, everything.

"Rhythm, if I'm a match, I've signed a form that will keep

anyone from knowing I'm the donor. For the time being, if you would—"

She reached out and took my hand. "I understand. You, Moses, and your mother's lives could all be in danger if anyone knew. And since I can't see Moses, I won't tell him over the phone or in my letters."

ACT 24
Waking Up
Moses

"Mr. King? Mr. King? Are . . . you . . . there? Can . . . you . . . hear . . . me?"

"Yes," I groggily said.

"Welcome back."

"From where?"

"You've been in a coma for three months."

"Huh?"

"Moses King, you were attacked, beaten, and repeatedly stabbed with some type of sharp object. As a result, we had to remove one of your kidneys, and a short time later, the other failed. If it weren't for an emergency last-minute donor, you wouldn't have made it.

"What?"

The last thing I remember was a blanket being thrown over my head, and feeling a sharp pain in my side. No, I remember a voice. Two voices . . . something about a message from Picasso and the Gangsta Gods for life. But why?

"Your fiancée has been here every weekend since the incident."

"I'm in a hospital?"

"Yes, sir."

"Every weekend? Rhythm? 'Fiancée'?" Rhythm, my fiancée. I smiled through the pain I felt in my back and midsection.

"None of that is important now, but what is, is you getting some rest. You've been through a lot."

"Can I make a phone call?"

"No. Not until you are transferred back to the prison."

"When will that be?"

"As soon as your vital signs are strong enough."

"You must be my doctor?"

"Yes, I'm sorry—Where are my manners?—Moses King, I'm Dr. Brinson, and you are on the tenth floor of Frazier Memorial Hospital."

A few days later, I was informed that my fiancée had been here again, and yet again she'd been denied access to my room. Some cornball, man-looking, fat, tight-white-dress-wearing nurse informed me that it wasn't the hospital's call, and that the Bureau of Prisons was denying any visitor access.

"You mean to tell me she has never been able to see me since I've been here?"

"No, she hasn't," the nurse informed me.

"What could I have done? I mean, it wasn't like I was going to jump up and run away. She travels here all the way from DC every weekend for three months, and y'all wouldn't even let her see me."

"Please, calm down, Mr. King. We are just doing our jobs. We don't make the rules."

I spent another month in recovery at Frazier Memorial in Atlanta, before I was transferred to the prison hospital at the Atlanta Pen.

After returning, the first thing I did was bum some stationery and a couple stamps from a convict orderly. It was a struggle to write through the pain, but Rhythm was on my mind, and I had to tell her how I felt and what I'd decided to do about us.

Rhythm,

    Queen, I appreciate everything you've done, but this is it. You have to stop. I can't and I won't put you through this any longer. I'm in prison, not you. I want you to live free. Find a love that you can touch. Find a love that you can feel with your arms and your heart. I'm only half of what you need. You deserve more than I can give. You've waited eight years too long.

    If I could go back eight, ten, twelve years, and I was given the choice to live my life differently, I would not change one thing.

    Without me being stripped of my freedom, and almost my life, I would've never found you, and without my Rhythm I have no soul.

    One day I'll have to check my soul in to God, but my heart will forever belong to you Rhythm. Goodbye.

One Love
Moses

Nine days later.

King,

    It's obvious that you've been so traumatized by the stabbing and beating you took, that you are not in your right mind. You know the song, 'Your mind is here with me, but your body's on the other side of town'? Well, your body is in that prison hospital, but I don't know where the hell your mind is.

    I can't believe you even put pen to paper and wrote that poetic garbage.

    You want me to find a love that I can touch. King, I feel you every second, minute, and hour of every day. Love is not a touch. It's a feeling, a state of being. Can't you see that I love you, Moses King?

I don't agree with some things you're doing, and the thought process behind them, and you know what I'm talking about, but I've stood by you.

And if you think that you're going to get rid of me after seven years, you better think again. You are my light, King. You are the reason I get up in the morning. You are the reason I breathe. You are the reason I fight. And if I have to fight you for your heart, you better strap up, 'cause I'm coming fast, hard, and strong to get my man that is lost somewhere inside your head.

So what? You've been in prison over seven years. Seven years ain't forever. Can't you see that what we have is so much more than ink on paper, and voices over a wire? What we have transcends space and time.

Those walls and bars that confine your body are nothing. They're not real. What is real, though, is truth, and truth was, is, and always will be.

At any given time those walls that hold you can come crashing down. Those walls were put together by man. What we have, no man can put together, no man can disassemble.

You say without Rhythm there is no life. I say, without my King I can't be Queen.

Oh, and lastly, Moses King, I am free. Oh, how I am so free. You gave me that gift when you came into my life and completed me. I love you, and as long as I breathe, I will move the sun and the moon for you.

Love and Life
Rhythm

ACT 25
Let That Be the Reason
Picasso

"Hello," Rhythm said, answering the phone.

"You 'sleep?" I asked.

"Pablo?"

"Yeah. What's crackin', big sis?"

"What time is it?"

"Two-thirty."

"What's wrong, Pablo?"

"Why somethin' gotta be wrong? I can't call my big sis?"

"Pablo, it's two-thirty in the morning."

"Yo, I can't sleep. I'm worried about my nigga. You know that nigga my heart, and he don't even know that shit."

"I wish I could tell Moses the truth. He needs to know how much you love him, Pablo."

"I wish you could too, but you know that can't happen. Remember the first time you told me you were going to write him, we agreed that you wouldn't tell him who you were, because of how much we looked alike?"

"I know. I know. I just wish we could've figured another way to get James without deceiving Moses."

"It's too late for that now. So, anyway, how's my man holdin' up?"

"His brother gave him a kidney. He's outta the coma, and the doctors say he is going to be just fine."

"That's word. All praise due to the Most High," I said. "So how you?"

"Losin' my mind, worrying about my little brother and my man."

"I ain't been little for a long time, but I'm chill. I'm just fucked up over all this. I can't even squash the beef the Disciples got with me, 'cause I'm fucked up with Mayor James and the feds."

"I still can't believe, after all the scandal he's been linked to, that his corrupt ass was elected mayor."

"I know. James think he pimpin' me for dead presidents, when I got his ass on tape like a mu'fucka, just like we planned."

"I still can't get any info on whether James is connected with the feds. I'm sorry I got you into this, Pablo."

"Don't trip. You ain't got me into nothin', big sis. I was a grown-ass man, when we both agreed that I'd be the one to get close to James. Hell, we got way more than enough to blackmail him into turning on the pigs that set Moses up."

"I know."

"We just have to see what's up with them damn feds, or whoever the cats are that keep sweatin' me for info."

"I've been inside the DC DA's office for well over two years, and I haven't been able to find any ties that James has with the feds. But, like I told you before, James has ties to something, and I think the supposedly FBI men that you're involved with are linked to James in some way.

"My security clearance just isn't high enough to find out, and I haven't gotten my boss comfortable enough with me yet to trap him into giving me what we need."

"Big sis, I have somethin' to lay on you—promise you ain't gon' trip."

"What is it, Pablo?"

"Look . . . I'm all right—I had on my vest."

"You were shot?"

"A couple weeks ago—"

"'A couple weeks ago,' and you just now telling me?"

"With everything goin' on with Moses, I didn't want to give you anything else to worry about."

"What happened?"

"Some Disciple niggas pulled up beside me at a stoplight and shot my Benz full of holes."

"How do you know they were Disciples?"

"They shouted, 'Disciples for life,' before pulling off. The day after my ride got shot up, I found out that the Disciples think I'm responsible for Moses getting knifed."

"Just like the Disciples that got killed a couple years ago. The feds made T-Hunt and the others think you did it."

"If it weren't for Moses convincing T-Hunt not to retaliate, a lot of Disciple and Gangsta God blood would've been shed. Moses was smart in preventing what was sure to be a war."

"You think the feds were trying to kill Moses?" she asked.

"Nah, they ain't got no reason. Moses ain't no threat. At least, they shouldn't think he is."

"Who do you think tried to kill him?"

"I wish I knew."

"I think we're about to find out real soon," she said.

"How?"

"I have a plan B, and I think we can put it into action."

"What is it?" I asked.

"Back when Moses got locked up, the feds stepped to Rev and scared him into submission. But after feeling him out at the hospital, I think that he would be down with us, if we had a plan to free Moses. And given the size of his following, we could definitely use him."

"So what's the plan?"

"I'm still working a few kinks out; give me a few weeks, and I'll fill you in. I just need you to get out of town, stay low, until I call you. I can't be losing a brother."

ACT 26
The Dead Zone
Moses

Although my body was in a messed up place, my heart was in heaven. I tried to let Rhythm go, but she wouldn't leave. She was in my mind and my heart every moment of every day, and the last letter she wrote was the motivation I needed to rise up and handle my business. That letter just motivated me to step my game up, but first I had to get out of "the dead zone."

I was told that the other section of the prison hospital was overcrowded; that's why I ended up in the dead zone. For ten days now, I'd been in here, trying to recover. The dead zone was what the cons called the prison hospital wing where sick cons were sent to die. It was more a morbid party wing hosted by Death himself, as opposed to a prison hospital wing. The caterers were the whacked quack doctors and the prison physician assistants.

The wing looked like a condemned "St. Elsewhere," with throwback equipment from a Frankenstein movie. Machines buzzed day and night, halfway keeping folks alive.

The conversation in the unit ranged from sad to sadder. Generic test drugs were administered like in the Tuskegee experiment. The sick cons that were in the dead zone wagered on who would be the next one carried out in a wooden box with handcuffs on.

I'd seen it several times over the years, but I still couldn't believe that when a con died, the body was taken out of the prison and to the morgue in handcuffs.

Fantastic Jones looked closer to sixty-five than forty-five. He was in the bed to my left, coughing up blood, waiting for the cancer in his body to finish him off. I prayed for his death, so he could be put out of his misery. It was sad to hear this man groaning in pain night and day, repeating the same phrase over and over. "Somebody, anybody, I don't know nobody, but, please somebody, come help me."

I was consumed with hate, listening to the hacks laughing and hollering across the unit for Fantastic to shut the fuck up and die.

"If just one of them sadistic bastards got close enough, I'd bite the dog shit out of his ass," Tony Mack would say.

Tony Mack was in the bed to my right, fighting death, like a washed-up fighter in a boxing match with a young Ali. Tony was dying of AIDS and hepatitis C.

It was 1982, and people were just finding out about this virus afflicting homosexual men everywhere. Tony educated me, and everyone else who would listen, about the virus, its effects, and his regrets.

I never thought in a million lifetimes that I'd look forward to seeing Juicy. He was the convict orderly sentenced to work in the dead zone. Juicy didn't refer to himself as a man, a sissy, fag, gump, or homosexual. "I am the queen bitch," he'd tell you in a minute.

"Momma's here, so get your asses up and talk to me," he would say at the beginning of every shift.

"Shut up, bitch," Tony Mack said.

"It's queen bitch to you, sissy," Juicy responded.

Oh, no! Not again.

Juicy and Tony would argue for hours. Although this was the best part of the day, my head felt like two professional wrestlers were getting it on inside my brain. I just wanted to sleep right now.

"Sissy, who you callin' a sissy?"

"Who answered?"

"Yo' daddy was a sissy, bitch!"

And the sparring began.

"I don't have time for this today. I have too many bedpans to empty, floors to clean, and intelligent conversation to partake of."

"Let me explain something to your gender-confused ass— I've been locked up most my life, twenty-two years—and I ain't took a dick nor sucked one. I'm a man." Tony patted his chest. "I get head, and I fuck 'gump pussy.' "

"Gump pussy?" Juicy put his hands on his slender hips. "Hmph! Gump pussy is male booty-hole—call it what it is, sissy." Juicy snapped his fingers in the air. "Don't make me read yo' ass . . . 'cause I'll read you like a Harlequin novel and throw you away when I finish, sissy."

"I done told you—"

"I know what you done told me, but let me tell you something—most of y'all—"

" 'Y'all'?"

"That's right—y'all—Did I stutter?" Juicy made an arc with his neck and placed his hands on his hips. "Y apostrophe A double-damn L." He drew out the letters in the air with a red-painted fingernail. "Y'all studs visit with your wives and family on visiting days. Y'all lift weights every day and talk about your manly exploits of women when you were in the free world. But, y'all come to momma for relief and release, when your little thing gets hard."

"So what?"

" 'So what' is . . . you, and all who are like you, live in denial." Juicy made a sweeping arc in the air with his arms. "It don't matter if you giving, getting or receiving, batting or pitching, you are having sex with another man—that makes you a certified, bona fide, card-carrying sissy, punk, faggot, whatever the politically correct term of the day is. You so much in denial; I bet you think you contracted the HIV virus from something you ate—Uhmm . . . sorry." Juicy smiled. "It don't work like that. You got it in prison, sticking your little thing in another man."

"Ain't nothin' little about me, sissy."

"Except the time you got left on this earth."

If looks could kill, Juicy would be dead and stinking, the way Tony stared at him.

"You need to make peace with who you are. I've accepted who I am, and it may not be right, but I can think of a whole lot worse things I could be. But you will probably die not knowing who you are. Physically, I am a man, more man than you or anyone like you could ever be, but psychologically, I'm all woman, baby"—Juicy snapped his fingers—"and I'm not ashamed. And you shouldn't be."

"Fuck you, Juicy!" Tony put the covers over his head.

"Moses, how you feelin', baby?" Juicy asked.

"Other than the two midgets fighting inside my head, I'd have to say I'm doing a lot better, but I can't let the doctors know."

"Why not?"

"Come over here." I beckoned Juicy to my side. "I'll tell you, and I need a favor."

I whispered in Juicy's ear.

"How much?" Juicy asked.

"I'll have five hundred put on your books, as soon as I get to a phone. I just need your inmate number."

"Because you cute and you ain't never cursed me or judged me, I'll get you what you want for two hundred."

"Juicy, you know I don't swing like that."

"Boy, I know that; I'm just messing with you. You ain't

even my type." Juicy waved. "I'll do it, but you make sure I get a money slip in the mail."

Three days later, Juicy gave me the names, the cell numbers, and the dorms of the three studs who tried to do me in.

Prison gossip spread quicker than a top story on Eyewitness News. It was all around the compound that I'd flew a kite, sent a note, whatever you wanna call it, to the lieutenant and the warden, requesting to be placed in protective custody.

A week later, I was in the special housing unit, better known as "the hole." My new home was a six-by-nine cell on the fifth of six tiers. For twenty-three hours a day I was locked in a rat-infested, cold, rusty-gray, metal cell, doing "half-ups" and baby crunches. (Half-ups were half-ass push-ups, and baby crunches were more stomach grunting than anything.) Being in the hospital so long atrophied my muscles considerably. I'd lost almost thirty pounds and had no wind. I would be target practice for anyone who wanted to "take me out" in general prison population.

By the time three months had passed, I was doing a thousand headstand push-ups off the wall and two thousand sit-ups five days a week. The only days I didn't work out were the two days I was allowed to take a shower. On those days I spent most of my time writing Rhythm.

I spent an hour a day outside in the winter Atlanta cold, running in a cage, clad only in my boxers and white Chuck Taylor Converse sneakers.

At the beginning of my thirteenth week, I flew another kite, requesting to be put back on the compound in open population. I sent word to Juicy to spread the news that I was coming back. I wanted to send a message to everyone that Moses King feared no man.

Ironically, one week later, I was put in the same dorm

where the studs who attempted to cancel me were housed. I kind of figured as much. It would be so much simpler for so many if I were dead.

Federal penitentiary cell doors all around the United States electronically opened at 5:30 a.m. every morning. My first morning back on the compound, I quietly jumped off my top bunk, leaving my new cellie to his dreams and nightmares. I opened my locker, moved some things around, and pulled out my bathroom kit. Next, I took out my red and white, twenty-ounce, plastic drinking cup and relieved myself in it. I didn't want to use the toilet in our cell and take the chance of waking my cellie.

I carried my cup and my toilet kit into the bathroom. After entering and putting the latch on the last toilet stall, I put the cup down and unzipped my bag. I pulled out the lone rubber glove I got from Juicy and put it on my left hand. With my other hand, I covered my mouth.

Without hesitation, I turned my head and put my gloved hand in the stopped-up toilet, reaching through toilet paper and feces, until I felt the tightly toilet paper-wrapped prison hospital scalpel, I'd paid Juicy to steal.

Two hundred dollars seemed to be Juicy's number. This had to be the highest price anyone ever paid for a knife. I could have made a shank out of a bedspring, a toothbrush, or a shaving razor, but I didn't want to take the chance on anyone seeing me.

After washing my hands, I went to the first cell. I was in and out in less than fifteen seconds. If his "bunky" saw or heard me, he didn't let on. Ten minutes later, the rubber glove was on its way to the city sewer, and I was showered, washed up, and back in bed.

"Emergency count in ten minutes. All inmates, to your cells. I repeat, emergency count in ten minutes. All inmates, to your cells," the voice boomed over the intercom.

I looked at my watch. It read 8:30. It was Saturday morning, no work call, cons slept in. I must've drifted off to sleep for a couple hours.

"Stand-up count. Everybody, on your feet in front of your bunks," a bull-horned voice shouted.

"Celly, get up. Stand-up count." I shook my cell mate awake.

Every day in the Atlanta Federal Pen, two hacks walked around through dorms and prison work sites and counted anywhere from the fifteen hundred to two thousand cons housed there.

At 4:00 p.m. every day, all inmates had to be in their cells, standing next to their bunks for the most important count of the day. Extra counts were held when there was an attempted escape or someone had been found dead. Unfortunately, in either case, the inmates were locked down, confined to their cells, until an investigation was completed.

The investigation process often turned up nothing. Three cons were found with their throats cut from ear to ear. Despite an intensive search and investigation, the murder weapon was never found. Although there were snitches in every prison, no one either saw anything or was willing to come forward in this particular case. I guess SIT (the Special Investigation Team) didn't think about putting their hand deep in a toilet full of shit.

The guards knew as much as the cons did about the goings-on. That's why I was questioned four times about the murders. They knew what these studs had done to me, and they knew I had something to do with their murders, but not being able to prove it made all the difference in the world.

It was still hard for me to believe that Picasso would order his Gangsta Gods to terminate me. It just didn't make sense, but not much did these days, I figured.

Shit was about to get real crazy. I wasn't worried, though. I could handle crazy. I'd done it for eight years now. The thing is; could crazy handle me? Obviously not—this time crazy failed and was going to continue to fail. The prison remained on lockdown for the rest of the week.

Once the lockdown ended, I saw Juicy, out the corner of my eye, making a beeline towards the toilet.

Thirty minutes later, Juicy caught up to me as I jogged around the quarter-mile prison track. The exchange was quiet and quick.

It was uncharacteristically cold that April morning, which made it the perfect morning. I was the only one on the track. I worked quick. I dug a shallow grave with my fingers. The guard tower with the best view of me was at my back. It took me only a minute to scrape out a hole and bury the tissue-wrapped scalpel in the moist, red clay, on the dirt side of the prison rec yard track.

I couldn't help but think, If Law were here, none of this would've happened. Law's reasoning was what helped me convince T-Hunt to get the Disciples to re-think taking Picasso out a couple years ago. And it was that same reasoning that I was going to use now. Which didn't mean Picasso couldn't be dealt with by an outside player.

ACT 27
Still a Man
Moses

It was times like these that I wished I had Law by my side. It was ironic that I'd replaced a strong, militant, revolutionary, scholarly, respect-commanding brother as my ride-or-die partner with a gay cat. I guess it wasn't as different as I first thought. Juicy was, after all, still a brotha. He was not Law One Free, but he was still ride-or-die to the end, like Law. And that was more important than his sexual preference.

Juicy and I had long conversations about an array of things. I no longer cared what others thought about us. Juicy was my friend, and as he once told another brotha, he was "more man than most." He proved that to me every day I rolled with him.

While walking the track one morning, I asked him, "Man, what made you . . ." I shrugged, trying to find the right words, ". . . choose your lifestyle?"

"I didn't choose to be gay; I am gay."

"I ain't tryin' to judge you, but I know you're a man of

God, I mean you go to Christian services every Sunday in the chapel."

"Go ahead. Don't stop now."

"Well, what do you think God thinks about your lifestyle?" I shook my head. "I mean, the Bible, Sodom and Gomorrah, procreating, laying with another man, all that—spiritually, where are you with that?"

"Moses, do you know why I've done what I have for you?"

"No, I don't."

"It's because you have never judged me. You speak to me like a person and not a thing. That's more than most people that I've known in this lifetime.

"You see, I grew up a single child in a loving Christian home on Atlanta's Southside. My father owned a barbershop slash church near downtown Atlanta, on Auburn Avenue, not even three blocks from Martin Luther King's Ebenezer Baptist Church." Juicy laughed. "You could say that my father was a preaching barber. His shop was called Pop's Shop. At Pop's Shop you'd get a sermon and a haircut at the same time. And my mother worked as a registered nurse at Georgia Baptist Hospital.

"We were never poor. Never struggled. I never wanted for anything, but to make my parents proud. I wasn't the child who became gay due to a traumatic experience as a child. I had never been molested or any of that stuff you hear as excuses from others who try to justify their gayness.

"I remember being in first grade and watching the girls at recess jump rope, dresses flying up, girlish laughter chorusing in the air. Tears would run down my face as I watched. Moses, I wanted to be free to play with them. I wanted to wear dresses and let my hair grow long, so I could wear it in a ponytail. But I couldn't. I was trapped in a male body. I didn't know anything about sex. I didn't like boys. I just wanted to be a pretty little girl. I was six years old then.

"As I got older, I went into a shell. I didn't want to play sports with the fellas, and I couldn't play dolls with the girls, so I lost myself in my schoolwork and books. I found freedom when I escaped into the pages of the works of James Baldwin, Richard Wright, Claude Brown, and Ralph Ellison. It was these times that I could be me without enduring ridicule and embarrassment."

"Didn't your folks realize how sad you were?"

"No, not really. My father was always at work. I think my mother may have somewhat noticed, but couldn't understand how an intelligent child with seemingly everything could be lonely and sad.

"As long as I didn't complain and I got good marks in school, everything was fine. My family was a proud one, and who was I to embarrass them? So I remained a turtle, hiding in my shell."

"Sounds like your folks were trying to be good people, giving you a nice home, toys, clothes, everything, but their time."

"I guess not." He shrugged. "They worked hard."

"Maybe so, but it seems their work blinded them, to what you were lacking. That's probably why you were so confused."

"I wouldn't say I was confused. I knew what I wanted to be. I just couldn't show it until I started college at Morehouse.

"My world disappeared, and a new one emerged in English lit 101 my freshman year. The class was given an assignment to read and do a report on Ralph Ellison's classic, *The Invisible Man*. The report had to coincide with our individual personalities and our perceived realities.

"I was excited, because I'd read the book and it was one of my favorites. But as I read it again, it was like I'd never read it at all. I'd always read novels for entertainment, never for education. Now I found myself searching for more than just things that were relative to my environment and me; I found myself searching for the meaning of life. It was in this book that I found out who I was." Juicy put a hand on my arm.

"Moses, I was the Invisible Man. For eighteen years I'd been "invisible." I was going through life afraid of being me, afraid of what others would say, what others would think—I was living a lie."

"Wow, that's heavy." I shook my head.

"This was my awakening. Ralph Ellison's book, *The Invisible Man,* brought me out of my shell, and I came out with a vengeance.

"I became involved with another male student. It was the early '70s. Our lifestyle led to fights, and ridicule by others . . ." He paused as if he'd forgotten something. "You know what, Moses?"

I was hanging on his every word. "What?"

"I had and I have no regrets. I was being me, and I was happy with the me that I'd discovered.

"I was a sophomore in college, when I told my parents that I was gay. Neither of them could accept my lifestyle at first. My father had never hit me until then. I guess he thought he could beat the gayness out of me. My mother had a crying fit."

I took a second to look up at the sky as we walked the track.

"But after that night, it didn't take long for my mother to accept me for me. My father told me that I was no longer welcome in his house."

"How'd you feel about your dad after that?"

"I cried. I was hurt. But James Jackson Junior was still my father, and I loved him."

"What about your mom?"

"It took about a week, but she came around. We actually grew very close in a year's time. We went for long walks, out to eat, to the movies, and through the joy that she heard in my voice as I spoke, she realized that she'd never heard or seen me truly happy until then. And you know what, Moses?"

"What?"

"I think she was happy that she'd gotten to know me. I mean, really know me. And when she did, I think she realized I was the same James Jackson that she had raised. The difference then and now is that she saw that I was confident and content with who I was. I was no longer that sad, little, quiet child she watched grow up.

"We laughed, we cried, we grew a lifetime as mother and son in that year we spent together."

"You keep saying that year. What happened the next year?"

He slowed down the pace and dropped his head. "She died. Heart attack. It was very sudden."

"Man, I'm truly sorry to hear that."

He shook his head as if to say, "Thank you."

We walked a half-lap around the track in silence.

"I'd like to think she died happy, or better yet, fulfilled."

I nodded. "I think she did."

"The funeral was beautiful. The inside of Ebenezer Baptist Church was surrounded with my mother's favorite flower: white roses. My father looked so sad, I just wanted to hold him forever. I was more sad for him than I was my mother. I knew my mother was at peace with God and resting fine."

"Ohhh."

"I hadn't seen my father since the funeral. A year had passed. I was a senior at Morehouse and it was April, a month before graduation, when I got summoned to the administration building.

"There, I learned that my father was in the hospital. I didn't ask for details, I just got into my Oldsmobile Cutlass and rushed to Georgia Baptist, where my mother had worked for so many years.

"Upon arrival, I was briefed by one of the barbers that helped my father run the shop. I still remember the conversation as if it were yesterday."

"Tell me about it," I said.

"Okay. Well, my father's best friend, Eddie was his name. I never knew his last name, but once I got to the hospital, he sat me down in the emergency waiting area, away from everyone else, and told me that Bony Tony the pimp came in the shop for a haircut while my father was talking about how smart I was and how I was the first Jackson to graduate college."

"I thought your mother was a nurse?"

"She was, but I think my dad meant his side of the family. Moses, I was shocked, because I had never known my father was proud of me. I thought he hated me."

I nodded.

"So next Eddie told me that Bony Tony started laughing and clowning my father in front of a barbershop full of regulars waiting for a cut."

"Clowning about what?"

Juicy stopped walking. A minute later we were both standing in the grass on the side of the track when he continued. "Bony Tony started ranting on about how I was gay and how I could make him way more money than his girls did. And after a while"—Juicy shrugged—"Eddie told me my father lost it."

"What do you mean, 'lost it'?"

"My dad dropped his clippers on the ground and took a run at Bony. That's when Bony shot him."

"Damn!" I shook my head.

Tears ran down Juicy's face. "The doctor interrupted Eddie and told us that my father was recovering nicely and he'd be released in another day or two. I left Eddie in the waiting room and went in to see how he was doing. When I got to my father's bedside, he held out his arms to me, and I leaned over and hugged him.

"While in his arms, my father said, 'Son, forgive me, and always remember that I never stopped loving you.' Moses, I swear, as soon as he said those words, his body went limp, and he died."

I nodded and followed Juicy, as we started walking the track again.

"I didn't cry, and I didn't grieve, until I hunted Bony Tony down."

"That's why you're in here, right?"

"Yep. I cut that nigga's throat right on the stairs of the 5th Precinct where he worked."

"I thought Bony Tony was a pimp?"

"He was, but he was also chief of detectives for the 5th Precinct."

"Dirty-dog pig," I said.

Juicy shook his head. "No regrets. My heart is at peace. I'm fine. So, to answer your first question—I believe that my actions and my thoughts are wrong in God's eyes, when it comes to my lifestyle, but that doesn't mean that I don't love and honor Him. I will always do that, and I will always be the queen."

"You's a fool."

"And you are the friend of a fool who loves you as the brother the fool never had."

Juicy had served six years and was up for parole in four.

He'd probably get paroled his first time before the board. Although he'd killed a cop, it was still a black cop.

There were five people in this world that I knew I could trust and depend on—Momma, T-Hunt, Law, Rhythm, and Juicy. If some heavy gangster shit ever went down and I needed some help, Juicy would be the first one I'd call. Killing a cop on the precinct steps was about as gangster as it gets.

ACT 28
Escaping the Future
Moses

"It's over, Moses. We gotta get out now, before we become statistics."

"How? I mean, what happened?" I asked. I was sitting in the visiting room with my boy, T-Hunt, stunned and confused.

T-Hunt crouched over towards me, his hands on his knees. "It's like this. Moses, we've lost too many soldiers to heroin, the penitentiary, and the graveyard. We've lost six Kings since you got stabbed almost a year ago; I don't see an end to the killing."

"Hold on, hold on." I shook my head. "What are you talking about?"

"I'm sorry, Moses. I forgot you don't know."

"Know what?"

"I didn't order it, and the Kings didn't sanction it, but a couple Disciples pulled up to a traffic light next to Picasso in broad daylight. One of them emptied a clip into his Mercedes."

"Was he okay?" I asked.

"Unfortunately, yes. But the Gangsta Gods retaliated, shooting a young Disciple in the head and leaving the body on his mother's doorstep."

"Why am I just hearing this?"

"Moses, you were in the hospital. You almost lost your life. I didn't want to bring any more undue stress on you. Besides, you have enough to deal with in here as it is," T-Hunt said.

"The war I tried to prevent has begun, huh?" I looked down at the red-and-black-speckled visiting room carpeted floor.

He nodded. "I'm afraid so."

"Damn!" I banged my fist on the table we sat at.

"Remember when we talked about changing the system, being a voice for black people everywhere, making sure that our kids would have the same opportunities as white kids?"

"Yeah, I remember," I sadly said.

"Remember when you would have everyone reading George Jackson, Diop, Clarke, Dr. Ben, Huey. You had all of us ready to die for our people. You had us feeling proud and good about being Black. Instead of our skin being our sin, you made it our power. Man, I would've stood in front of ten trains for you. I can't do that now."

"I'm sorry, T. I really am." I paused. "But when I stepped down, you took over. You're King of Kings. The Disciples may have been my baby, but you're the father now. It's up to you to take them in whatever direction they're going. You know I have your back, but you have to realize, things are much more complicated than they were when I was King of Kings."

"I realize that, but I have to go with my heart in order to save my soul. Man, I love you, Moses, I love the Disciples, but I love me too." He pointed to himself. "You taught me what it was to be free, to be strong, to be Black and proud. You taught us this. I was happy, with little to no money, struggling. I felt then that I was the richest, poor man in the world."

"You're still rich," I said.

"No, I'm not. I own a four-thousand-square-foot high-rise condo in downtown Chicago, a summer home in South Beach, and more cars than I can drive. But I have never been as poor and unhappy as I am now."

"I understand the way you feel, T, and I respect what you're saying."

"Do you really understand?"

I put my hand on his shoulder. "Yeah, I think I'm beginning to." I looked him in the eyes and nodded.

"What do you want me to do with your cut of the money I've been saving for you these past few years?"

"How much do I have?"

"Thanks to your buddy, Law, you got 1.3 in an account in Zurich, and 1.4 in Grand Cayman, and one million buried in a graveyard plot I purchased in your name three years ago at Crown Cemetery in Indianapolis."

"Law buried my money?"

"You know how Law is. After all he's been through, you really can't blame him for all his conspiracy theories."

"Yeah, I guess you're right . . . but a graveyard. I wonder how the hell he pulled that off."

"I don't know, and I didn't ask," T-Hunt said. "Let's just hope he knows how to dig it up, when the time comes."

"So what about the Disciples? What will happen to them?"

"I've divided the Nation into six sets, and I've given the Kings their independence."

"So you've already told the Kings you're out?"

"Yeah, I had to."

"And what was their reaction?"

"They were messed up about it, but when I laid everything out, they understood."

I put my head in my hands. "Man, what have I done?"

"You followed your vision."

"Man, I just thought that we could make all this money and go back into the community, clean it up, and build from there."

"I ain't blamin' you for shit. We made a lot of money. I lived a lifestyle that most Blacks can only dream about. We both had big dreams, but everybody don't dream in the reds and blues that we do. Our people complain all day long about being oppressed, but Black folk just haven't sunk deep enough to be willing to do whatever to change conditions. Hell, look how hard it was to get the Disciples to start reading. You know if we won't even lift up a book, we won't lift up another brotha."

"I wish I had seen that a long time before now."

"Yeah, me too," he said. "Me too."

"So what's your next move?"

"I'm gon' let the government take my homes, the cars, furniture, and all that material shit, and I'm taking Zion to Toronto."

"'Toronto'? Man, what you smokin'?"

"Moses, I gotta make some moves quick, or we'll both be dreaming from jail."

"Whachu' mean by that?"

"Well, I got a message stating that I'm about to be indicted on everything from racketeering to murder. I believe it. Whoever left the message knew too much of my business."

"Do the Disciples know?"

"The six Kings do. That's why they understand why I have to leave."

I was all messed up inside. I felt like I'd let my best friend down. Whether T-Hunt wanted to admit it or not, this was all my fault.

"We've been through a lot together. No matter where we

go, which path we travel . . ." I squeezed my eyes shut. "I love you, man." I got up and hugged my boy.

"I love you too, Moses. And don't trip. I'm gon' be all right. You know how I do?"

"Yeah, I do. That's why I'm calling Law first thing in the morning and telling him to dig the money up and give it to you. I want you and my godson to have it."

"Moses, man, I'm good. Keep your money. I got a couple million already waiting for me in Toronto. I've already arranged for mine and Zion's deaths. I got new birth certificates and socials for both of us to start a new life with."

"So this is goodbye?"

"Yeah." He nodded before putting his fist over his heart and saying, "For life, baby."

"For life."

We embraced. Nothing more had to be said.

I'd lost my father, Solomon, Picasso, and now T-Hunt. And I could understand how I'd lost all of them, but I couldn't figure out where Picasso and I went wrong.

ACT 29
A New Understanding
Picasso

Rhythm and I sat in Law's office on the sixteenth floor of the Eidelman building, downtown Chicago. At first Law wore a confused look on his face, when Rhythm and I told him we were brother and sister, but after I explained why we kept it a mystery, he just said, "That's some helluva love."

We laughed a minute before getting back to the business at hand. I sat in a black leather office chair in front of Law's desk, and Rhythm sat next to me while I spoke.

"After some Disciple niggas tried to bury me last year, shit got crazy. I went down to New Orleans for a month to lay low and wait on my big sis to get a handle on some FBI shit, and when I got back in town the Gangsta Gods and the Disciples were at war.

"But yo, Law, I ain't had nothin' to do with Moses gettin' shanked. Those cats that tried to off Moses weren't even Gods. Yeah, they knew the gang signs and the Gangsta God constitution, but they were not Gods. If Moses didn't handle them, we would have."

"If the Gangsta Gods weren't behind Moses' attack, then who was?" Law asked.

"Hell if I know?" I shrugged my shoulders.

Rhythm straightened out a crease in her pants suit as she stood up. "I'll bet my life either Richard James or the FBI were behind it."

"I'm big on government cover-ups and conspiracy theories, but I don't see why the FBI would exert their energy on Moses," Law said.

"It's not about Moses; it's about divide and conquer." She walked over to the wall-sized window looking over the city. "Picasso, major drug dealer, millionaire, head of a five-thousand-plus-member gang. T-Hunt, leader of an even larger drug, street gang."

"Where does Moses fit in to this theory?" Law asked.

"I'm getting to that; just follow me a minute." Rhythm walked around the office. "Rev's story about his run-in with the feds years ago has led me to believe that they still have their eyes on Moses, and we know they have my brother on what they think is a tight leash. And if they have their eyes on Moses, you know they're watching the Disciples. And if this is true, they must think Moses is still running the Disciples from the inside. If not, they wouldn't be planning on indicting T-Hunt this early."

Law said, "Next year's election. James runs for governor, gets elected while a gang war is going on. While in office, he does something like spearhead a gang task force. He's already kept tabs on the Disciples and the Gangsta Gods, so he takes down their leaders, sweeps the streets for gang members, and ends the war, setting him up to run for president in the following four years."

"Wow! How the hell did you get all that out of what she said?" I asked.

"History. It's already been done," Law said.

"When?" I asked.

"The American Civil War. Seventy-five of the first hundred years the president came from the South, and the South was building up momentum to leave the Union and form its own government. Freeing the slaves was the only way to take money and power away from southern plantation owners. So, you see, it's all about votes and power. We, like then, are just chess pieces in a much bigger game," Law explained.

"Ah shit! It all makes sense now." I nodded my head. "James and the feds are in bed together. Them mu'fuckas been playin' me the whole time. They didn't care if I gave them shit on the Disciples; they just wanted niggas to think I was a snitch. And when killing the two Disciples, making it look like I did it, didn't start a war, they tried to have Moses offed, making it look like my Gods did it . . . all to start a gang war."

"I wish so bad that I could tell Moses what's happening, but I can't," Rhythm said.

"That's right, big sis. I already risked too much, sending someone to warn T-Hunt about the sealed indictment James slipped up and hinted at."

"Yeah, but what's done is done, and you had to do that," Law said. "So let's move on."

"Moving on ain't as easy as that. I'm running out of moves."

Rhythm interrupted. "Richard James was the police commissioner for ten years before he was elected mayor, and now he's thrown his hat in for next year's governor's race. Now is the time we have to strike."

"What do you mean?" Law and I asked at the same time.

"Congressman Perry Homes spearheaded and headed up the commission that was investigating police corruption in the city of Chicago and, specifically, inside the police commis-sioner's office."

"The congressman that Moses was accused of killing?" Law asked.

"The one and only. That's the motive we need to support the theory that James had Congressman Perry Homes murdered," she said. "With the support of Moses' brother, Reverend King, what Picasso has on tape, and what I've put together working in the DA's office in DC, we can take James down and get Moses exonerated. It'll be dangerous, and some of us may lose our lives, but it's a risk I'm willing to take for 'my king.'"

ACT 30
Momma King
Moses

A cheerful-sounding female voice answered, "Mr. One Free's office. May I help you?"

"May I speak to Mr. Free, please?"

"I'm sorry, he's unavailable. May I ask, who's calling?"

"Yes, ma'am. Can you tell him that Moses King called?"

"Oh, Mr. King, I've heard so much about you."

"Don't believe everything you hear."

"Mr. One Free has only had great things to say about you."

"Oh well, in that case, do believe everything you hear."

"You are so crazy." She laughed. "Please hold. I'll put you through."

Five minutes later, Law came on the line. "Youngblood, I'm sorry 'bout that. I was wrapping things up with a client. Anyway, how the hell are ya, and what took you so damn long to call a brotha?"

"I've been waiting on you to slow down."

"Oh, you wasn't ever gon' call me then, huh?"

"Come on, Law, you know better than that. Man, I'm proud of you. You've been out a little over a year and you got your own practice in downtown Chicago and a sweet-sounding secretary."

"And you know she's chocolate fine."

"Man, you better be careful; don't want yo' old ass havin' a heart attack."

"You mean, you don't want me givin' that sweet young thang no heart attack and end up back in there with you for 'sexicide.'"

"Hell, I wanna be just like you when I grow up," I said. "So tell me about your practice."

"I got a window office overlooking the Chicago skyline, thanks to you, our Nicaraguan friend, and a few others, I'm maintainin'."

"I don't know how. Knowin' you, you probably workin' pro bono and fightin' for folks who you know can't pay."

"Youngblood, you know me well, don't ya?"

"Yes, I do. Law, you just don't know how it makes me feel to hear the happiness in your voice."

"Yeah, I'm happy, and I just wanna tell you thanks for everything." He paused. "Youngblood, I've been keeping tabs on you. I know everything. I had trouble sleeping for months. Youngblood, if it weren't for your woman, I'da done somethin' we both would've regretted. Boy, she's the truth."

"I know. Believe me, I know."

"So much has happened in a year. I have so much to tell you."

Phone conversations were monitored in prison. High-profile convicts were scrutinized intensely. Since the murder of the three cons who failed to finish me, I was watched even closer than I was before.

Law knew the rules. I knew he wanted to say so much more, but he couldn't.

"Moses, we have our work cut out for us, and you are the key to us completing our mission."

"I would have called sooner, but by the time your number was placed on my calling list, I was put on phone and commissary restriction. I was lucky they didn't throw me in the hole while they had me under investigation."

"Hmph."

A quiet minute passed, before Law broke the silence.

"Your mother is a wonderful woman. I see where you get your drive," he said. "Momma King accepted me like I was one of her own."

"That's Momma." I smiled. "She's always taken strays in. Even my enemies love Momma. She always seems to be able to bring out the good in people. She never worries about things she can't change. Always has food for the hungry, medicine for the sick, and happy words for the sad."

"I don't see how that woman does it. She has more energy than a Kenyan marathon runner."

I smiled as I thought about Momma givin' Law several of her "Jesus Lawd, Lawd Jesus" speeches.

"When I first met her, she had me laughing and crying all day and half the night as we told stories while eating ice cream and drinking coffee. She was listening mostly to stories about you. She never judged—"

The phone went dead. I didn't want it to end, but I knew it was coming. A new phone system had been put in all around the prison system. All phone calls were limited to fifteen minutes, and instead of being able to make collect calls, convicts had to pay for their own calls.

The Bureau of Prisons and the Justice Department figured out just one more way to profit off prisoners. It was bad enough that prisoners were forced to work for twelve cents an hour, manufacturing everything from mattresses to helicopter harnesses.

Damn phone. Damn prison. Shit, just when we were talking about Momma. I was relieved to hear someone else besides T-Hunt telling me about Momma. But I knew Momma was okay. She was strong, much stronger than she looked. God, I missed her so much.

T-Hunt had been keeping me abreast as to her condition and state of mind all these years. I was just glad she understood why I cut off all contact with her. I just couldn't bear her seeing me in prison. I felt like, if I let her come, then I was accepting the fate the courts gave me. I just couldn't do it.

Besides, Momma knew I was innocent. She knew I didn't have anything to do with killing that congressman and his wife. I just wished my brother Solomon had half as much confidence in me as Momma and Rhythm did.

ACT 31
Rhythm and Soul
Rhythm

Having grown up in middle-class suburbia, Queens, New York with my mother and stepfather, and not having rats didn't mean that I didn't know how to catch them. When it came to the crooked politician species of rat, you just needed a larger block of cheese. Being an assistant United States Attorney in the politician rat capital, Washington, DC, gave me plenty opportunity to see how rats are trapped and how they trap themselves.

I spent another two weeks of research and planning after Picasso met Law. I couldn't help but be nervous as my flight landed in Chicago. I don't know why I was nervous; I knew Solomon wanted to help. I just didn't know how far he was willing to go.

"Rhythm, nice to see you again." Solomon gave me a hug and loaded my small carry-on bag in the trunk of his blue Lincoln Continental.

We made small talk during the twenty-minute drive from the airport to the King estate in the "artsy-fartsy" Chicago suburb, Buffalo Grove.

First thing I thought upon stepping onto the white marble foyer was that he definitely had arrived.

"Rhythm, I want you to meet my fiancée, Sunflower Jones," Solomon said.

"What a unique name."

"I don't know if that's good or bad," Sunflower said.

"Oh, I'm sorry. It's just that the word sunflower is so beautiful."

"Well, thank you, Rhythm. My grandfather was a chief in the Inca tribe of the Sequoia nation. He gave me the name. The Incas revered the sunflower. They believe it promises power, warmth, and nourishment."

I looked around the expensively decorated den.

"Rhythm, can I get you something to drink?" Sunflower walked from the spacious den overlooking a beautiful lake off the manicured, treeless back yard.

"No, thank you. I'm fine."

"So I take it, this is not a social visit," Solomon said.

"Not exactly."

"So what's going on, Rhythm?"

"I haven't been totally honest with you, Rev. There is a lot you don't know about me."

He crossed his legs and leaned forward. "I'm listening." He tapped his manicured nails on the crystal coffee table in front of him.

I sat down in the saddle-brown leather high-back chaise to his left. I took a deep breath. "I don't know where to start."

"The beginning is always good."

"Okay, here goes. My mother was an elementary school teacher before she met Chaka Nkrumah. He was a leader in the African Political Revolutionary Party, before his group merged with the Black Liberation Army. Chaka ate dinner with Adam Clayton Powell Junior and lunched with Father Divine.

He came to the States as a foreign exchange student from

Senegal. While studying for his Ph.D. in psychology at NYU, he became fascinated with the plight of Blacks in America. He couldn't understand how we could just accept being treated like animals in America."

"He sounds like Moses."

I shook my head. "He was far from being like your brother. Anyway, while in college he met some revolutionary followers of Marcus Garvey. While they felt that Blacks should return to Africa, he debated that Blacks had just as much stake and claim to the soil they were forced to toil for three hundred years.

"'Why go back, when you can go forward?' became his war cry. His motto was soon adopted by several students who wanted change, but didn't want to leave America to get it."

"I like that—'Why go back, when you can go forward?' I'll have to steal that one," Solomon said.

"Anyway, my father was speaking at Abyssinian Baptist Church on West 138th Street in Harlem, when my mother, Portia Azure, fell in love with the tall, clean-shaven, burnt-coal-black Senegalese leader. After only knowing him for two weeks, they married. She soon found out that he was into a lot more than leading a revolutionary party for change."

"Really." Solomon uncrossed his legs.

"The first time she questioned him about the late hours he kept, and all the money he always seemed to have, to be able to afford the fancy Cadillacs, the expensive clothes, and the upscale apartment they lived in, he beat her."

"Noooo."

"Yes, and she was more in shock than in pain, when he first hit her in the jaw, knocking her to the floor. While on the floor, with her hand on her jaw and looking up at him in shock, it all came together. The glassy eyes, the guns, the late hours, the money, it all added up to one thing—drugs, she surmised.

"After regaining her footing, she ran to the kitchen and

got two knives from the dish rack and sliced him from his Adam's apple to his belly button."

Solomon whistled. "Your mother didn't play."

"No, she didn't. After cutting him, she told him that if he ever raised a hand to her again she'd finish the job."

"Did he?"

"Are you kidding? The man was a drug dealer and a lot of other things, but he wasn't crazy. My mother told me that was a turning point in their marriage. He hardly touched her at all after then. She told me that I was a miracle child because she and Chaka were only together once after she cut him.

"She figured the drugs he was using suppressed his sexual desire. They were together two years before she found out that he had kidnapped a young girl from Havana, Cuba to be his sex slave. When she found that out, she was pregnant with me."

"Tell me she didn't go after him with a knife again."

"No—this time a gun. She was six months pregnant, when she popped up at his other apartment with his sawed-off shotgun. His Cuban mistress cowered in a corner of the front room, while my mother explained that she'd kill him if he ever showed up near her door, and before she left, my mother offered his bruised and beaten Cuban mistress safety if she left my father and came with her."

"Did she go?"

I shook my head. "No, but a couple years later the timid little Cuban woman showed up at my mother's home in Queens with a little baby boy. She introduced herself as Naiaria."

" 'Naiaria'?—That is a beautiful name," Solomon said.

"In choppy English, she explained that she wanted her son to know his family. I was only twenty months old at the time, but my mother says my baby brother and I bonded like we were twins. She said it was uncanny how much we looked alike; I was just a few shades darker than him."

"Pablo!—I knew you looked familiar." Solomon jumped up and pointed. "Pablo Nkrumah is your brother?"

I smiled and nodded. "Since I can remember, the only thing that separated Pablo and me was space. I loved my little brother like no other. We saw each other every weekend, and we cried when Naiaria picked him up and took him home for the week."

"Wow! I didn't meet your brother until after Moses went to prison. If it weren't for Pablo's large donations, there probably wouldn't be a New Dimensions First Church of God."

"I bet he's never stepped foot in the church."

"I don't think so; that's why I never understood why he gave so much."

"Rev, my brother does a lot of wrong, but he has a good heart. He believes in supporting Black business, and since he loves Moses the way he does, he wanted to help his family."

"I thought they were rivals."

After explaining the rest of the story to Solomon, he was momentarily in shock.

"The whole thing sounds like the movie of the week," he said. "So let me get this straight, Pablo's mother shot and killed your father, Pablo was sent to live with your father's sister in Chicago, and the mother died in prison."

I nodded.

"And you said you talked on the phone and wrote each other every day. And before you even spoke to or wrote Moses, you felt you already knew him."

"Yes, Moses was my Black 'Superman.' His case led me to change my major from African-American studies to law."

"I bet you never told Moses, did you?"

"Never. Rev, you know how it is—when you tell one lie, you have to tell another one to cover up the first, and so on."

"That's what they say. I wouldn't know, you know. I'm like George Washington—I never told a lie." Solomon laughed.

"Yeah, right. Anyway, Moses thinks I heard about his case through my college roommate, who I told I was from Chicago."

"You're telling me all this for a reason, obviously."

"Yes, I want you to know everything about me, and Pablo. You need to, if you decide to help us free Moses."

ACT 32
Writing Rhythm
Moses

Rhythm,

Queen, I hope this letter finds you in better spirits than I am. Queen, tell me, am I going through some type of paradox in time or what? I mean, I've been off the streets for nearly nine years. And I can hardly believe the transformation that brothas and sistahs have gone through.

The world has changed so much in just a decade. Jheri curls and silk shirts have replaced Afros and dashikis. It's hard to tell the brothas from the sistahs these days.

Back when I was on the streets, brothas threw fists in the air and eloquently spoke of Black power and explained the beauty that was in Blackness. Now, a decade later, those fists have turned into limp corporate handshakes, and "Black is beautiful" has been replaced with skin-bleaching creams, blonde wigs, and blue contact lenses.

In the '70s, Ron and his brothers were singing about fighting the power, Sly and his family were bringin' folks to the "Family Affair," and Marvin was asking, "What's Goin' On?"

Now I turn on the radio and all I here is bumpin' and

*grindin', freaks comin' out at night, and rap music degrading
sistahs, and glorifyin' gang-bangin', and dope dealin'.*

*I know I'm probably a godfather in this movement; for that
I accept responsibility. I never would've thought it would have
come to this. Queen, I've made a lot of mistakes in my life, but
none as big as choosing a path to lead our people, without
knowing where the road would go.*

*I have to do somethin' about this madness. What, I don't
know, but I have to right my wrong.*

*One love
Moses*

Ten days later.

Moses my King,
    *Revolution. Revolution starts in the minds of the people,
and no revolution has ever been successful without economic
empowerment and mental emancipation of the few who lead it.
And it is all sparked by a driving thought from an ambitious
few.*

*Moses, the revolution has to be televised and visualized in
the minds of the oppressed. We have to make the people, not our
people, but the people understand the condition that we, and
they, are in by not knowing the truth. We have to make them
see that land barons who are only interested in keeping the
masses in ignorance, disarray, and confusion control the
world they live in.*

*I know what you've been told, but we don't have to be like
them to overpower them. Remember, if God be for you, no man
or government can come against you. I am not trying to sound
preachy. But, as you say, it is what it is, and it ain't what it
ain't. It's up to us to implement change and make it do what
we want it to do.*

*The movement has to start with the faith of at least a mus-
tard seed, and then the truth has to be told. Bombs, bullets,*

*and missiles can't penetrate truth. Remember, truth is reality.
But the key word is,* remember. *That's what we've forgotten.
We have to make people remember the past, remember Harriet,
Frederick, Nat, Denmark, Du Bois, Thurgood, Elijah, Marcus,
Asa, Malcolm, Martin, Assata, and Huey.*

*But first, Moses, before you can be instrumental in even be-
ginning to orchestrate a revolution, you have to revolutionize
your own thinking. Re-evaluate the things you are into and the
things you believe.*

*Love and Life
Rhythm*

ACT 33
Baiting the Hook
Solomon

"**O**kay, Solomon King, you're a man of God, not a man of man. Be strong. You're doing this for Moses. You're doing this for justice. You're doing this for God," I said to myself.

I picked up the phone in the church office. Why am I so nervous?

Over the last month, Rhythm, Moses' friend, Lawrence, Pablo, and I went over what I called "Operation Fight Corruption and Free Moses." Now was the big morning, and I had to make the first play.

I took a deep breath, hung the phone on the wall. I picked it back up then dialed the number.

"Good morning. Richard James for change. My name is Melissa Brand, you've reached the Richard James for governor campaign headquarters," a cheery voice announced.

"Well, good morning to you, young lady. I'd like to arrange a fund-raiser for the future governor," I said.

"I'm sorry. Who's calling?"

"Reverend Solomon King of New Dimensions First Church of God."

"'The soul King'?"

"That's what some call me."

"Please hold one minute, Mr. Soul—I mean, Mr. Reverend, sir."

The girl was so excited that she forgot to press the hold button. I heard her telling someone she had the soul King on the line. I heard another voice telling her to get a number, that Mr. James would want to take the call himself.

I still found it amazing how the media could make or break a person. A little media exposure and you could command an audience with the president. I thought back to a few months ago when several networks covered the "Reverend Soul King Call to Stop Gang Violence and Start Gang Love." The event went well, and we received an overwhelming amount of support from community leaders and business owners.

A female voice interrupted my reverie. "Reverend King, is there a number where you can be reached? I'm sorry, but Mayor James is unavailable at this time."

"Sure, my number is 576-1576," I said before hanging up.

Confident now that I had made the call, I thought that this might just work. Rhythm was an amazing woman. And I'm not just saying that because she was doing a "Winnie Mandela." Nine years is a long time to stand by someone you've never touched or seen. And to risk her career, her freedom, and possibly her life for Moses spoke volumes.

I hoped Moses realized what type of woman he had. And when he found out that she was Picasso's sister, I hoped he'd understand why she never told him. After all she was risking for him, he'd better understand.

I'd known Pablo for, I guess, about seven years, and I still couldn't believe that I didn't notice the resemblance when I met his sister at the hospital.

The resemblance was uncanny. They both had long black

hair. Rhythm's locks fell over her shoulders; Picasso wore his in a ponytail. They had the same eyes, nose, and facial features. He was much lighter, and had her by almost a foot, but other than that, they looked very much alike.

Pablo wearing a wire to record his exchanges with James was dangerous and ingenious. I wondered how he pulled that off for so many years without detection. The payoffs, the incriminating conversations, they were on seven-year's-worth of tapes.

On each tape, Pablo somehow included the dates of almost every conversation. From what I understood, if the feds hadn't gotten involved, Rhythm and Picasso would have used the tapes long ago as leverage to get Moses' case overturned.

I just wish I had known about the tapes way before now. I guess, if I had, I couldn't have done anything. My church congregation wasn't large enough, and I didn't have the influence I had now.

Picasso and the police commissioner, now mayor, usually met in public restrooms or on back roads on the outskirts of town. That was smart.

But after listening to some of the tapes, it was hard to believe the things Richard James bragged about to a person he was extorting. A man of his background had to know better. I guess, he thought Picasso was too dumb to record him.

The ringing of the phone brought me out of my thoughts.

"Hello," I said, hoping James' greed would make him overlook the fact that I was Moses' brother.

"Yes, this is Richard James. I'm calling for Reverend King," a strong, confident voice replied.

"Mayor James, as you know, my name is Reverend Solomon King. I'm the pastor over at New Dimensions First Church of God."

"Everybody knows the soul King. You've got over fifteen thousand members."

"You've done your homework."

"That's my job."

"As you said, I have over fifteen thousand members and at least another thirty to fifty thousand brothers and sisters that faithfully watch my services on television. I can be very influential in getting you elected."

"I'm happy to hear that you're interested in politics, Reverend."

"I'm interested in community and doing the right thing."

"As I am too. The city of Chicago needs more public servants like you and myself."

"I couldn't agree more." Jesus forgive me, I silently prayed.

"Well, how can I be of assistance to you, Reverend?"

"Mayor James, I'd like to sit down with you and see how we can help each other. I have the people's ear. I just need reassurance that you are the right candidate for the Black community to throw their support behind."

"I always can and do make time for the people."

"Exactly. That's why I need a couple hours of your time to discuss matters of community."

"Let's see . . . I'm looking at my calendar. I can move a couple things around, and I could meet with you, say, tomorrow at noon."

"Noon will be fine, Mr. Mayor."

"How about lunch at the Plaza Hotel?"

"Tell you what—let's meet at my church. I'll have lunch catered, and we can talk in private."

"Looking forward to it."

"Barbecue chicken, macaroni and cheese, and collard greens fine with you?"

"I was raised on soul food; I can hardly wait."

The lies just flowed from his mouth so smoothly. I could just picture him now, barbecue sauce around the mouth of his cone mask, the fans in Momma Tee's rib shack making the sheets him and his Klan brothers wore, while they sat at a bench table in the little rib shack on 10th and Clover.

"Did I say something funny?"

I must have laughed out loud. "No, I'm sorry. I got distracted. I'll see you tomorrow at noon, Mr. Mayor."

After hanging up, I dialed one more number.

"Hey, this is Solomon. We're on for noon tomorrow at the church. We have to work fast."

"I'll be there in an hour," Law said.

I hung up and called the others.

ACT 34
Home-Field Advantage
Solomon

"**B**lessed are the peacemakers, for they shall be called the children of God," I said to myself shortly after I asked the Lord to guide me. I was in the church study, waiting for Picasso to radio me from his perch on the second floor.

A second later, Picasso radioed me. "Here he comes. He's pulling up in a black limousine, over.

I ran my hands down the legs of my black slacks, adjusted my white collar, and headed to the front.

"He just let down his window. It looks like he's arguing with someone while talking on a car phone," Picasso radioed back in.

Before I stepped out into the Chicago April sun, I radioed back, "I'm up front. I'm turning off my two-way—oh and how about those M-1's?" I was referring to the battery-operated, high-powered binoculars Pablo was using to watch Mayor James' every move.

Mayor James was much shorter than he looked on TV. He couldn't be more than 5'7", I thought, as he stood outside the dark Lincoln, saying something to the driver.

His beady little eyes, long chin, and sunken cheeks made him look like a white weasel in a tailor-made suit. He looked as confident as ever, as he walked to the church front doors.

"Governor, I'm glad you could come." I extended my hand.

"'Governor'—I like the way that sounds, Reverend." He reached out and took my hand. "Let's just hope I have enough constituents in nine months that feel the way you do." Richard James followed me deeper into the church.

"We'll talk and lunch in the church study," I said, opening the French double-doors and stepping aside.

The room was more a high-tech library than it was a church study. The room boasted twenty-four-foot walls, accented by a colorful, stained-glass ceiling depicting African-American angels riding in a circle on horse-like clouds through the sky. The dark-green, leather, high-back chairs that sat around the long oval-shaped conference table matched the thick carpet that covered the study's floor.

Remote-controlled skylights and Victorian lamps provided the lighting. A ten-by-ten-foot theatre projector screen along with a walled-in sound system took up one wall, and a library of books took up two others.

Soft jazz piped through the church intercom system as we took a seat opposite each other at the blonde wood conference table.

"Very impressive." James seemed to be admiring the wall that led to the church congregation area. On it was a mural of a large, graying, dread-headed, dark-skinned black man walking through a desert, leading several tired followers to a land of clear waterfalls, fruit trees, and grassy hillsides. The caption above the fifteen-by-fifteen-foot mural read: AS I'VE PROMISED.

"Thank you." I sat back in my chair and crossed my hands on my lap. "Richard, let me tell you what you're going to do."

"Excuse me?"

"You will convince your friend, President Reagan, to issue a full pardon for my brother, Moses Toussant King." I crossed my legs and rested a hand on one knee.

For a minute he seemed to be thinking. Then all of a sudden he burst out in laughter. He pointed to me. "At first, I thought you were serious."

"I am." I uncrossed my legs and leaned forward. "Let me tell you how serious. I'm serious enough to not only ruin your career, but I'll have you indicted and convicted of everything from extortion to murder."

"Reverend, with no due respect—and I mean no due respect—this meeting is over." He rose to leave.

I pulled out my radio, switched it on, and pressed the talk button. "Play the tape."

James was halfway to the door, when he heard his voice over the intercom.

"Pablo Picasso—what a name! If they call you Picasso, then people should call me Houdini, the way I make people and problems disappear."

"I didn't have a problem with the Disciples, you did."

"Oh, but you do now. All you had to do was give them something, but noooo, you had to play games."

"You takin' out Herbert and Big Ben was some dumb shit. Now I really can't give you shit on the Disciples."

"I don't see why you're so upset, Pablo; now you got your chance to take out the rest of the heads of the Disciples. Like I said, with them out of the way, you and your gangster goods can rule the Chicago drug trade."

"Gangsta Gods."

"Whatever."

"What about the feds? You know they sweatin' me, and now since you done made it look like I killed the two Disciple cats in Miami—"

"You have nothing to worry about. They were just two

Blacks with gang affiliations. The FBI will forget about them in a few weeks. They can't tie you to any bodies found in Miami."

James was now sitting back at the table across from me, his face expressionless.

"It don't make any difference what they can tie me to, and you know it. It's the fact that they are probably watching my every move. And what about the Disciples?"

"What about them?"

"I gotta do something about the shit storm that gon' come behind this bullshit you done started with my Gods and the Disciples."

"Yes, you do. Looks like you have to take care of them before they take care of you. Oh, and don't even think about coming clean to Tharellious Hunt. Remember what happened to the two Disciples in Miami?"

James put his arms behind his head and leaned back in the chair, a smile plastered on his face.

"Stop the tape," I shouted into the two-way.

"Why stop now? It's just getting interesting."

I couldn't figure this guy out. We had the goods on him, and he was steady smiling.

He got up, put his arms behind his back, and walked over to the Black Moses on the wall next to the French double-doors. He nodded. "Interesting picture." He turned towards me.

I hadn't moved. I was still sitting in the chair.

"You know what, Sol, ol' boy?" He laughed, his face glued to the mural in front of him.

"It's obvious that you haven't listened to that tape." He nodded. "Granted, it sounds like me on the tape." He put his index finger in the air. "But if in fact that voice is mine, I have admitted to no wrongdoing." He turned to face me. "Reverend, how can you call yourself a man of God, huh?"

Before I could answer he added, "You sit here in a church and try and blackmail me into using my influence to free a murdering, rapist drug dealer. Somehow you've managed to manufacture a recording of someone that sounds like me speaking to a notorious gang leader and drug dealer, and you think you can use that against me?" He looked me up and down. "And you call yourself a minister; you're no better than your vermin brother and the rest of his Chicago gang-member friends."

I had to pray for guidance, because I was one second away from giving in to the temptation of putting my fist in his mouth. I had to sit on my hands, so he wouldn't see me trembling.

I closed my eyes and counted to ten. After opening them, I took a deep breath and stood up. "You're right." I nodded. "I'm no better than them; I'm one of them. And we're not vermin. If you opened your eyes . . . oh, that's right, you can't . . . you're blind."

"It's you who are blind."

"As I was saying, we're not vermin, we're all God's children. But, I understand your misunderstanding. I know a lot about snakes—they're blind and use their sense of smell and touch to stalk their prey."

"You've wasted enough of my time with all your empty threats. The difference between you and me is that I don't make threats. I deliver results. I'll be seeing you real soon, boy." He turned and walked towards the French double-doors.

I took a step in his direction. "Okay, well, hear this boy." I spat the word boy out of my mouth like it was sour milk.

Continuing, I said, "You will bring Lieutenant First Class Edward Porter and retired detective Samuel Lester up on charges of murder, police corruption, false imprisonment, tampering with evidence, and rape."

"What? What are you talking about?" He took his hand off the knob and turned back to me.

I took another step. "Don't play stupid. You know damn well those two were the arresting officers in my brother's case. But if you would rather take the fall, that'll be fine too."

He waved a finger in my direction. "You don't know who you're dealing with. Tell you what—I'll look over this conversation. You give me that tape, and we'll forget about this whole thing."

"And obviously you don't know who you're dealing with. I have over twenty thousand soldiers in God's Army ready to go to war at my word. Now who do you really think will go down, you or me?"

"I think I'll take my chances. As I've said, I'm innocent of any wrongdoing." James turned back towards the door.

All of a sudden, the French doors burst open, hitting James in the face.

"No," Picasso exploded. "You gon' sit yo' punk ass back down and do as you're told. Yo, I don't 'ho' for you no more. I liberate myself right now, mo'fo'."

"You piss ant, I'll crush you like the snail you are," James fired back.

"And if you do, your fat, funky wife, Elizabeth, your two big-legged, freckled-face daughters at Princeton, your old, shriveled-up, prune-face mammy, and your blonde-headed whore-mistress will come up missin'. And to show you that I mean business, look at these." Picasso threw a handful of pictures on the table.

I was just as shocked as James was. No one told me about the pictures now scattered out on the table.

Richard James' eyes grew twice their size, as he looked through the pictures taken of his family in his home, at school, in the bathroom, and everywhere that was supposed to be private.

"And, oh yeah, ain't none of my boys gon' do the job. I

done hired the best killers—White killers." Picasso looked at me. "Yo Reverend, sorry about the pics and the language, but I gotta speak 'snake' to a snake."

Then he looked at the mayor. "That tape you just heard, fool, I got a lot more with all kinds of good shit on 'em."

"Okay, you win." James shrugged. "It may take some time for me to figure this all out."

"That's not acceptable. Time is what we've wasted for over nine years. The time is now. You have one week to expose this scandal. You have another to orchestrate a media blitz of my brother and his unjust imprisonment. Four months from now, on the first Sunday in July, my brother better be sitting"—I pointed to the ground—"in this church."

ACT 35
Discouraged and Encouraged
Moses

Rhythm,

Queen, I hope this letter finds you in the best of health and spirits. It's hard to believe that it's 1984. In two months, on May 17th, I will have been in here a decade. So much has changed. I hate to sound like a broken record, but I'm just amazed on how far we've gone backwards.

Just the other day, after Solomon's Sunday morning church service went off, a brother in the TV room got up and turned to BET. The lead story was on. Marcus Johnson was hosting a panel that consisted of two college professors, a Baptist minister, and a senator. By what they were saying, you would have thought they were White.

After listening and watching the thirty-minute program, I was left wondering what planet they had lived on over the last fifty years. Rhythm, they were all speaking of how far we as a people had come over the last fifty years.

Had the panelist forgotten that the Civil Rights Movement went from being a proud-to-be-Black and Black empowerment freedom movement to a Black-on-Black, happy-to-be-a-slave, hate movement.

I've been doing a lot of reading and research on land development. It's very interesting how White flight is starting to take place from the suburbs back into the cities.

Remember the time when there were no Blacks in the suburbs? Remember when it wasn't even safe for us to go into the 'burbs at night? Have you noticed that all the Black-owned businesses in our community have closed, with the exception of barbershops and beauty salons? Pretty soon, they too will be White- or Korean-owned, if we don't do something now. But did the panelist speak on this?—No.

I know, by my words, it seems as if I'm angry, and got a lot of hate in my heart. I am angry, but not at White people, not at the system. I'm angry with myself. I'm angry that I have become worse than the system that created the condition that the Black family is in.

Queen, I know we've exhausted most of my appeals, but I know there is something. There just has to be something out there that we've missed.

One,
Moses

One week later.

King,

I just read your letter. It's about 10:00 p.m. I'm lying in my bed, and I'm thinking, this man is my lion. I gotta free him from those cages, so he can roar. I'm thinking that I am head over heels in love with a man that I have never touched. I'm thinking of how God has let you touch me in such a way that my soul is burning and my heart is on fire.

I'm wondering what would happen if there were a thousand Black men that understood as you do? What would happen if a hundred Black men had the passion that you possess? What would happen if ten Black men had the intestinal fortitude that you exhibit?

Moses, my King, I am your Queen. I am your lioness. I'll roar for you until I can make the bars of Babylon crumble, and crumble they will.

Trust me, King, I'm coming to get you real soon, so don't sleep.

Love and Life
Rhythm

ACT 35
God's House
Solomon

"Not good morning, but—" I extended the microphone in the direction of the congregation.

"God's morning," the congregation shouted.

I pulled the microphone back to me. "How y'all feel this morning?"

"God," they responded.

"Well, all right now. God is what?"

"Good."

"When?"

"All the time!"

I felt good on this Sunday morning, standing at the New Dimensions podium. I smiled as I looked into a sea of smiling faces. There wasn't an empty seat on the ground level. I looked up into the balcony; it looked full as well.

I looked around the church. "I wanna thank everyone for praising with us this morning. I see so many old, and new, beautiful faces."

God is truly good. Last week, I challenged the congregation to bring at least two guests, and obviously they'd met the challenge. I promised a God party like never before; now I had to keep up my end of the bargain.

"Oh, we gon' get down this morning. Are you ready to do the 'God thang,' family?"

"Heaven, yes," they shouted.

"Maybe y'all didn't hear me." I took off my purple robe and turned to my right. "Percussion section, can I get some bass?"

"Boom——boom-boom-boom/boom/chick-boom-boom."

Turning to my left, looking over at the horn section, I said, "Break me off some sax."

"Are y'all ready to do the God thang?"

"Heaven, yes!" they shouted several decibels higher.

I turned back towards the rest of the New Dimensions Praising Him twenty-piece orchestra and gave them the signal to cut.

I started to walk around the pulpit's massive stage. "I wanna tell y'all a story this morning . . . a story about love."

"Take your time, Reverend," someone shouted.

"You see, there was this brotha who started a gang. Now this brotha feared no man. He had a message and wasn't gon' stop until that message was heard. He recruited twelve lieutenants who traveled with him. Many thought the brotha was mad, because he was bucking the system. Now, back then"—I shook my head—"no one bucked the system unless"—I held my index finger in the air—"they wanted to get strung up and crucified on the side of a highway.

"When someone asked this brotha what he was doing, he would respond with something like, 'I'm doing God's work.' They'd ask, 'Aren't you afraid of what will happen if they catch you spreading this Word?' And the brotha would respond with something like, 'No, I'm afraid of what will happen if I don't spread the Word.' And when asked, 'Who are you to come here trying to change things?' the brotha would smile and respond, 'I am Jesus of Nazareth, Son of my Father, God.'"

"Well, all right now," a woman shouted.

"Preach on, Reverend, preach on," Deacon Grant shouted from behind me.

"Now this man Jesus bucked the system. A system of oppression, a system against God. See, Jesus wasn't scared. He let no man put fear in His heart. His lieutenants bucked the system right along with Him. I mean, these twelve brothas were straight ride-or-die, as you young folks would say. They were no-limit soldiers for God.

"When folks started seeing and hearing this long dread-haired, bronzed man who wasn't afraid, they felt hope. And when they started seeing Him heal the sick and feed the poor with knowledge of self and of God, word spread fast that a leader, a Savior, was among them. They started to believe."

A woman jumped up and shouted, "Hallelujah!"

"See, Jesus was a 'show me' type of brotha. His lip service was followed by action. The revolution was one of action and words, and it was rising. But, still, many were still in disbelief.

"Now, let me tell you another story, one similar to the one you just heard."

"Take your time, Pastor."

"This is a story about another revolutionary. Back in the early '70s my brother, Moses King, started a street gang called the Disciples. At some point most of you have heard or read about them.

"Ummmm-hmmmm," someone said.

"Well, at the gang's inception, Moses and the Disciples gave back to the community. They fed the hungry and clothed the poor. They organized book drives. They headed up reading groups, promoting positive African-American cultural study material. And still, my brother left the Disciples to go and work with children at a Help Center.

"Almost ten years ago, on May 17th 1974, Moses was arrested and, eight months later, convicted of the rape and murder of Fiona and Congressman Reverend Perry Homes.

"Now I know I've never spoken to you about my brother. Why?—Because I was afraid. Afraid, because powerful men dragged me into a room at O'Hare Airport after Moses' arrest. They told me if I ever stood up for Moses, they'd kill my mother, Moses, and me.

"I knew Moses was innocent, but what could I do? I had no proof. But now I do. I can prove that Moses was set up by local law enforcement. Men hired to protect and serve. Men who lock your children up daily were responsible for the murders of Reverend Perry and Fiona Homes.

"In six weeks from today, on Easter Sunday, the New Dimensions First Church of God family will hold services in the streets outside of the Atlanta Federal Penitentiary. We will demand freedom for our fallen brother. I'm chartering as many busses as I can to make the trip. After service, anyone interested in going to Atlanta on the bus can see an usher, to be placed on the sign-up list.

"I am sending out a call around the nation to stand with me as I fight for justice. Dr. Martin Luther King said, '. . . An injustice anywhere is a threat to justice everywhere.'

"I need soldiers in God's Army who are not afraid of Pharaoh. I need soldiers who are tired of being abused by a cold just-ice system, instead of a fair justice system. I need soldiers by my side who are tired of seeing and hearing the stories of young black men being savagely beaten by police. I need soldiers who are tired of paying first-class taxes and being treated like third-class citizens. I need soldiers who are tired of seeing more young men go to prison than college. I need soldiers who will stand up to the call and say, 'I ain't scared.'

"For every one that is tired of being sick and tired I want

y'all to say"—I pointed the microphone at the congregation—"I ain't scared."

"I ain't scared!" the church shouted.

"When Pharoh's army tells you to go home, what are you
gon' say?"

"I ain't scared!"

The whole church was on its feet. Thousands of parishioners were shouting at the top of their lungs.

"When they tell you to lay down or we gon' lock you up
and throw away the key, what you gon' say, family?"

"I ain't scared!"

ACT 37
Rat Trap
Law

All the years we spent together in the penitentiary, and Youngblood ain't never warned me about the Chicago cold.

Windy City is an understatement. Chicago should be called the windy, wet, cold city. If God was trying to drown Chicago, he was well on his way to doing just that. Three weeks of rain. And by the look of the early spring March sky, I'd say the rain was about to start again any minute.

My teeth chattered, while waiting at 10th and Michigan for the WALK signal to light up. Just as it did, I stepped out into the street—and damn near ended up being roadkill.

Some nut blasting classical music from a new-model Ford Bronco went speeding by, splashing water all over my London Fog long coat. The fool had run the damn light right in front of the police precinct. Every damn cop couldn't be at the Dunkin' Donuts.

I jogged across the street.

"Lieutenant Porter, wait up." I waved and called out to the back of his head, as I jogged into the police station parking garage.

He turned around right as I caught up to him. "Yeah, what can I do for you?—Make it quick; I'm in a hurry."

"My name is Lawrence One Free. I'm an attorney, and I have something I think you'll be interested in."

I placed my black briefcase on top of his dark-blue Chrysler. I popped it open and handed him a manila envelope with several pictures in it.

"What are these?—I told you I was in a rush; I don't have time for games—And please get your briefcase off my car." He started unlocking the door.

"These are pictures of a meeting that took place a few days ago between the mayor and the Reverend Solomon King," I hurriedly said.

"Who cares?"

"You should." I pulled out a mini-recorder from my inside coat pocket. "Listen to this." I pressed play.

"Okay, well hear this. You will bring Lieutenant First Class Edward Porter and retired detective Samuel Lester up on charges of murder, police corruption, false imprisonment, tampering with evidence, and rape."

"What? What are you talking about?" the voice of Richard James said.

"Don't play stupid. You know good and well these two were the arresting officers in my brother's case"—I pressed the STOP button.

"I know you're in a rush, but I have a lot more for you to hear. As a matter of fact, I have James on tape agreeing to bring you and Lester to justice."

Switching gears, I asked, "Would you like to come to my office?"

"Look, I really don't have time for this. If this is a joke—"

"Mr. Porter, did that tape really sound like a joke?"

"Get to the point—What do you want?"

"Richard James." I handed him my card. "Look, I'll be at my office until ten this evening. I would advise you to make it your business to come see me before you talk to anyone else." I turned and walked out of the parking garage.

As soon as I made it to a pay phone, I deposited a quarter and made the call.

"Hello," a voice answered.

"Rhythm, this is Law. I think I hooked Porter."

"How do you know he won't try and contact James?" she asked.

"I don't. But let's just pray he believes that James is coming after him."

"Sounds good, but it's still risky."

"Risks are a part of life," I said.

"Who knows what James is gon' do? He's gone two weeks past the ultimatum Reverend King and Picasso gave him."

"I know. That's why Porter is our ace in the hole. I got this, Rhythm—you have to just put a little trust in old Law."

Back at my office I made sure I had a loaded clip in the .45 Picasso gave me. I could never be too careful. No telling what Porter or any desperate man would try and do.

I was lying on the black leather couch in the reception area, drifting off to sleep, when footsteps outside the door startled me out of my haze. I looked at my watch. It was a quarter to eleven. I eased off the couch and walked towards the door. I got to get me some softer shoes.

The knob slowly turned.

My heartbeat raced as I pulled out my gun and aimed.

The door eased open.

A second later I was staring into the barrel of a .38 police special, while Porter stared into the barrel of my .45.

"Mr. Free, it's me, Detective Edward Porter." He lowered his gun.

I relaxed and put my piece back into my suit jacket

pocket. "Please come into my office." I led him into the spacious black and gray room, with a wall-sized window overlooking the Chicago skyline.

"I'm here." Porter sat in the leather chair facing my desk in front of the window.

"I represent someone who has been extorted for several years by Mr. James. I have access to a mountain of incriminating evidence that would put Mr. James under the jail."

"How do I know that you're on the up-and-up?" he asked.

"You don't. But I'll tell you this—without me you don't have an ice-cube's chance in hell. We both know that Mr. James is a corrupt and very dangerous man with friends in high places who will go to extremes to control any major damage done to him and his career."

"Why would James even entertain the idea of bringing up any skeletons of the past?" Porter questioned.

"What do you mean?"

"You tell me," he said.

"You mean the Homes case? Think about it. His hand's been forced. Moses King's brother, the Reverend Solomon King, obviously has some heavy shit on James. He must've threatened to go public with what he has. The Reverend has a large following, and with that comes power. And James is not in a position to, let's say, diffuse the Reverend.

"From my understanding, the Reverend just wants his brother freed, and he knows that James is the key to making that a reality."

"For argument's sake, let's say Dick James were to incriminate me in some type of wrongdoing."

" 'Let's say.' "

"By incriminating me, he incriminates himself."

"Not exactly." I pointed a finger in the air. "Not if he destroys all ties linking him to the King case and he makes a deal first. Right now, time is of the essence. I'll give you this tape. Go home, listen to it, and meet me back here at 8:00 a.m.—no attorneys, just you."

Without shaking hands, Porter got up and started walking toward the door.

I told him, "One more thing—any plans you had for tomorrow, cancel them."

ACT 38
The Deal
Rhythm

It was warm for mid-March in DC. Two joggers ran past me. But not warm enough for shorts, I thought.

Traffic was gridlocked as usual. Thank God the Federal building where I worked was only a twenty-minute walk.

After entering the building, I made a beeline to "the Babe's" office. My boss, Bill Powell, had won more cases for the prosecution than any other DA in history. Hence, he was christened "the Babe," after Babe Ruth.

"Good morning, Bill," I said.

"What makes this morning so good?"

"The sun is shining. God allowed me to wake up; He allowed you to wake up."

"On the wrong side of the bed, with the wrong damn woman."

"Bill, you're always complaining about Marcie. If she makes you so unhappy, why don't you leave her?"

"Hell, I can't afford to. Her and the kids would milk my salary dry. I'd end up living in some cramped-up efficiency in Georgetown, straining to watch football on a thirteen-inch black and white. And besides I've gotten used to Marcie's bickering. It puts me to sleep at night."

"Bill, you are very special."

"Aja, this better be good. Not even God gets up this early. Now can you explain to me again why I'm here at six in the morning?"

I explained to him in careful, rehearsed detail what was happening in Chicago. I could see the cogs turning, as Bill's methodical mind went into motion as I spoke.

"Okay, so tell me again—why are they coming here and not to the DA's office in Chicago?" he asked.

"Trust—they have none."

"Aja, something tells me this has something to do with all the vacation and personal days you've been using lately." He frowned and shook his head. "Don't we have enough cases to prosecute here in the nation's capital?"

"Bill?"

"Don't Bill me. You've gone outside your jurisdiction, Aja."

"Technically, I haven't. In criminal cases involving elected city and state officials, a governing body outside that city or state can investigate and prosecute those officials," I said.

"Yes, but that call has to be made by the DA."

"I'm sorry."

"I don't need a character reference."

"So what now?" I asked.

"You're one of my best attorneys, we're friends, and most importantly, this is an election year for me. When the media gets wind of this, I wanna be in front of it. And, Aja, you better not make me regret this."

I jumped up and ran behind his desk and gave him a hug. "Oh, Bill, thank you, thank you, thank you."

"If you really wanted to thank me, you'd go to Mc Donald's and get me—"

"Two egg McMuffins, coffee, two sugars, no cream." I headed for the door of his office.

"Don't forget—"

"I know, two ketchups and two strawberry jellys," I said. "I've been getting you breakfast for how long now?"

Porter sure doesn't look the way I imagined, I thought, as Law and Lieutenant Porter walked in Bill's office a little before noon.

"Hello, Ms. Azure, so nice to see you again." Law extended his large hand towards me.

"Likewise, Mr. One Free." I shook his hand.

"Lawrence One Free, this is Bill Powell."

"Call me Bill. Heard a lot about you, Lawrence," he lied as he shook Law's hand.

"Bill, Aja, this is Lieutenant First Class Edward Porter of the Chicago PD," Law said, introducing the gray-haired, broad-shouldered, Herculean-built white guy.

The meeting was very productive. So productive, that Bill called in a stenographer to take shorthand. After a couple hours, a deal was worked out that would grant Porter immunity and leave him with half his pension. Of course, Porter's retirement would be effective immediately.

Judging by Porter's lack of resistance to the proposed deal, it seemed testifying to a grand jury and, quite possibly, at the Richard James trial, was a small price to pay to stay out of prison.

All we needed now was for whichever judge that would be appointed to try the case to sign off on the plea agreement.

And so far, in the five years I'd worked for Bill, I never saw a plea agreement that left our offices come back denied.

Before Law and Porter left a half-hour ago, Bill called his old golfing buddy, Judge Frank Dugan. Dugan told him to send the warrant right over and he'd sign it.

It was going on 4:30. Bill had just finished filling out the arrest warrant for James, and I was about to run it over to the Evergreens Country Club for the judge to sign, when Doris Baker, Bill's personal assistant, interrupted us.

"Bill, Judge Dugan is on line one. Would you like me to take a message?" she asked.

"No, I'll take it." Bill picked up the phone.

Then his eyes widened, and his face turned red.

Uh-oh, must be bad news.

After hanging up, he inhaled.

It's definitely bad.

He inhaled again. "We have a slight problem," Bill said. "It just so happens that less than fifteen minutes ago Richard James held a live press conference in Springfield, Illinois, on the capitol lawn."

ACT 39
Playing the Game
Moses

"Twentieth Century Fox, big-legged 'ho's and cocaine rocks." My domino partner slammed the domino down on the stainless steel common area prison table.

"Damn, Rock, you sweeter than bear meat," one of the players said to the brotha who set my partner up for the twenty points he'd just counted.

"Yo, Moses, they talkin' 'bout you on CNN," one of the old heads shouted outside one of the four TV rooms in the dorm.

Everybody got up and jetted into the almost empty TV room.

"Just to recap the latest developments," the news anchor announced, "Chicago mayor Richard James, the frontrunner in Illinois' gubernatorial election this fall, shook up Chicago with a surprising turn of events at a press conference he held earlier this afternoon. We're now taking you live to the capitol in Springfield, Illinois."

One of the fellas asked the old head, "Old School, I thought you said they was talkin' 'bout Moses?"

Old School threw his hands up in the air. "Just listen, will you."

"Rock, turn it up," I said.

"Thank you all for taking time out of your busy schedules to attend this press conference this breezy, sunny afternoon," the mayor said. "As you all know, I am, and have always been, a servant of the people. I left my government job and took over as police commissioner in the city of Chicago in 1972. My goal has always been to protect and serve the people, as our motto states."

"Protect, hell," I said. "The only thing he protects is that false image he represents—I'd like to serve my foot to his ass."

"Shhh." Old School turned, looked at me, and put a finger to his lips.

James continued, "I wouldn't be doing my job as a public servant if I stopped now. I am very sad to say that we've uncovered police corruption and a police cover-up.

"New evidence has just come to my attention in the 1974 murder/rape case of Congressman Perry Homes and his wife Fiona. As police commissioner back then, I made a promise to the King family . . ."

"What?" I jumped up and shouted.

". . . that if there was corruption in my police force, I would uncover it, and the individuals responsible would be prosecuted to the fullest extent of the law."

I pointed to the 19-inch television mounted at the top of the wall. "Lyin' mutha." I laughed. "I ain't believin' this shit."

"And I intend on making good on my oath." He looked into the microphone.

I can hear Momma now, "A lie don't care who tell it," she'd say.

A Black female reporter asked, "Mr. James, wasn't this case

the one that put community and gang leader, Moses King, behind bars for life?"

"Yes, ma'am."

"Mr. James, what evidence, if any, have you uncovered to exonerate Moses King?" another reporter asked.

"We've uncovered information that has led us to the murder weapon used in the killings, and we are investigating other evidence recently uncovered that could possibly vindicate Mr. King."

"Mr. James, what is going to happen to Moses King now?" another asked.

"I don't know; that's up to the courts."

"Why was Moses King framed, and who killed the Homes family?" another asked.

"No comment. Thank you for coming, everybody. Good day." He walked off the capitol lawn, smiling and waving at the cameras.

"Moses, looks like you 'bout to go home," Old School said.

"Yeah, right."

"The man said he done found evidence that prove you ain't killed them folks. Nigga, you oughta be on yo' knees, instead of gripin' 'bout petty shit you can't change."

"They got you fooled, Pops. I done fell for the okey-dokey too many times over the last ten years, filing appeal after appeal, and each time being denied—"

"But the man just said—"

"I don't care what he said. All I heard was a man lying and trying to cover his own ass, trust me when I tell you." I put a hand on Old School's shoulder. "There's a lot more to that press conference than what we heard."

I looked at the fellas standing around the TV, and then back at Old School, who had sat back down waiting for us to leave, so he could continue watching CNN.

"Believe me when I tell you that the man has no intention of lifting a finger to get my case thrown out."

"Why not?" Rock asked.

"The man is evil, not stupid. He knows that if I ever hit the bricks, I'll come after him."

ACT 40
God's Army
Solomon

I'd just come from teaching Wednesday night Bible study at the church. Tired was an understatement for the way I felt. I didn't know how I was going to keep my eyes open for the rest of the drive home.

The last month had been crazy. Since the Atlanta movement had started, I stayed busier than a one-legged midget in a butt-kickin' contest.

Because of the gang truce that was sparked by the announcement of the upcoming rally in Atlanta, gang members all around the city were worshipping together at New Dimensions. It was unreal. I had to put loudspeakers outside the church the past couple of Sundays. And I loved every minute of it.

People that hadn't been to church since their diaper days were at New Dimensions First Church of God on Sunday for the celebration of life and God. As the young folk would say, "I was bringin' the noise."

My sermons were unedited. I didn't bite my tongue. I dealt with issues we faced everyday as a people and related them to issues that were spoken about in the Bible and sometimes even the Koran. And I provided solutions to these issues.

I was referred to as a cult leader in the Chicago Daily newspaper last week. Another newspaper reporter said in an article that I was the "Big Brother" of the convicted murderer and rapist, drug gang founder, Moses King. I didn't mind that part.

Unfortunately, that was true. Even the part about me bringing all the cities' gangs together to form one large gang was true. But the part about me preparing young men and women for some type of prison takeover was insane.

Despite what was being reported and written, I still allowed the media into New Dimensions Sunday services. Obviously, the reporters didn't realize that the negative publicity brought more people out on Sunday than the positive did. I loved it. Absolutely loved it.

Because of the New Dimensions Sunday morning traffic the last few weeks, Chicago's finest went from just directing traffic in and out of the church parking lot to now directing traffic on Benjamin E. Mays, two streets over from State Street, where the church was located.

The last couple weeks, parking was atrocious. If you didn't get to the church at least an hour early, you likely had to park your car two or three blocks away. In just two weeks, the church had sold and taken orders for over twenty-five thousand God's Army T-shirts to help sponsor the trip.

I'd gotten calls from across the nation from other religious leaders, asking what they could do to help. "Pray and spread the word," I told them.

The motion lights that lit up my driveway came to life as I pulled in. What I wouldn't do for one of Sunflower's backrubs. Unfortunately she had to go home to the small village of Chimbote in Peru to tend to her ailing mother.

I pulled into the garage and got out of old faithful, my nine-year-old Lincoln Continental, the only car I'd owned since coming home from the Army.

Eleven days. Eleven days before Easter Sunday. Eleven days before we rallied outside the Atlanta Federal Penitentiary.

I was so exhausted, after putting the key in the door, I could barely turn the knob. The three hours of sleep I'd gotten the last three and a half weeks had finally caught up to me.

I could've sworn I set the alarm before I left. I passed by the white keypad on the wall.

The speaking engagements, television talk shows, radio interviews, and all the activities the church was sponsoring to build momentum for the freedom movement was the reason I could barely make it up the stairs to my bedroom.

I maneuvered my way to my bedroom bathroom in the dark, like I'd done so many times in the past.

After turning on the shower, I felt that something wasn't right. I couldn't say why or how, but I felt like I wasn't alone.

I stepped out of the bathroom, still fully dressed and walked to the wall at the bedroom entrance.

After turning on the bedroom ceiling fan lights, I froze.

"Hello, Solomon. How are you this evening?" an average-looking White man, wearing blue jeans and a black sports jacket, asked.

He stood, leaning against my beige recliner in the bedroom sitting area; another guy, wearing a black Blues Brothers suit, sat in the chair with his legs crossed and a hand on his knee.

"Exhausted. I've had a long day, to say the least."

"'And it only gets longer as night's serenade gets louder and sleep becomes a dream.' I believe that piece was written by Robert Underwood," the guy in the chair said.

"No, I think that was 'Night Serenade' by Uhuru," I said.

"You are quite the calm one . . . for a man who comes home and finds two strange men lounging in his bedroom sitting area," the one wearing blue jeans said.

"It's called faith," I said. "Nothing can happen to me unless it's in God's plan."

"Is God bulletproof?—Because if He is, you may be all right," he replied.

I just smiled and nodded as if to say that God indeed was bulletproof.

He got up and started to walk slowly towards me. He stopped to admire the African tribal masks and other Afrocentric pieces strewn across my bedroom walls. "Do you remember what you were told years ago in that small cubbyhole office at O'Hare Airport?—Oh, I'm sure you do." He took another step towards me. "Your God wouldn't let you forget that, now would He?" He walked closer.

These are not the men who stopped me at the airport all those years ago.

"After all, if your God planned so well, He surely wasn't one to forget things, huh? You were told not to make any noise. You were told that if you did, you and your mother would face an untimely death."

For some reason I wasn't afraid in the least as the man speaking raised the silenced handgun and pointed it at my chest.

Other than misquoting the short poem, his partner didn't make a move or say a word, until now. He got up from the chair that Pablo and I brought up from the downstairs den a week ago. He too raised a silenced gun and pointed it in my direction. "The good news is, we have decided to let your mother live; the bad news is—"

ACT 41
A Time for Prayer
Picasso

"Picasso, a couple of suits are leaving the King estate," the cop I hired stated.

"How the hell did they get in the house?" I asked.

"They must've already been inside when we pulled up behind Mr. King."

"Do not—and I repeat—do not let them out of your sight. I wanna know every move they make."

I had an eerie feeling. Something definitely wasn't right. James would be crazy to take the Reverend out. He'd already covered his ass, so it couldn't be that. But then again James wasn't playing with a full deck.

"They are getting into a white Chevy Monte Carlo SS," my guy said over the car phone.

"I don't care if they're in a spaceship—don't lose them."

After I put the car phone back into its cradle I whipped my beige Mercedes around and headed towards Buffalo Grove.

My phone rang. "Speak," I said into the receiver.

"You want me to run the tag?"

"Nah, I want you to get on a loudspeaker and ask them

who they are and where they're going—hell yeah, I want you to run the damn plates."

This fool had a degree in criminology, and was a detective on the Chicago police force, so why in hell did he ask me such a silly-ass question.

"I want to know who they are, where they live, when they take a shit. I wanna know how many times they take a breath in a minute's time."

After hanging up from the clowns I hired to keep watch on the Reverend, I dialed his number. On the seventh ring, the answering machine picked up.

"Yo Reverend, pick up. Reverend, it's Picasso. I'm on my way. Call my car phone if you're okay."

I tried to break the land speed record, racing over to the Reverend's spread.

Why didn't I have the clowns go see if the Reverend was all right instead of following the suits that came out of his crib? Or better yet, I should've had one of them stay behind and look in on the Reverend.

I made the thirty-minute drive to the Reverend's spread in fifteen. After jumping out the Cadi and running up the cobblestone walkway, I rammed my shoulder into the door. "Damn!" I shouted, holding my shoulder. The large oak doors didn't budge.

I was about to bust out one of the stained-glass windows in the door, when I decided to try the knob. It was open. "Reverend!" I ran around the first level of the house.

"Reverend King." I turned on the foyer light and ran up the stairs, taking them three at a time.

"Reverend," I cried out as I saw his silhouette from the hallway of his bedroom. As I came closer I saw that he was laid out between his bathroom and the bedroom floor, blood everywhere. "Oh, no! Reverend?"

I picked up the phone from a nightstand next to his bed. Tears were streaming down my eyes. I dialed 911.

After hanging up I stepped over to him and dropped to my knees, cradling his head in my arms. I looked up at the ceiling. "God, you know how I roll. I don't ask for nothin'. But now I need You like I've never needed You before. I know I haven't talked to You much since Moms passed, but if You could help me out now, I'd appreciate it. You took my Moms; please don't take the Reverend.

"If it weren't for him and his brother Moses, I know I'd be dead or on skid row. I know I ain't no helluva somebody, but the Reverend is good peoples. He's down here representin' You to the fullest. I'm dependin' on You. Amen."

Ten minutes after I dialed emergency, the paramedics arrived.

After the paramedics removed his jacket and shirt I was surprised to see that the Reverend had on the bulletproof vest I gave him. I guess all the blood on the carpet came from somewhere else.

I made several calls after arriving at Northwest Memorial. The first was to Rhythm. I told her what had happened. She listened attentively, trying to console me in the process.

A few minutes after hanging up she called back to tell me that she'd be on the first flight out of DC in the morning.

Next, I called my peoples.

"Yo, this Picasso. What's the deal?"

"The two men split up. I've got a line on both of them. I'm just waiting on a call back from headquarters."

"For what?"

"I ran the plates. The car was registered to a ghost corporation, so I had the tax records pulled for the houses they went into. Female names came back on both. I'm digging into their histories, you know, finding out if they're married, have family, whatever."

"Call me back when you got more." I said.

"This could get expensive."

"Muthafucka, how long I been using you?"

"Around four, five years now."

"In that time, have you ever had a problem gettin' paid?"

"No."

"All right then. Call me when you have something." I slammed the hospital pay phone down.

I had drifted off to sleep, when a white coat came up to me.

"Are you the immediate family of Solomon King?" he asked.

"Yes, I'm his brother," I said, wondering why the hell I hadn't called Momma King.

"The police will need to talk with you. They're on the way."

"Hold on," I grabbed the doctor's white coat. "Is the Reverend going to make it?"

"Hard to say. He's lost a lot of blood, and the excess fluid around his skull is putting a lot of pressure on his brain."

"What are his chances?"

The doctor put a hand on my shoulder. "Not good. And if he does pull through, he'll need special care for the rest of his life."

"'Special care'?—What does that mean?"

"He won't know who he is, or where he's—"

"You mean to tell me the Reverend is gon' be a vegetable?"

"I'm afraid so."

ACT 42
The Family Glue
Rhythm

I'd only known Momma King for a short time, but that short time felt like forever. She knew how much I loved Moses, and she never questioned me about how I met him, why I loved him, anything. She just accepted me with open arms.

She nodded here and there, but for the most part, she didn't move while I explained in detail what had happened to Solomon and what we were doing to get Moses exonerated.

Momma King was sitting beside me on the gold couch in her living room. She reached for my hand. "Rhythm, baby, God has a plan for both my boys. Now I don't know rightly what that plan is, but I just don't believe it involves the graveyard, or life in prison."

With one son in prison serving a life sentence and another in the hospital fighting for his life, I don't know how she stayed so optimistic.

"Rhythm, now let me tell you a little story." Momma King looked into my eyes. "My father raised me after my mother died giving birth to me. He was a hard-working man of God, who never compromised what he believed; I loved him for that. I buried him when I was eighteen." She paused and shook her head.

"I buried my Herbert, twelve years after I buried my father. I fell in love and married that man, because he too was a God-fearing man, and a good husband and father. He may have given in to me, but I was the only one.

"Herbert was stubborn as ten mules, when it came to a cause he believed in." She smiled, remembering. "One of the first things that I fell in love with was his spirit to fight for what he believed in. He had that same spirit my father had."

I nodded as Momma King took a breath. I wanted to say something, but I didn't know what, so I just kept quiet and listened.

"Because of what I learned from my father and Herbert, I was able to raise my boys to be like them."

Using her fingers to get her point across, she continued, "Have faith only in God, be God-fearing, and fight like hell for whatever you believe is the core message that I instilled in my boys. 'Giving in and giving up is failure, and trying until there is no more trying is victory,' I told them."

"I agree."

She squeezed my hand. "See, Rhythm, no matter what, I have to believe that Moses and Sol got more tryin' than a little left in the both of them. Like I taught my boys, have faith in Him and Him alone. That's why I don't look to no judges, or no doctors to tell me the plan for the men that Ruth-Ann King brought into this world."

Now I see where Moses gets his determination from.

"I've never for one moment worried about my youngest, and I won't start worrying about my eldest now. They need my support, not my sorrow. Now, baby, let's go see Solomon." She patted my hand.

We took a cab to the hospital.

The doctor there explained that we couldn't see Rev because he still hadn't regained consciousness.

That's when Momma King made the doctor slowly explain everything they had done for Rev and what was being done in terms of his recovery. She wanted to know the meds he was on, how his body was reacting to them, what machines he was hooked up to, and what they did. She wanted to know everything.

And when the doctor tried to tell her his chances of recovering, she waved him off and explained that she didn't want to hear percentages and numbers.

Very polite and straight to the point, she said she was only interested in results. As soon as she finished talking, we headed towards the exit doors.

"Baby, you mind taking me to the church?"

"No, ma'am, not at all."

We rode the rest of the way in silence.

Once we walked inside, she pointed to the podium and said, "Baby, that is where I want you this Sunday."

"Excuse me, Momma King?"

"Baby, I want you to listen closely to what I am about to tell you?"

"Yes, ma'am."

"The time a man needs a woman most is when he's hospitalized, sick, or in prison. Any other time, he can pretty much make it on his own. Maybe not well, but he can make it."

I nodded.

"One of my boys is in prison. The other's in the hospital. By everything that I've heard from the both of them and your brother Pablo, they all think you the Queen of Sheba.

"As that Queen, you must speak. Now, I need you, my boys need you, your brother needs you. Colored folk everywhere need you to speak. Speak to us with your heart. Lead the congregation. Lead the viewers from all over the country that tune in on Sunday mornings. Lead them to the promise land." She paused. "Baby, don't let 'em give up the dream."

ACT 43
Helplessness to Faith
Moses

"Name and number!" a guard shouted, and banged on my cell door.

"Yeah," I shouted, wiping sleep from my eyes.

Again, the guard shouted, "Name and number!"

"Moses King, 24147-028."

"Get dressed. The chaplain wants to see you."

The chaplain wants to see me! Oh nooooo! Lord, please don't let it be Momma, I prayed. I put on my prison greens.

The only time an inmate was summoned to the chaplain's office was when something terrible happened to a family member. Dread fell over me as I was escorted by a prison guard to the side of the education building where inmate and religious services were held.

Father Mahoney rose from his desk, put his hands behind his back, and walked around to greet me.

"Mr. King . . . please." He gestured towards a comfortable-looking chair.

"If it's all the same to you, Father, I'd rather stand." I tried to brace myself for whatever he was about to say. I closed my eyes and started praying like I had never prayed before. "Our Father, who art in heaven . . ."

The chaplain put a hand on my shoulder. "Your brother, Solomon King, was shot six times last night."

"No! God! Please, no!" My legs gave out. I was on the floor, and my head was spinning.

"Moses, Moses, son, can you hear me?" The chaplain shook my shoulders.

My eyes were closed when I asked, "What happened?"

"The authorities think your brother may have been the victim of a gang-related shooting."

"Nooooooooooooooooooooo!" I screamed.

"I'm sorry, son."

"Everybody loved Solomon. No, no, no!" I said, shaking my head. "'Gang-related'?—They're wrong." I rose to my feet and grabbed the gray-haired Irish-Catholic priest by the arm.

"They're wrong, Father! Do you hear me? They're wrong."

Out the corner of my eye, I saw the prison guard quickly approaching.

Father Mahoney shook his head. "Officer, everything's fine." He turned back to me. "Son, I understand how you must feel, but you have to let go of me before the officer restrains you."

I took my hands off him. "Father, did you hear me?—I said they're wrong. My brother is a reverend; the gangs in Chicago love him."

"Obviously, someone didn't. I know this is difficult for you, but it is believed that someone didn't like the message your brother was sending."

"'Message'? You don't have any idea." I covered my eyes and crumbled to the floor. "Father, would I be able to attend Solomon's funeral?"

ACT 44
Sunday Service
Rhythm

Nervous doesn't even begin to describe what I was feeling, as I sat next to Momma King on the front row of the church. How was I going to get up on that stage and speak to thousands of people I'd never even met? Oh, well, it is what it is. I shrugged. "Rhythm, you can do this," I said to myself, as the junior minister took the stage.

"Thank you, Sounds of Grace. How about the New Dimensions concert choir?" he asked, leading the applause.

"God is good when?" He leaned towards the congregation, his hand to his ear.

"All the time," they chorused.

"And all the time?"

"God is good," the congregation replied.

"This is a sad Sunday. A Sunday for mourning and a Sunday for praising. As you all know, Reverend King is in critical care at Northwest Memorial as a result of multiple gunshot wounds suffered at the hands of unknown assailants that broke into his home Thursday evening."

Sighs, gasps, sniffles, and silent sobs came from the congregation.

"Reverend King needs our prayers, and for our faith not to falter. His condition is unknown as of now; all we know is that he is day-to-day. But he is a rock, and if anyone can survive such an ordeal, he can."

For a brief moment the crowded church was deathly silent. Not only was every theatre seat in the church occupied, but the two large tents outside the church were also packed with concerned folks, anxious to hear and see what our next move was. I was glad Rev had the foresight to lease the loudspeakers and the tents for our pilgrimage to Atlanta.

The young junior minister wiped his eyes with a white handkerchief. "The King family appreciates the flowers and all the cards you've been sending.

"We regretfully inform you that due to the shooting, instead of making the trip to Atlanta, we will be holding a weekend lock-in prayer vigil for our beloved fallen leader at the church this coming Easter weekend.

Prayer vigil? What?

"Now, I'd like to bring up a very special lady, to say a few words." He extended an arm in my and Momma King's direction. "Momma King has told me that this woman is amazing and is very close to the King family. Without further ado, I introduce to you Ms. Rhythm Azure."

I was greeted with timid applause. A silent calm had fallen over me as I rose from my frontrow seat. I felt a million eyes on me as I made my way to the large stage.

Once I reached the podium, I grabbed hold of the microphone so tight that my hand started turning red. I looked into the eyes of thousands of starving faces, and thousands of hungry eyes stared right back. Their eyes were burning my soul as beads of sweat started to form on my forehead.

Even though I'd rehearsed over and over what I was going to say, I now stood there frozen.

"Please bear with me; I've never done anything like this before."

"Take your time, child," someone shouted.

I closed my eyes and took a couple of deep breaths. "I've been blessed to know both men in the King family. Determination, perseverance, faith, and community are the first words that come to mind, when I think of Moses and Reverend Solomon King."

"Girl, you doin' just fine," someone else shouted.

I smiled at the vote of confidence. "As a little girl in Sunday school, I remember learning the story of Moses. I remember thinking that if I'd climbed a mountain, talked to the Creator, and had been given a back-breaking rock tablet with commandments from God to carry back down the mountain for the salvation of the people and the appreciation I got was everyone acting a fool, doing everything against God, I probably would have given up on them and asked God to give me another group of people to save.

"And then you had Solomon. Out of anything I could wish for, out of anything I could ask God for, wisdom would not be in my top twenty."

Several people laughed.

"Solomon didn't ask for women, gold, or chariots. He asked for wisdom, and God made him the wisest, richest man in the Bible. Now you put these two men together and what do you have?—You have freedom. I mean total and complete freedom that comes from determined wisdom, faith, and the love and betterment of man and community."

"Amen," reverberated throughout the church.

"Bishop Solomon King is a true lover of God and God's people. Do you remember when this man was in the streets, holding church in neighborhoods where police wouldn't even go into? Do you remember what you said? Don't be shame. You remember saying or thinking that this man had to be out of his ever-loving mind?—Ain't none of these thieves, hustlers, gamblers, addicts, and dealers interested in God.

"You probably thought that no one was going to take the brother of a murderer and rapist seriously; you all know what you said better than I do. And despite what anyone said, Reverend King never became discouraged. He never gave up on you, so why should we give up on him?"

One of the deacons behind me shouted, "Whip 'em, girl, whip 'em."

"Reverend King said we are going to Atlanta to bring about a new day, and I am still going, because I believe in the right to freedom, I believe in justice, and I believe in you." I pointed at the church congregation.

"Sistah, you ain't goin' alone," a heavy-set, older woman stood up and shouted.

"I believe in the future, and the future is now. The future is not a man, but the future is manifesting the message of love, unity, truth, and freedom. This is the message Reverend King was—is trying to spread."

An older man stood up. "I don't think they heard you, sistah; tell 'em again."

"Now that the shepherd is sick and he needs the sheep, it's up to us to be his disciples and carry his message to Atlanta. The Reverend wouldn't want us to be cooped up in this building for an entire weekend praying for him. He'd want us to fight." I threw a fist in the air. "He'd want us to carry on what he began.

"If we don't go to Atlanta, if we don't stand up now, we will continue to fall for anything. Reverend King's in the hospital fighting for his life because of you, me, Atlanta, Moses, justice, freedom, and God, the type of true justice that African-Americans and third world peoples have never seen in this country."

"Ain't that the God's truth," another woman stood up and shouted.

I shot a fist in the air. "Justice for Moses will set a precedent. It will show the powers-that-be that there is a power much stronger than what they and us can see."

A young brother stood up and shouted. "Speak to 'em, woman."

"I don't know about any of you,"—I made an arc around the church with an accusing finger—"but I am a soldier in God's Army."

I took off my jacket, ripped off my blouse, and threw them both to the floor.

SOLDIER was stenciled in bold white letters on the front. I turned around to expose the words IN GOD'S ARMY on the back. "Are we going to stand up, or are we going to stay seated?"

Pablo stood up in the front row. "I'm standing up, big sis."

Suddenly, the double-doors in the rear of the church opened. Every one turned around. I could hardly believe what I was seeing. He was risking his life and his freedom being here. He was supposed to be on the run.

"And I'm standing up with my people for my people," T-Hunt said. He walked down the middle aisle until he was face-to-face with my brother. "I love you, man, and for the record, ain't no beef with us. He shook his head left to right. He hugged Pablo. "This is my brother." He turned towards the congregation.

I smiled. Law is amazing. I don't know how, but he must've found T-Hunt and explained everything. All I wanted to know was, why he didn't tell anyone?

I leaned over the stage and gestured for T-Hunt to come and get the mike.

He took the mike from my outstretched arm. "The war ain't between the Disciples and the Gangsta Gods, it's between right and wrong. It's between justice and injustice, good and evil. It's between us and the CIA, FBI, Chicago PD, and the US Justice Department."

The church exploded with applause.

The tears that threatened to fall when I first took the stage were raining from my eyes now. I looked at Momma King. She nodded, tears flowing from her eyes.

Everyone was on their feet, headed towards the stage to show solidarity. People who were standing in the streets outside the church were coming in to stand with us, until not another soul could fit in the fifty-thousand-square-foot facility.

ACT 45
Who Did It
Picasso

I hated doing this kinda shit. I pay a king's ransom to a Chicago police detective and his partner to find out the identity of two muthafuckas, and I couldn't get shit.

The pigs got technology out the "ying-yang," and they can't even tell me about these two funky-ass crackas. Now I had to go and get gangsta on they monkey ass.

"Law, you sure you down for this shit?"

"Youngblood, I did seventeen years in hell for watching a redneck pig kill my father and pee on my mother—now you tell me if I'm down with making a pig pay."

"Enough said. Do me a favor?" I asked.

"Yeah."

"Get that suitcase out the back seat, open it, and tell me everything that's in it. We need to make sure I'm not forgetting anything."

Law pulled the small black carry-on bag from the back seat of the stolen Bronco we were riding in. "Okay, we got one Black and Decker electric saw, a case of saw blades, a 35 mm camera, a nail gun, a box of nails, a silencer, and a .45 Magnum pistol."

"That's everything."

"What we gon' use to tie 'em up with, Youngblood?"

"Already taken care of. That's the least the dirty pigs I got on my payroll could do."

"How many in the house?" Law asked.

"We'll find out soon enough," I said as we pulled up to a department store parking lot. "Let's go."

We jumped out the stolen truck and got into a white van.

"Picasso, you didn't say anything about bringing anyone," one of the cops said.

"What? You thought I was goin' in the muthafucka's house solo?" I shook my head. "Don't even play yourself like that. Now, is everything taken care of?"

"Yeah," he said, pointing to a note pad with a layout of the house. "You got the perp, a woman, who must be a wife or a girlfriend, and there's a little girl about six or seven in the house."

"Ahh, fuck!" I slapped my palm against my forehead. "I didn't even think about kids."

"Nothing to worry about. The kid is tied and gagged in a bath—"

"You didn't hurt the kid?"

"Other than having bruised wrists from the duct tape, she's fine. Now as I was saying, the perp and the woman are duct-taped and gagged in the kitchen. I have a man sitting on them until you arrive," he said.

I turned to Law. "Let's roll."

"What about the other perp? You still want my people to sit on him?"

"Nah, you can cut him loose. I got enough info to make my plan work, and if I need the other one, I'll call you."

He pointed to the gym bag slung over my shoulder. "Is that—"

I removed the black strap from my shoulder and slung the bag in his lap. "Thirty-five thousand—count it."

"No need," he said. "I know where to find you." Then he and his partner wiped down the dry cleaning delivery van and jumped out.

Law and I rode in silence down I-94. We took the Lincolnwood exit. The North Side and the South Side of Chicago were as different as night and day. While the streets were newly blacktopped and clean on the North Side, you had to drive an obstacle course to avoid all the potholes on the South Side.

After pulling into a dark, short driveway, I said, "Time." I put on my ski mask.

Law looked at his watch. "Two-thirty a.m." He put on his black ski mask.

"Showtime," I said as we jumped out of the van.

We ran through the small yard up to the front door. I knocked three times and rang the bell twice.

A large ski-masked White cat let us in the new-looking, two-story, bone-colored brick home. He pointed down a long hallway in the direction of what must've been the bathroom where the little girl was. Then he pointed to a bound and gagged couple strapped to two kitchen chairs beside a winding staircase.

After signaling the cat to leave, Law and I walked into the spacious, post-modern decorated kitchen. I couldn't believe this shit. I walked up to the perp, and the mu'fucka was light-bright, close to white, but he was definitely a nigga.

The two Starsky-and-Hutch wannabes I'd hired told me the mu'fuckas was White. Fuck it. I shrugged. I snatched the tape off of his oreo, sellout-ass mouth, while Law approached us with my .45 aimed at his head.

"What do you want?" the perp confidently asked.

I ignored him. I just shook my head in disgust. I grabbed the bag from Law and put it on the kitchen floor next to the trembling, wide-eyed broad.

"This white 'ho' your wife? If so, she's a big pretty muthafucka. And if she ain't, she's still a big pretty muthafucka," I said as I worked.

"What is this?" he asked.

I ignored him. "The Bears are clicking, and even the Bulls are showing signs of life. What ya think about them Cubs?" I put a nail in the nail gun.

"What are you talking about?" the perp asked.

"The Cubs, you know . . . baseball." I plugged the extension cord into the wall socket.

"What are you doing?"

The woman was silently going crazy, wiggling like a big-ass pink worm.

"What am I doing? Oh, nothing really." I plugged the nail gun into the extension cord. "Just trying to verify the information I got from your partner before he went into cardiac arrest from the pain. I made the mistake of torturing his dumb ass, instead of one of his loved ones; you know the sayin', dead men can't talk," I said with a snicker in my voice.

"What the hell are you talking about?"

The loud pop the nail gun made after inserting a nail into the kitchen countertop caused both, him and her to jump.

"You know the Reverend Solomon King—your partner told me everything. And I mean every muthafuckin' thing. I could hardly believe the things he told me." I shrugged. "I just don't know if everything he said was on the up-and-up, so I figure I'd nail this bitch's hand to the kitchen table and start cutting off each finger until you talked or until she went into shock or cardiac arrest, whatever the fuck came first. And then I'll go get the little girl out of the bathroom and start on her, and if you still don't talk, well, I'll just have my partner shoot you in the head.

"Torturing you would be a waste of time, don't you think? I mean, if you didn't talk by the time we got around to you, you probably wouldn't."

I took a couple steps towards the woman, maintaining eye contact with the perp. "By the looks of it, I know you really can't tell, but I really don't dig this torture shit."

The woman squirmed in front of me and my nail gun.

"What did he tell you, my partner? What did he say?"

I shrugged my shoulders. "That doesn't matter. What matters is what you tell me and if it coincides with what he said. 'cause if it doesn't, everyone in this muthafucka gon' be fertilizer."

Law started stroking the side of the perp's head with the gun barrel.

"You know what? This bitch is too hysterical. I doubt if I can control her enough to nail her hand into the table. I'll just have to nail her hand to the chair since she tied up to it already. Yeah, that'll be easier." I nodded and dragged her chair from the table and over in front of the perp.

"How do I know you won't kill us after I tell you what you want?" he asked.

I shrugged. "You don't." I brought the nail gun down fast and hard, inserting a six-inch nail through the woman's hand. I could see the veins in her neck come to life as she squirmed. She looked like a blowfish, the way her cheeks puffed out trying to release a scream through the duct tape covering her mouth.

Then I heard a streaming noise. I looked at the kitchen floor under the woman and noticed that she had pissed herself. I hated to do it. I had never laid a hand on a woman in my life, but I had to do what I had to do.

After seeing what I had done to his woman, the perp caught an instant case of diarrhea of the mouth.

It took thirty minutes for me to record everything. This shit was much deeper than I'd first thought. But now it all made sense.

Before we left, we removed the nail from the woman's

hand and cleaned her wound. I'd nailed the meat between the thumb and the forefinger, so there would be no nerve damage.

Thanks to the picture over the fireplace of him and his partner shaking hands while graduating from the FBI academy, the camera I brought wasn't needed.

ACT 46
Miracle at Revolution Boulevard
Rhythm

"**B**aby sis, we have a slight change of plans." Before I could ask what, Pablo continued, "Law and I have something to do. Leave without us. We'll be there by morning." He hung up the phone before I could protest.

We left Chicago Saturday morning on the first of twelve buses. People were carpooling and making last-minute plans to follow our caravan. We'd chartered twelve buses, and that still wasn't enough.

I hated turning people away, but we were forced to. Every bus was filled to capacity, and just like Black folks, hundreds of our people were trying to get a seat at the last minute. Large black-and-white banners with the words God's Army were plastered on all of the buses.

Reverend Jesse Jackson and The Honorable Minister Louis Farrakhan were the keynote speakers at the event.

We were picking up mini-caravans of carpoolers on the highways as we passed through Kentucky and Tennessee. By the time we hit the Atlanta area, our army of vehicles must have grown by twenty at least.

Seven downtown and surrounding area hotels housed the people in our large group.

Our bus pulled up to the Marriott Marquis around 10 p.m. I didn't know about everyone else, but I was bone-tired. My neck and my back were killing me from all that sitting. I could hardly wait to take a hot shower and fall into bed.

I wasn't expecting them to be in town until morning, but it would've been nice if Law or Pablo returned my calls. I guess I just had a case of the worries.

"Rhythm, baby, you look like you have something heavy on your heart. Anything you want to share with me?" Momma King asked.

"No, ma'am, I'm fine," I lied. I pulled the covers over my head.

It seemed like I'd just gotten into bed, when the hotel phone rang. "Hello," I said.

"This is your 5 a.m. wake-up call you requested," the voice on the other end replied.

After wiping sleep from my eyes, I pulled back the curtain and looked out the 10th floor window. The moon was full and shining bright.

A little over an hour later, Momma King and I were riding in a limousine, courtesy of the Reverend Arthur Evans from First Corinthians, located in Stone Mountain, Georgia.

Vehicles coming anywhere near the prison were being re-routed by police. Orange and white police barricades were all over the streets. The city had obviously prepared for our arrival.

I'd heard that the state had tried to block our rally. But by the time news of the rally hit Atlanta and the time the powers-that-be took the news seriously, it was too late. They didn't have enough time to file an injunction to stop us.

As we passed the huge Grant Park picnic area up the street from the prison, I was in awe, when I saw Winnebagos, vans, tents, and a variety of vehicles, with plates from as far as California to New York, camped out in the park.

I closed my eyes and smiled, thinking this was the hand of God at work. Thanks to an outpouring of support from Black clergy all over the nation, the call was indeed answered. This was going to be much bigger than, I was sure, even Rev imagined.

We pulled into Mrs. Winners Chicken parking lot, where a temporary headquarters had been set up. Mrs. Winners was located directly across the street from the humongous, Gothic-looking, gray prison.

A tall, slim, middle-aged brother introduced himself as the Reverend Jake Boyce of New Life Ministries and greeted Momma King and me. He explained that he and Rev had been friends for years, and that his ministries were in Spartanburg, South Carolina.

Reverend Boyce was also responsible for the sound system that was being expanded, as we spoke. He explained that the speakers were wireless and that sound was distributed through them through a high-powered radio frequency.

As he spoke, I couldn't help but wonder where Law and my brother were.

By ten in the morning, the streets were crowded with supporters and street vendors selling knock-off God's Army T-shirts, food, and all sorts of things.

The Atlanta police kept busy re-directing traffic and putting up more barricades as supporters continued to flood the area.

Due to security reasons, we were told that we weren't allowed on prison grounds, so we set up a stage next to the prison on the Four Seasons housing grounds.

Four Seasons, Thomasville Heights, and Grant Park Village were project housing developments that sat directly to the right of the prison.

Several local Chicago and national news agencies were covering the rally. There was even a Goodyear blimp filming from the air.

Tears started to form in the corner of my eyes as I saw thousands and thousands of people flooding the streets wearing black God's Army T-shirts.

The Reverend Jake Boyce opened the service with a prayer.

It was around one o'clock, when the Minister Farrakhan got up to speak. By then, the sun was smiling, the warm weather dancing off the skins of thousands of Black folks for miles around.

Large video screens had been set up as far as six blocks away, so everyone could see and hear the speakers. As the Minister started to speak to an excited and hyped crowd, his voice was drowned out by the loud whirring sound of a Huey helicopter flying overhead.

The crowd moved back to make room for the large helicopter landing on a large dirt area a couple hundred yards away from the stage. Everyone's attention had been diverted to the helicopter. People were climbing on each other's shoulders, trying to get a look at the people getting out of the Huey.

ACT 47
God's Time
Solomon

I didn't walk through any long tunnels with bright lights at the other end. No dead relatives called to me. There were no flower gardens with beautiful people singing from them.

The last thing I remember before the lights went out was a series of loud noises and me getting pounded in my chest with something pointy and hot.

I remember waking up thirsty and disoriented with a headache from the tightly wrapped bandages around my head. I remember my arm hurting from the IVs in them. And I remember my mouth being dry as sand paper.

Before I had a chance to locate the nurse call button, a beautiful young sistah walked through the door, carrying a metal tray.

"Excuse me, sistah," I said. "What is today's date?"

The sound of glass breaking and metal clanging to the floor assaulted my ears.

"Oh, my God." She put a hand to her mouth.

"Not even close," I joked.

She pointed. "You're talking, oh my God."

"Sistah, relax."

She started crying as she walked towards me. "Reverend, we thought you weren't going to make it, but they were wrong." She sniffed before raising her hands in the air. "Thank you, Jesus. Thank you, Lord."

"I'm sorry, Reverend, but if it weren't for you, I would still be hooking out on Michigan Avenue, or worse, in prison or dead. You just don't know what you mean to me and my two girls."

"Thank you, sistah . . ."

"Brown. Mary Lane Brown."

"Thank you, Sistah Brown, but all praise is due to God. I'm just the tool that he used to speak to you."

"I'm sorry, let me get the shift nurse," she said, turning to leave."

"I thought you were a nurse."

"I am—I mean, I will be in six months. Right now, I'm just a tech. I take vital signs and clean wounds." She headed towards the door.

"Wait."

She turned back around.

"What time is it, and what's the date?"

She looked at her watch. "It's 3:45 a.m., Saturday, April 4."

"Good Lord." I sat up and swung my legs over the side of the bed. Before I knew it, I was on the floor.

She rushed to my side. "Reverend, you been out for nine days; you can't just pop up like that."

I felt dizzy. And I was starving.

"You pulled your IV out."

"I'm sorry, but the rally is tomorrow. I have to get out of here."

"There is no way the doctor will release you that soon. You suffered brain damage, at least that's what they thought."

After she helped me to my feet, I begged her to help me.

She watched me push my catheter machine around the room and had me answer a battery of questions like, "What's your name? Who's the president?" etcetera, she agreed to help me. The only stipulation was that I had to get back in bed, let her re-insert the IV, and pretend I was still asleep, until she came on her next shift that night at ten.

Right before she left the room, I gave her Law's and Picasso's phone number and asked her to call and tell them that I was fine and not to leave for Atlanta without me.

After Sista Brown had gone, I realized that I didn't even ask her if the rally had been cancelled. Lord, I hope not. I lay in bed, thanking God for sparing my life, praying that the rally hadn't been cancelled.

Around twelve that evening, Sistah Brown escorted Picasso into my hospital room. Picasso's eyes watered as he dropped a black bag slung around his shoulders to the hospital floor.

"I knew you were going to pull through," Law whispered into my ear, while we hugged each other.

"I brought you a pair of pants, a sweater, and some shoes." Picasso pointed to the black Nike gym bag on the floor.

"Thank you." I unzipped the bag and took out the clothes.

A few minutes later, I was dressed and ready to go.

"Where's Law?" I asked.

"He's down in the car."

"Thanks for everything, Sistah." I gave the young sistah a big hug before we left.

I looked like a Black Arab, with my head bandaged up, but other than my sore ribs, I felt fine. No headache or anything.

Three men from three different backgrounds and three different religions sharing one love, one God, and one reason for living, I thought, as I got into Picasso's white Rolls Royce.

ACT 48
Big Love
Moses

Every television room inside the penitentiary was tuned in to the rally. I can't even explain the feeling of joy and relief that fell over me, when Solomon first spoke out about my case during one of his Sunday services last month. If I died right then, I would've died a happy man.

Even if this rally didn't get my case back in court, I'd be happy. Happy because my big brother was back.

"Lord, they can have my freedom, they can have my life, but please spare Solomon. Please, Lord, bring him out of the coma and send him back to the people." I was steadfast in prayer, when the TV room erupted.

"What the hell," one brotha shouted.

I opened my eyes to see a large helicopter on the TV screen landing in the middle of the crowd, not too far from the stage.

A brotha in the TV room shouted, "Whoever them fools are gotta be out they damn minds."

"They lucky they didn't get shot down," another said.

I didn't know where the no-fly zone began, but I knew

there was a no-fly zone around penitentiaries all over America.

After the helicopter landed, Black men outfitted in black leather combat boots, black fatigues, black God's Army T-shirts, and black hats that read FOI (Fruit of Islam) on them emerged to massive shouts of, "Revolution!"

Fists were in the air everywhere. It looked like the parting of the Red Sea, as these men jogged to the stage. As the FOI security force of the Nation of Islam dispersed to the side of the stage, pandemonium erupted. I jumped out of my seat and dropped to my knees, crying and thanking God.

People were crying, screaming, and shouting as Law, Picasso, and Solomon took the stage. Minister Farrakhan and Solomon embraced, and the Minister handed over the microphone.

"Ain't nothin' like a party, but a soul King God party. Everybody, let me hear it now," Solomon said, as he rocked from side to side, shocking and surprising the nation.

"Ain't nothing like a party, but a soul King God party," the crowd sang.

"That's right, that's right. I'm here. They threatened me . . . they tried to kill me . . . but let me tell you something, family—I wasn't scared . . . 'cause I knew God had my back. And if I died that night, well, that would've been just fine, because Jesus died, Martin died, Malcolm died, and so many others died for freedom; for us to be able to live another day to fight for justice. But I didn't die; God wasn't ready for me to go. And you better damn well believe, I ain't goin' nowhere until God's ready."

Applause erupted on the project grounds, in the streets, and in the TV room, where I and every inmate stood on our feet. I could barely see the television for the tears that welled up in my eyes.

Almost five minutes passed before over six blocks of supporters calmed down enough for Solomon to continue.

"The revolution is here and now, live and in color." He pointed to the news reporters and cameras at the foot of the stage. "And it is being televised."

Solomon turned to his left and pointed. "The brotha to the left hanging up that massive poster is Lawrence One Free."

Somebody standing behind me shouted, "That's my nigga."

He pointed to the prison. "He served seventeen years behind those very walls, before his case was overturned by the United States Supreme Court. Seventeen years for a crime he didn't commit."

"Oh, hell yeah, Law said he wouldn't forget us," another inmate shouted.

"And behind me, the men you see on the projector screens are the men who represent the system of government that destroyed Lawrence's family and took his freedom. These men"—He pointed—"are the men who broke into my home and shot me six times. Six times, because I would not heed their earlier threats and back away from pursuing justice for my brother, your brother, Moses King. These men are FBI.

"This is our government. This is our justice. Are we going to sit for this any longer? I say, hell no. We are going to stand and fight for real justice against their tyrannical, Hitler-like 'just-them' system."

"Hell yeah, preacher man, talk that talk," someone behind me shouted.

"We, the people are going to put our differences aside, and we're going to unite through our likenesses. No longer must we divide ourselves from our Muslim brothers, our

Catholic brothers, our Baptist brothers, our Methodist brothers, or our Jewish brothers.

"There are four words that bring us together—Belief in one God. There are five words that bind us—Children of the one God. There are six words for which we should die fighting for—True freedom, true justice, true equality."

The crowd went crazy as Solomon shot a fist in the air.

He continued, "We must be our brother's keeper and stop letting a system of injustice control our thinking, what we believe, the way we believe, and we must stop them from choosing our leaders."

"Moses, your brother gon' end up right in here wit' us, if he keep talkin' 'bout buckin' the government," a brother behind me said.

"I say to all of you today, I'm Muslim, I'm Christian, and I'm Jewish; we're all are in one Army—God's Army—because we believe. I said, 'We believe,' say it for me, family."

"We believe," echoed for however many blocks brothers and sisters lined the streets.

"One day I woke up and I said, 'Loose me, Satan—I ain't scared.' I realized that as long as God be for me, no man or army can stand against me. That's right—I ain't scared." Solomon pointed to the TV cameras. "You hear what I'm saying FBI, CIA, CPD? Understand this—I'm a SGA, soldier in God's Army, and I ain't scared. Say it with me, family."

The words "I ain't scared" broadcast all around the nation on that day, at that moment.

Crackerjack Jackson, an old head that had been down over twenty years said, "He say that now . . . wait 'til the boys in blue put his ass in handcuffs and pull out they nightsticks."

"Nigga, shut the hell up," Mookie Williams told him. "They done shot his ass six times and the Reverend on TV callin' they ass out." The ex-leader of one of the biggest street gangs in LA was down with Solomon too.

"We're not asking the courts to free Moses King; we tellin' the courts to free Moses King. We will no longer ask for justice—If we don't get it in the courts, we will take it in the streets."

Solomon again pointed at the cameras. "America, history has shown us that you can't stand an internal revolution. It will cripple your economy. The government of England couldn't withstand the American Revolution. The Russian regime couldn't withstand the Russian Revolution. The King couldn't withstand the French Revolution."

"Hell, the government gon' definitely kill him now," Crackerjack said.

"So, America, I stand here with God's Army." He nodded. "Yeah, you see us, and we will only grow like a cancer. A cancer that will continue to eat away at the fabric of racism that this country's system of government is built on, until there is nothing left but the crumbs of true justice that we will build on."

Applause and cheers exploded through the crowd as Solomon handed the microphone over to Picasso.

"My name is Pablo Nkrumah. It is said that I am the head and founder of the Chicago street gang, the Gangsta Gods, but that is neither here nor there. I'm here to make a plea. I'm making a plea to the Crips, Bloods, GDs, Vicelords, and every gang in America—Stop killin' our people; stop fightin' over street corners that you don't own; stop pushin' that poison to our mothers, sisters, and brothers.

"Get incorporated. Pool all that dope money and turn it into hope money. Devise a plan. And buy some land, re-develop your community and bring the unity."

Everyone in the TV room turned their attention to Mookie Williams. The metal folding chair he sat in fell over after he jumped up all excited.

He pointed to the TV screen. "I ain't never picked up a book, but if God's Word can inspire a movement this deep, and have real niggas talkin' like this, I gotta go check that Bible out right now for myself." Mookie Williams left the TV room.

ACT 49
Soul on Fire
Moses

The Friday after the rally I was cuffed and taken to the warden's office. In nine years of being at the pen, I'd never been into the warden's office. I didn't ask any questions. I just went quietly with the guards that escorted me. I wondered what was being pinned on me now.

Upon entering, the guard removed the cuffs.

The warden motioned for me to have a seat, while he finished filling out some paperwork.

A few minutes later, the warden pushed some papers across his desk and motioned for me to take his pen and sign them.

I slid my seat up to his desk and quickly read over the first paper. I got dizzy reading the presidential pardon signed by Reagan himself.

Is this for real? It's gotta be.

I scratched myself, making sure that I wasn't dreaming. Words couldn't and wouldn't describe how I felt.

No matter what these papers said, I knew I wasn't free until I was outside the penitentiary walls. After leaving the warden's office I was escorted back to my cell to pack.

It must have taken me all of ten seconds to gather my bed linen for the prison laundry.

In less than two hours, I was on my way out. At Receiving and Distribution, where inmates were processed in and processed out, the guard gave me a brown T-shirt and some old jeans.

I saw their lips moving. I knew they must have been speaking to me, but I couldn't hear anything the cons and guards were saying as I walked through a series of security checkpoints.

I knew my legs were churning quickly, but my mind was playing tricks on me. As I walked, I looked around and everything seemed to be in slow motion. It was like I was high on Thorazine or Valium.

The last set of doors opened, and the sun's rays hit me like a cannon. I fell to my knees. While on the ground, I blinked several times and shook the prison haze from my mind before getting back to my feet.

"Moses," a woman's voice called out.

I carefully and slowly started descending the seemingly never-ending prison stairs.

"Moses?"

I stopped moving and looked up. At the bottom of the stairs stood living verification that God was real.

With hands and arms extended towards me was an angel without wings. "Moses," she said once again.

Her burnt-almond skin glowed in the sunlight. The breeze seemed to dance off of her white form-fitting flowing sundress. Her hips, her legs, her shoulders started to dance as she started to slowly ascend the stairs towards me.

I could even see the ripples of her stomach muscles dance to the rhythm that her body was moving to. Her midnight-sandy, reddish-brown dreads cascaded down to her shoulders, bouncing as she moved. Her hair and her bright teary eyes were twins in color. Her smile was electric diamonds. Her lips were richer than her skin tone and full like a fulfilled lover's moan.

I left prison on April 10, 1984 with rhythm in my soul, and Rhythm in my arms.

ACT 50
Loving, Holding, Touching
Moses

We had just finished loving each other. The moon's shadow glided over the dark, rippling waters of the Caribbean. I figured it was somewhere between three and five in the morning as Rhythm lay in my arms in the moonlight out on the beach.

"Moses, I have so much to tell you."

I stroked the dark dreads in her head. "My ears are all yours."

She turned to face me. "Pablo Nkrukmah is my brother, and he has never done anything to you but love you while you were inside."

I smiled and nodded. "I know."

"What? You knew? Why didn't you?" She punched me in the chest.

"Shhh." I grabbed her and pulled her close to me.

After Law got out, I had him find everything out about Picasso. I had him go back to the day he was born.

"Once I found out that you were his sister, it scared me at first, but only for a minute, because I knew you loved me and you wouldn't do anything to hurt me. Still, things didn't make sense. There was still a missing link, so I dug deeper. And before I had Law hire a private detective, you and Picasso went to him and told him everything."

"But the prison phones, the mail . . . how do you know what we told him?" she asked.

"Of course, Law couldn't tell me over the phone what you three talked about, but he did assure me that Picasso had been on our side since day one. That's when I told Law how to find T-Hunt. I didn't care if anyone was listening. One, because we spoke in code, and two, I just told Law how to find T-Hunt, not where to find him."

"Oh, now I get it. That's why T-Hunt came in the church and reached out to Pablo."

The next day I went to Grand Cayman International to move some money around, so I could make a move on some real estate ventures I had Law looking into back home.

While waiting to see a personal banker, I started watching the television monitor hanging from the ceiling in the waiting area.

"Rumors of extortion, bribery, and murder have threatened to bring the city government of Chicago to its knees. Although front-runner gubernatorial candidate Richard James has been rumored to be heavily involved in police corruption, he has staunchly denied any rumors of misconduct, calling them ridiculous lies.

"Still, James is adamant about keeping his promises to clean up corruption and crime once he's elected governor.

"We caught up to Mayor James a little while ago coming out of the state department, and he refused to comment on the rumors," the voice said over the flashing headlines.

ACT 51
The Beginning of the End
Moses

The week had been ice cream and pecan pie and neither of us wanted it to come to an end, but after seeing that news brief, we both knew we had to get back.

Something was going down much different than Rhythm planned. From what I got from the news brief, it looked like James was escaping prosecution, and instead of his approval rating plummeting, it was up.

Rhythm and I split up at the airport. She had to get back to her job in DC so she could try and get a handle on the situation.

As soon as I touched down at O'Hare, I flagged down a taxi.

Solomon really went all the way out for Momma, I thought, as I entered the secured high-rise apartment building Momma now lived in.

She was at the door waiting, when I got off the elevator. It was uncanny how Momma always knew when she was having company. And I thought I was surprising her. I even gave the concierge a ten-spot not to tell her I was coming up.

She held her arms out to me like I was still a child, and I

ran into them like I was one too. We hugged, we cried, and
we enjoyed each other's company for all of twenty minutes
before she had me call my brother.

"What's up, big brotha?" I asked when he answered the
phone.

"Moses! Oh my God!"

"No, not quite."

He laughed. "Still the joker, huh?"

"Always."

"Where are you?"

"Momma's."

"I'm on my way."

Wow! Solomon must have a red cape and a blue suit, as
quick as he got over to Momma's. It hadn't even been ten
minutes since we got off the phone.

Tears were in his eyes as he lifted me off my feet. "I've
been wanting to tell you this for a long time now, little
brother—I'm proud of you, always have been. I pray for you,
and I thank God for you, every day. Forgive me, for waiting
so long to come and get you. I love you, little brother."

"I love you too, man, and I understand why you did what
you did—and thanks for the kidney."

He nodded.

"Rhythm told me everything. I'm glad you didn't put
Momma in harm's way.

"Get your stuff. You staying with me. Pablo and Law are on
the way over to the house. You've got very little time to learn
a whole lot."

Fifteen minutes later, we were pulling into Solomon's driveway.

"Man, your front yard looks like something out of a land-
scaping magazine," I said.

"You like what I've done with the azaleas?" He pointed to

the small bushes and lights that surrounded both sides of the driveway.

"Yeah, but the floral arrangement around the well in the middle of the yard is the bomb."

The doorbell chimed repeatedly, while Solomon was in the middle of giving me a tour of his four-bedroom, three-bath custom home, overlooking a private lake in the back-yard.

"All right already, I hear you," he said as we walked down the stairs to the front door.

Picasso almost knocked Solomon down, trying to get to me. As we embraced, he said, "Moses, my nigga, look at you, baby boy. Yo, I missed you, god.

"Follow me, I got something to show you."

"Good ta see you, Youngblood. Told ya before I walked out of prison, we'd find a way to get you out." Law put his arm around me as we all followed Picasso out the front door.

It feels good, damn good, to be back with family. I checked out the new Black-ice blue 84 Fleetwood and the new "big-daddy," triple-light, bright-white SEC 560 Benz.

Solomon's big blue Lincoln was almost ten years old, but it was clean. Picasso walked passed it and opened the driver's door, revealing the bedsheet-white leather and sand-blond beige interior of his Benz.

"Catch!" Picasso threw a key to me.

I caught it.

"Whachu think?"

"Picasso, this has got to be one of the coldest Benzos on the street. And white too—man, you know white is my color."

"I know. That's why I had this one special-ordered and rush-delivered, just for you, baby boy." He smiled.

I threw my hands up. "Man, I don't know what to say."

Picasso came around the car. "The expression on your face says it all."

A few minutes later, the four of us were sitting outside on Solomon's rear deck.

Picasso stood up. "I want everyone to dig what I'm 'bout ta say. You"—He pointed to me—"T-Hunt and everybody thought I was on some power trip, when I left the Disciples. Yeah, I wanted to be King of Kings, no question, but that was because I knew I, we, had to stack some mad paper. And I just felt that getting in the dope game was the way to go."

"You didn't think about the lives you'd be destroying?" Solomon asked.

"Yeah, I thought about it, but I also figured Black folks were so messed up as it was, that I wasn't going to make it much worse?"

"I don't understand," Solomon replied.

"Studying Karl Marx and Lenin, and seeing how Lenin and Stalin took down the Russian regime made me think that I could use the capitalist concept of wealth building. And once I acquired enough wealth, and had enough crooked politicians in my pocket, I could successfully fund and start a mental revolution, to free the masses. The few that I was killing with my heroin were, unfortunately, casualties of a war that I didn't start."

"I know T-Hunt is your man and all, Moses, but I couldn't see your vision, our vision, being manifested with him at the head, so I did what I had to do. I had to make five times the noise the Disciples were making so the dirty-dog-pig police would step to me before they stepped to T-Hunt. I just couldn't trust that he would know how to handle the shit if the pigs would've stepped to him first."

I interrupted. "I know. Rhythm explained all this to me last week. I don't know if I would've done what you did, but it is what it is, and I'm thankful. I owe you, man."

"Naw, Moses." He pointed a finger at me. "The only thing

you owe me is to finish what you started when you first made me a Disciple."

We all talked and planned from early afternoon to well into the night before we put a blueprint of a plan together. Law and Picasso caught me off-guard when they explained how deep the conspiracy was.

ACT 52
A Woman's Fury
Rhythm

I was standing outside of my brownstone in DC. "Bill, what the hell is going on around here?" I said out loud to myself.

Richard James' wrinkled-up smile greeted me at my door on the front page of the Post, shaking hands with the director of the FBI, President Reagan, and my boss. The caption read "Justice United Against Crime."

I walked into my apartment to find my multi-colored tangs and my two lionfish floating at the top of my seventy-gallon saltwater tank. What else could go wrong? I shook my pounding head.

It was apparent that my neighbor had not fed my fish while I was gone. Whatever. I'd have to kill her, er, I mean deal with her later.

I dropped my suitcase on the hardwood foyer floor, turned around, and headed right back out the door. *What the hell had happened the two weeks I'd been away on leave?* I sped out of my driveway.

Needless to say, me being mad was an understatement as I

stood in Bill's office fifteen minutes later, tapping a hole in the floor with the heel of my shoes.

"Aja, you have to calm down," Bill said with his arm extended out.

"'Calm down'? Bill, how can I calm down?" I dropped the paper on his desk. "What are we doing here, Bill? I thought we were the good guys."

"Edward Porter disappeared not long after you left. He never even showed for his grand jury testimony. No one's heard from nor seen him. While searching Porter's home, the detectives noticed that someone had packed and fled in a hurry. Later on that same day, Porter's 1984 Jaguar was found in an airport parking lot."

"C'mon, Bill, that's bullshit, and you know it. Somehow, James found out about Porter's testimony and had him killed."

"Watch it, Aja—you can't go accusing a high-ranking official of murder without any evidence."

"They got to you, didn't they?"

"No, no one got to me, Aja. I received a call from the president requesting that he, the director of the FBI, and Richard James meet here at my office. Of course, I agreed.

"During the meeting, Richard James went on record, as he recounted the story of overzealous, corrupt rogue cops in the Fifth Precinct during the early to mid '70s."

"Let me guess, James failed mention that he was at the head of all the corruption, right?"

Ignoring my outburst, Bill continued, "James also introduced a box of phone records and illegal wiretaps linking Edward Porter and Samuel Lester to the murder of Congressman Homes and his wife."

"Bill, do you hear yourself?"

"What do you mean?"

"'Illegal wiretaps.' You didn't say, 'James introduced wiretaps,' you said 'illegal wiretaps'; you just substantiated my theory."

My boss sat back in his chair and crossed his arms. "And what theory would that be?"

"Congressman Homes spearheaded and headed up the committee that was charged with investigating police corruption in 1974. Obviously, James had something to hide, so he and his men placed illegal wiretaps around the congressman in hopes of getting some dirt on the man." I placed my arms on Bill's desk and stared him in the face. "I think you can figure out how James planned to leverage the dirt they got from the congressman."

"If James went through all this trouble, why would he need to have Homes killed?"

"Think about it, Bill—the pressure was building with each day that passed without getting anything on the congressman. The committee must've been getting close to finding something, so James somehow killed the congressman and his wife, making it look like Moses did it. Not only would this get Homes out of the way, but capturing the congressman's killer the same night would make James look like a hero.

"After all of this, the committee wouldn't dare continue the investigation after their leader's killer was brought to justice by the very people they were investigating."

"Interesting theory, but that's all it is, Aja—theory."

"But—"

"But what, Aja? You know that evidence and witness testimony is what yields convictions, not theories."

Unfortunately, Bill was right, but that didn't mean I was wrong. "Okay, what about Lester? Have you brought him in?"

"Lester washed ashore just this morning. We're waiting until morning to release his identity to the media."

"Why?"

"We want to notify his next of kin first."

"Come on, Bill, you and I both know that's bullshit. You can notify them within an hour of the body being identified." I pointed a finger at my boss. "The reason they're keeping Lester's identity so tight-lipped is because they want to have their stories together in case Porter pops up, or washes ashore."

"Who is they?"

I threw my hands in the air. "FBI, CIA, NSA, I don't know."

He just gave me one of those "what-could-I-do" shrugs.

"Who found Lester?"

"Some kids skipping school."

"Where exactly was the body found?"

"On the shore of Lake Michigan. He was shot in the head three times. Ballistics matched the bullets that were extracted from his head with—"

"Let me guess—Porter's service revolver."

His silence confirmed that I had hit the nail right on the head.

"This has set-up written all over it, and you know it, Bill."

"What can I say?" He shrugged. "What can I do? My hands are tied. The case, if any, is back in the hands of the state of Illinois. The president personally asked me to drop the investigation on James after he came forward and willingly cooperated, answering all of our questions."

"I'd like to see those questions," I mumbled, as I stormed out of the DA's office.

"Let it go, Aja, and that's an order."

ACT 53
Wake Up Call
Rhythm

As soon as I got home, I started making calls. I tried Picasso's phones, no answer. When I called Law's office, I was told that he would be in court all day. I called Rev several times before I called Momma King, and she'd told me that Moses and Solomon were out together. I couldn't get in touch with anyone.

I was so frustrated and my head hurt so bad, after taking two Tylenols, I balled up and fell asleep on the loveseat in my sunroom.

When I woke up, the moon was shining through the sunroom glass. I must've slept for hours. What time is it?

Before getting off the loveseat, I grabbed the cordless phone off the floor and took it with me into the kitchen.

After I got a fresh bottle of White Zinfandel out of the rack and poured myself a glass, I dialed Rev's number.

"Hello," a drugged-like Rev answered.

"Rev, this is Rhythm. Is Moses there?" I savored the wine's soft texture.

"Hold on."

"No, don't put the phone down; you need to hear this. Can you just have Moses grab another phone?" I asked.

"What time is it?" he asked.

"I don't know? Eleven, twelve, maybe." I could hear him slowly moving around.

"Moses, pick up the phone."

"Good morning," a cheery-sounding Moses said.

"'Morning'?" Rev yawned. "What time is it?"

"Five thirty-five, good to be alive," Moses said.

Five-thirty. I must've really been tired to sleep for twelve hours.

"I don't even wanna know," Rev said, still half-sleep.

"I do. What are you doing so wide-awake this early in the morning?" I asked.

"I just finished meditating. I wanna take advantage of such a clear morning and go running before the smog-mobiles get on the road and poison my lungs," Moses said.

"Listen to this—Richard James, President Reagan, the director of the FBI, and, get this, my boss were on the front page of the Post. James killed Porter and Lester and made it look like Porter killed Lester, and Porter is missing, and has been, since a grand jury was sequestered to get his testimony as to the extent of James' involvement in everything."

"Slow down, Rhythm. What are you talking about?" Moses asked.

"Edward Porter has disappeared, and Samuel Lester was found dead this morning. It just seems to me that James is behind Lester's death and Porter's disappearance."

"I haven't heard any of this," Rev said. "Surely Lester's death should have made the local news."

"Uhh, it did—you just didn't know it. Lester's identity is being released sometime today. And get this—the president himself told my boss to lay off James.

"This is much bigger than we thought. Think about it—

this is an election year, and the president's involvement changes the game and the stakes."

"Breathe, Rhythm. Baby, take a breath, calm your nerves," Moses said.

"Everybody is telling me to calm down. How can I calm down? Did you hear me?—Knock-Knock, hello, is anyone home?"

"It was hard keeping up, but I assure you we heard every single word," Rev said.

"Rhythm, today the fellas got together and put all the information we'd gathered together, and we have almost everything figured out. Nothing you've said is surprising. In fact, it only verifies what we already know.

"Tell you what—I'll fly up this weekend and fill you in on everything. For now, just please relax and go about your normal routine as if everything is fine. Because, trust me, it will be. We have a plan; just sit tight. Moses King is up from under the bars of Babylon. You've fought hard to get me here. Now let me carry the sword for a while, okay, baby?"

ACT 54
Forum of Gods
Picasso

"I called this forum of gods because we're about to embark on a new day. We've been bangin' strong and wrong for far too long. Everybody know my man out now, and we need to not only continue the gang truce, we have to do more than unify; we got to defy and rectify our differences and become one family."

I pointed to the three stacks of papers piled on the mahogany conference table inside the Bishop's meeting room in the church.

"I want everyone to fill out these papers and pass them out to all the gods."

My fifteen lieutenants were shiftily nervous but remained quiet.

I continued, "These papers are applications for a name change. I'll pay for everything, but we gotta become, as I said, one fam. The Disciples are doing the same thing as we speak. Everybody will keep their first name. The fam's last name will become One Free."

"No disrespect, Picasso," one of my lieutenants said, "but you askin' a lot. I mean, you gotta think about our families and shit. It's chill what you doin', but everybody don't feel the same way you do."

"Check this—if it wasn't for Moses, none of us would be here clockin' like Citibank. Moses is the godfather of grip, when it comes to the gang thing, ya dig?

"He made me who I am today." I patted my chest. "Everyone should want to be like the man. And everyone should want to be a part of one big-ass ride-or-die fam. I mean, I want all y'all to feel me, when I say I understand your doubt, your reservations, and your loyalty to your immediate kinfolk.

"And loyalty should be part of the reason why you should want to strengthen the chain of brotherhood, ya dig?" I penetrated the eyes of all fifteen heads in the room. "Imagine how strong we would be if we had a gang of, say, fifty thousand gods all bearing the last name One Free.

"And imagine the feeling, when kids ask you what One Free stands for and you can proudly say it represents the freedom and mental emancipation of each individual who bears this name like a cross, crossing over from slavery to freedom."

Changing tactics, I said, "Y'all watch TV and listen to Black radio. What is the war cry of the Black politician?— Get out and vote, right?"

"Right," a few answered.

"Now imagine what a family of fifty, seventy-five, a hundred thousand Black folks with the same name could do. Talking about power, we'd redefine the word."

"No disrespect, boss," one of my lieutenants interrupted, "but we can't get fifteen niggas to agree on one single issue. How you expect to get fifty thousand niggas to change they family name?"

"The same way Mr. Cadillac gets fifty thousand niggas to buy his cars when they livin' from check to check in some ol' raggedy-ass apartment. The same way Mr. Klein, Mr. Levi, and Mr. Jordache got a million niggas wearing they names on they asses." I paused to let what I just said set in.

"All we have to do is do it. We over five thousand strong. If we, the gangstas, change our names, young 'uns that want to be like us will think it's cool, and hip. So what do they do?— They come to us, or the church, and they follow right behind us. Before you know it, the 'One Free' revolution will be a reality."

"I don't know," the same god said.

"What? You don't know that politicians will be walking around wearing kneepads, kissing our asses for support. Or is it, you don't know that we gon' rock the boat—hell, we gon' drive that bitch until the engine falls off."

I was on a roll. I just hoped my lieutenants were starting to feel me.

"Imagine how we could decrease the Black-on-Black violence in the community over the next couple generations. All these cousins and One Free relatives standing together, fighting against outside oppressive forces, instead of killing each other."

The room was quiet. I had everyone's attention now. I could almost see the cogs turning in the heads of my soldiers.

"That leads me to my next resolution—As of the end of the month, we out the dope game."

"Picasso, you got to be kiddin'," one of my lieutenants said.

I shook my head. "No, the hell I'm not. Everyone down with getting paid on the legit tip can follow me, as I invest in buying up the community and building shopping complexes, malls, restaurants, and nice affordable housing for our people and shit.

"No longer will you have to sleep with a gat under your pillow. No longer will you have to get nervous when five-0 pulls up behind you.

"Now, for all y'all heads who ain't trying to be with me, then I want you to understand that you're against me and what is soon to be the 'First Family.'

"I'll tell you this now—Moses and I are stopping the dope game on the South Side. I want everyone to ride with me. You know I wouldn't run you off no cliff. As long as I'm around and got one breath in my body, I'm gon' take care of fam, and until you say otherwise, you gods are my fam."

"Why now?" another god asked. "Why this moment? Why not last year or next year?"

"You heard the phrase From Niggas to Gods, right?" I asked.

The god said, "Yeah."

"Right now, we ain't nothing but niggas pretending to be gods. A god is going to live in the light of the Father, the one God, the Supreme Ruler and Creator and Sustainer of the universe. Right now, we are funning in the devil's playground. We pushin' the devil's potion. We done got paid, our pockets are fat, but our souls are empty. Believe the hype, when I tell you I can get us paid like Rockefeller, without slingin', H, yayo, or herb.

"We gon' incorporate our gang, our fam. We'll begin pooling our bank together, so we can start buying up Chicago and re-developing the city. Afterwards, we gon' lease that shit right back to the city, the banks, our people, everyone.

"Personal percentages will be reflected and calculated by how much each family member puts into the pot. Furthermore, family will get first dibs on the jobs that we'll provide. Do y'all muthafuckin' feel me or what?"

A few nods, and tentative "Yeahs" rang around the room.

"I don't know about y'all, but ain't no cracka done gave me nor my ancestors forty acres and a mule. Interest done compounded like ten mu'fuckin' times ten since the signing of the Emancipation procla-damn-mation.

"It's time for us to fight over land we own, instead of corners we don't."

I faced a barrage of questions and opposition after speaking to the gods. I tried to remain passive, but after an hour, I became frustrated with their limited thinking.

After two hours, everyone at least came to terms and agreed to take the name-change papers to the rest of the gods and to get the ones who wanted to become a part of the One Free family to return them this Sunday after church service.

ACT 55
And Still I Rise
Picasso

"**D**amn, a nigga need a massage," I said to myself as I pulled up to the front of my building. When I get in the crib, I'll play with Fluke a few minutes, feed him, send for one of my grade A four-star cuties, and finally, I'll take a hot shower and wash all the hate off me that I felt earlier from the gods.

Carlos, the valet, opened my car door. "Mr. P, what's shakin'?"

"I can't even call it, baby boy." I rolled off a ten-spot and handed it to the young Hispanic valet.

"I don't know why you can't. I ain't seen this one before, Mr. P." Carlos ran his hand across the convertible white top of my two-year-old, bookshelf-brown Bentley.

"It's old. I picked it up a few days ago."

"Mr. P, this ride is butter." Carlos got in and sat on the baby-soft, camel-brown calfskin driver's seat.

I walked through the buildings revolving glass doors.

"Good evening, Mr. P. Would you like your mail?" the concierge asked.

"Not right now, Ron." I waved. "So how's everything today?"

"Same ol', same ol', different day."

I walked on the plush red carpet walkway heading towards the bronzed elevator doors.

I was about to get on when Ron's voice stopped me. "Oh, yeah, Mr. P., I forgot." He jogged in my direction. "Earlier, about one or two, a couple of unfamiliar professional-looking gentlemen came around asking questions about you."

I frowned. "What sort of questions?"

He shrugged. "They spoke to my supervisor, and next thing I knew, they got on the elevator."

"Any idea where they went." I peeled off a twenty from the roll of cash I took out of my pocket. "Or who they were?"

"No, sir, but I didn't see them leave. They could have, though, maybe through the garage or a fire exit. Or maybe they got by me when I was busy with another resident."

After handing Ron a ten-spot behind the twenty I peeled off, I got on the elevator. He was lucky I gave him that. The information he gave me was not the least bit helpful; matter of fact, it was borderline gossip.

"One or two o'clock, he said." That had been six hours ago. Ron was probably just trying to get a tip. The two cats could've been anybody, if there were even two guys. I got off of the elevator at the penthouse.

I pulled my pearl-handled, lion-hunting knife from the case I wore on my side and put it in my front pocket. I really shouldn't be worried. If any strange muthafucka got into my crib, they wouldn't live to tell about it. Fluke would have they ass for lunch.

Timidly, I opened one of the French front doors. *Where the fuck is my dog?* "Fluke!"

I pulled my knife. I had a mind to turn and run, but I

couldn't. I was tired of running. Tired of looking over my shoulder. I was sick and tired of just being "plain old tired."

Fuck all that—this is my mu'fuckin' castle, and it just gone have to be what it gon' mu'fuckin' be.

I switched the oblong fluorescent light on the hall and turned around. Suddenly I found myself staring into the barrel of a silenced revolver.

Then I heard the front door close behind me.

I turned and saw Fluke. The sick sons of bitches killed my baby.

"Search him." The gun-wielding suit ordered someone I couldn't see.

As soon as I felt hands on my body, I bent over and coughed, feinted to my left, did a tuck and roll, while a hot intense pain exploded in my right shoulder.

I came up in a kneeling position, my pearl-handled hunting knife in hand.

One of the suits made himself a perfect target, standing in my face with his gun pointed at me. I cut the wrist that held his gun, causing him to drop it on the elevated black marble foyer floor.

The gun backfired, as it slid off of the foyer and onto the carpet.

The other suit fired off a shot and missed. One or both of the bullets shattered my saltwater fish tank that was built into the living room front wall.

One hundred gallons of water, rocks, and fish gushing out into the sunken den onto my golf-course green, two-inch-thick carpet was all the distraction I needed to slice a wide smile across one suit's neck. In less than a second I threw my knife into the other suit's chest.

"Fuck!" I looked at my fish flapping on my ruined ninety-pound carpet. I arched my back at the sticky pain I felt in my shoulder.

I turned to look at the control panel on the wall. I was relieved to see that the green light was still flashing. I couldn't remember how many backup tapes I had behind it.

I gingerly walked over to the wrought iron-and-glass terrace French doors and picked up the wet gun that was on the carpet near the suit with a knife sticking out of his chest.

"Bitch, you done fucked with the wrong one for the last wrong mu'fuckin' time." I brought the butt of his gun down on his wounded chest.

That shit had to hurt, but the Flintstone barely made a sound. Oh, he winced and cringed, but he didn't scream.

"That vest is the only reason you still breathin', bitch. I guess you didn't anticipate my knife when you put that shit on this morning," I said, my hand on his throat.

"You won't make it out of here," he said.

"I can't mu'fuckin' tell." I held the gun's silenced barrel and slammed it into the suit's nose.

I heard the bones crack in his nose. He was definitely a professional, the way he took the pain, with only a grimace on his face.

"I'm gon' ask you one time—Who sent you?" I held up the gun butt in the air, ready to take another swing at his already broken nose.

"I did," a familiar voice said from behind me.

I was about to turn around.

"Ah-ah-ah, don't move a single, solitary muscle, Pablo." The person removed the gun from my hand.

"Takin' a big chance, aren't you, James?"

"Not really." His shoes made a squish sound on the carpet behind me. "See, I'm not here. I'm in the poverty-torn Niggerville town of East St. Louis campaigning. As we speak, everyone thinks I'm resting at the Radisson Hotel in South Illinois, where several of your dumb watermelon-, fried-chicken-eating Sambo brothers saw me retire to this afternoon to finish preparing a speech I'm giving at the East St. Louis 'Niggers, alligators, apes, coons, and possums NAACP leadership conference tomorrow morning," he said, laughing at his own dry humor.

"You can kill me, but it won't stop me. I'll come back from the grave to crush your world."

"Dead men can't talk—or didn't you know that?"

"I promise you, I'll be on trial with my right hand up swearing to tell the truth and nothing but. And I will identify myself as Pablo Guerva Nkrumah, co-head of the Gangsta Gods under your tutelage."

"Yeah, and I'll be there to admit to all the murders I committed in the past for 'Part Two,' and the conspiracy to stop niggers from ever getting the noose from around their necks."

"Part Two, the second coming of Cointelpro. I know all about the government-sanctioned, secret FBI organization to exterminate brothas before they rise to power—"

"And?"

"And I guess you forgot the hit I have out on your family?"

"Of course not. Now that wouldn't be White of me to forget something like that, now would it?

"It took me a while to find out that you hired the Bartoli brothers to take out my family, but find out I did. You cost me a significant amount of cash, but who cares? It's over. I'll charge it to the job."

"I guess you killed Porter and Lester, huh?" I had a feeling James was arrogant enough to brag on his being a tough guy.

"Fucker tried to turn on me . . . after all I did for him. I would've taken care of him. He would've only received a slap on the wrist, but no, Porter tried to cross me. No one will ever find him, unless they can find his head and his hands, which should be shark bait by now. I told you long ago, 'No one fucks with me, not even your God.'"

"You sick bitch-ass cracka, I know all about you and your Cointelpro, FBI past. And I know all about Part Two as well."

"I'm impressed—Too bad you won't live to tell about it."

"What I don't understand is, why did you go to so much trouble to get Moses King off the streets?"

"Once the Counter Intelligence Protective Agency of the FBI was dismantled in '71, a few top agents, like me for example, were put into high-ranking city and state government positions in major cities around the country to monitor and diffuse of anyone threatening to become another Martin King.

"Now if you would be so kind as to strip—NOW!" He shouted. "You think I'm stupid, don't you? I swept this place for bugs before you got here. You got me on tape one too many times."

I'm glad my back was turned to him. He couldn't see the smile on my face. I didn't have my place bugged, at least not in a way he could detect.

"Take them off too," he said.

"I hope you are enjoying the show, freak." I removed my boxers. "Satisfied?"

"I will be in a few minutes."

"Until then, you mind finish telling me what this shit is all about?"

"Now that I see you're not wearing a wire, I guess I can give you this one last wish.

"Over the years, Homes became the voice of the nigger in the state of Illinois, and his support from White liberals in the state was rapidly growing. After Homes was given the green light to assemble a committee to investigate police corruption in the city, I was ordered to do something about the bastard, and Moses was just the right pigeon at the right time."

This cat is dumber than I thought. How he made it so far in his profession, running off at the mouth like he did, I'd never know.

"You see, we were watching Moses too. He was stirring up some noise in the nigger community, but he was never a real threat. So before he ever had a chance to become a threat to the White power structure, as you call it, I decided to have my men frame him.

"I thought this would be a great way to divide the niggers. Y'all can't seem to do anything even halfway right, unless you have some sense of solidarity. Funny thing is, when Porter and Lester killed that nigger, Homes, them dummies had to fuck his young wife.

"Porter called me, telling me how pretty the little whore was. I was in the area, so I came and got a piece of the bitch too. You should have heard the whore. 'Quit! Please! No! Don't!' That black bitch knows she wanted some milk in her coffee. She probably had never had a White man until that night. After I came, she went with the bullet I put in her head."

"I can't believe you're telling me all this."

"Why not?—It's not like you'll tell anybody our secret, except maybe the worms." He laughed.

"So what's gon' happen to Part Two now?"

"Nothing. It will always exist. The name may change, but there will always be a government-sanctioned organization around to prevent the rise of any minority in this country. The only niggers we will allow to become leaders in the nigger and spic communities are the ones that we can control."

"So why am I still livin'?"

"First, because I want those tapes. And secondly, I want to show you that your nigger God bows down to me."

"God don't bow down to Satan, and I won't bow down to you either." I turned and lunged at him.

A succession of hot pain exploded in my chest and stomach, while I scrambled towards him. I was getting dizzy. So much pain. I coughed as I moved. "Even in death, I will haunt your nightmares and slaughter your dreams," I said.

He backed up into a wall, as I reached for him.

My mother smiled. She reached out and took my hand. "Mommacita," I cried.

ACT 56
How Long? Not Long
Moses

Although I'd been out of prison for a month, it seemed like a year instead. I never thought I would've attracted so much media attention. After a month, I was still getting calls to appear on a wide variety of television talk shows. I'd done a few, but I had to turn down more invitations than I could accept. I was too busy these days, trying to orchestrate a large land acquisition and development deal, among other things.

I'd just left the judge's chambers, getting my name change signed off on. It felt good to finally liberate myself from my slave name. I was now officially Moses One Free. I felt like this was just the beginning.

"I guess I have to call you Youngblood One Free now." Law ran up to me as I was coming out of the courthouse.

"One Free for life." I shot a fist in the air.

"You ready for some more good news?" Law asked.

"Always."

"A couple weeks ago, I gave our real estate attorneys over at Tate, Long, and Wiley, the go-head to hire a commercial development research firm to put together some numbers and revise our strategy to buy the seventy-five-acre Ida B. Wells project housing development on the South Side."

"Okay. So have they come up with anything?"

"No, not yet, but they've assured us that the Chicago Housing Authority will get behind us if we can show how we can revitalize the community and increase the city's revenue."

"How would we be increasing the city's revenue?"

"Eventually, the city would have to do something about the condition of the apartments. When they do, they would see that they would have to tear them down and relocate all those people and build another low-income housing project."

"Exactly what we're going to do," I said.

"Right. But we're going to do it right. And the city won't have to pay for shit, and they make money by selling us the current structure."

"Of course, they'd be more worried about money than the five thousand people, and the sixteen hundred and sixty-two families who are herded together, living in the sub-standard rat- and roach-infested housing development."

"We knew that from the beginning," Law said. "The good news is, one, I got your corporate resolutions papers and your state seal for the company, two, all parties involved with making this project a success think the company is owned buy a group of White investors who want to remain anonymous."

"How is that good news?" I asked.

"You know the socio-consciousness of America is racist," Law said.

"Yeah, and?"

"Okay, so now they think White folks stand to benefit off the urban-revitalization project that we came up with. So when it comes down to getting grants and loans to complete the project, once we acquire the property, it will be a cakewalk."

"Smart."

"You know . . . what can I say?"

"So what do our attorneys and the research firm think our chances are of making our dreams a reality?"

"They think it's a no-brainer for the city to approve. Our project relieves the Chicago Housing Authority and the city from being eventually forced into doing something about the dilapidated seventy-five-acre deathtrap that they've turned a blind eye to for so many years. And if we fail, they'll be able to say they tried to re-develop the community before we came in and took over the project," Law explained.

"This is a helluva power move we trying to pull for our first real-estate venture."

"That's the way we gotta roll, Youngblood." Law's stare became much more intense. "We free today. We gotta set our people free tomorrow, and only with us showing them that we can take back our community and successfully control and increase the economy in it can we motivate others to do the same—"

I cut him off. "And we make a statement by buying the Ida B., the first project housing development in Chicago."

"And the nation," Law added.

"Next thing you know, we'll own the whole South Side."

"Talking about making a statement, shit, we writing a new chapter in urban renewal and development. We are going to re-educate the urban nation."

"Let's just hope Picasso can re-educate the Gangsta Gods," I said.

"Getting them and the Disciples to align themselves with the One Free movement will be a defining moment in history."

"I can't even imagine how many young cats will follow

them into the One Free family," I said, before we both got into my car.

It wasn't like Picasso to pull a disappearing act. No one had heard from him for a couple days now. Rhythm called me at two something this morning, worried about her brother. She told me that he was supposed to fly into DC yesterday morning, but he never showed and never called. She said she had tried calling him on all his numbers.

Before hanging up, I told her that Law and I would swing by his apartments when I left the courthouse.

ACT 56
Finding Picasso
Moses

The tires on my Benz screamed as we bent the corner at North Street and pulled up to valet parking at the Grand Plaza.

I almost banged the door into the bookish-looking Hispanic valet as I jumped out the car. Law was limping and on my heels, as I threw the keys to the valet before hurrying through the revolving doors of the apartment building.

"Excuse me, gentlemen," the "Hulk-Hogan-in-a-suit" concierge said, "But can I help you?"

We stopped and explained that we were there to see Mr. Nkrumah in suite 2500.

After the concierge took our names, he called up to Picasso's penthouse apartment. He quickly informed us that there was no answer.

He smiled. "You're welcome to wait in the lobby or the library." He extended an arm in two different directions.

"Thank you, but we'll come back," I replied.

"We could've easily tricked that big-ass farmer. What's the deal, Youngblood?"

"We gotta play it cool. No need to attract attention.

Remember, I got a spare key. We can park around the corner on Michigan Street, and we'll sneak in the building through the parking garage."

Thanks to Law's broke-down feet, it took us all of fifteen minutes to get back to the building. He complained about his corns the whole two blocks he limped back to the building.

"Shit! I'm getting too old for this 'Shaft' shit. Youngblood, remind me to get some Dr. Scholl's shoe pads."

"Yo' old ass need a wheelchair."

"Fuck ya! And will you slow the fuck down . . . before I shoot you in the damn leg."

We approached the keyed entry elevator foyer.

"If I was one of those booty-skirt-wearin', big-tittied, fine-ass Soul Train dancers, I bet your ass wouldn't be complainin'."

"And if I was a fifth, I'd be too fucked up to complain. But if is just that—it's a two-letter word that doesn't begin to stop the howlin' my dogs are doing in these damn shoes." Law hobbled to catch up.

"Old man, bring yo' ass on." I held the elevator open.

"And again, I reiterate—fuck ya."

We got off on the twenty-fifth floor and were at Picasso's door in no time.

I knocked. No answer. I pulled out my gun and motioned for Law to do the same.

Something was definitely wrong. I listened to the door another minute. Fluke wasn't behind the door growling. That dog was so mean, he didn't bark, he just growled.

Fluke and I were cool, but I still was scared of his big, black ass. I took a deep breath as I turned the key in the knob. I pushed the door open as far as I could. Something behind it was preventing it from opening all the way.

"Fluke, it's your uncle, Moses. Where you at, boy?" I shouted out and whistled before timidly stepping inside the

hardwood wrought-ironed railed foyer. "Let's go," I whispered, signaling Law with my forty-five.

As soon as I walked inside, my nostrils were assaulted by a
sickening odor. The smell of fried shit in garlic was like in-
cense, compared to the smell of death.

I held one hand over my nose and looked to see what had
prevented the door from closing. I just shook my head. "I
see why Fluke wasn't on top of us when we opened the
door."

Law walked around me. "Damn! Pray we don't find
Picasso like his dog." Law shook his head in disgust at the de-
composing, bloody dog sprawled behind one of the front
doors.

Enunciating my words slowly and clearly, I said, "Oh . . .
my . . . God!"

The dark-green-carpeted den was a damp mess. Glass, colored rocks, coral, and dead fish were on one side of the
room. A broken glass table, furniture, and Jet and Ebony
magazines were on the other. This is some super-thick carpet
to absorb all this water, I thought.

All of a sudden I was a kid again. T-Hunt and I had just
watched this little slick-tongued Hispanic-looking kid stand
up to the Goliath-like bully, Big Dino Banks, and his band of
flunkies. I was thinking, this kid was crazy, or he had a sui-
cide wish.

Then something weird happened. I looked into the kid's
eyes at a distance that was too far for most people to see another's eyes. It was in the eyes that I saw what was in his soul.
I saw a will to stand up and fight, like none I'd ever seen before.

I took another step on the damp, squishy carpet, before I
again re-visited that childhood day.

I saw a will to be free and a will to be without judgment.

Squish. I took another step.

I saw a will to die, if it meant compromising his freedom.

Squish. I took another.

I saw Moses King in this kid.

Squish. I dropped to my knees.

The words "I'll never forget" played through my mind as if the kid had just said them yesterday. And then, for a minute, I was looking down on Picasso kneeling over my body as I lay in my own blood.

"I'll never forget," I said, returning to reality. I cradled Picasso's head in my arms and closed his eyes.

"I'll never forget," I said again, more to myself than to him.

I was rocking back and forth, forth and back, shaking my head. The feeling was agonizing. He was part of my family. A part that died, and yet a part that would live in my mind and heart forever.

Law's hand was on my shoulder. "He's gone, Moses."

I shook my head. "No! No! No!"

Law got on his knees and put his arms on me as I grieved. "Come on, Youngblood, let him go. We have work to do."

I gently laid Picasso's head back down on the wet carpet and let Law slowly help me up. Once I got up, I wiped my eyes and walked to the alarm control panel on the wall beside the door.

I felt hope, as I saw the green light blinking on the panel. I reached in my pants pocket and pulled out my keys. Next, I used the edge of my key to turn the loose screws on the panel until I'd removed the four screws that held it in place.

Upon removing the panel, I took out the five fancy-looking recorders.

A couple months ago, when I first got out of prison, I remember thinking that Picasso had taken paranoia to a new level. Then, I chalked his paranoia up to too many years looking over his shoulder. He had the feds to contend with, as well as the robbing crews out there waiting for a chance to hit a lick.

He'd explained to me that he'd had all his apartments wired with an elaborate system that recorded everything. The system was disguised as a simple home alarm. And since he used ordinary stereo speakers as microphones, a debugging system couldn't detect it.

Funny thing was, he'd gotten the idea when Richard James replayed bits and pieces of incriminating conversations that he'd had with the West African from New York who got him started in the dope game.

According to Picasso, James flipped the West African, known simply as Li'l Daddy. A couple months later he was found on a park bench in Harlem, with his tongue in his hand and his dick in his mouth. Picasso went on to tell me that James explained that he, Picasso, would suffer a similar fate if word got out that he was a snitch too.

I wasn't the least bit surprised, when Picasso told me that it was James' people that got word to West African Archie that Li'l Daddy was an informant. Although Picasso never said it, I believe that he played James' game so long because he didn't know how to get out without getting killed.

Keep your friends close, but keep your enemies closer. I grabbed the tapes and the recorders.

About fifteen minutes later, Law and I pulled up to a corner store back on the South Side. While Law went to a pay phone and made an anonymous call to the police, I went inside and purchased twenty AA batteries for the dead recorders that were about to be brought back to life.

Once I got back into the car, I called Rhythm on her cell and told her to drop everything and come to Chicago.

"Call me once you've found out which flight you'll be on and what time it will get in," I said, before hanging up the phone.

It must've been the urgency in my tone that caused her not to ask any questions.

Next, I called Solomon. His voicemail picked up. "Bruh, 911, I need you to call me immediately," I said.

Since we were already on the South Side, Law and I decided to go by New Dimensions in hopes of finding Solomon there.

Law was finishing putting the batteries in the recorders, when I broke the silence.

"As bad as I want to hear what's on those tapes, I think we should wait for Rhythm," I said.

"Man, it might be too much for her. You know how close she and her brother was, and besides, she's a woman," Law said.

"Yeah, maybe so, but don't forget who we're dealing with here."

"What do you mean?" he asked.

"She is a Black woman who knows who she is, where she came from, and what she has to do to get to where she needs to be."

ACT 57
Hours Later
Moses

Law and I paced, prayed, and waited in the church study for a little over three hours before Solomon barged in.

"I just came back from the Memorial General Hospital madhouse. Do you know that I was there for six hours? And in six hours, five people were turned away and sent to the city hospital because they didn't have adequate medical insurance.

"Brothers are dying of AIDS, sisters are suffering from cancer, children are being born drug-addicted, and hospitals are turning our people away simply because they can't afford or don't have medical insurance. The system just makes me sick to my stomach."

I extended my arm towards his favorite chair. "Solomon, please have a seat. We have something to tell you."

"I'm sorry, Law, Moses. I'm just so frustrated. Every single time I volunteer at the hospital, I come back feeling like I'm not doing enough."

"Welcome to the world of trying to save the world, big brother."

Solomon took a seat in the study facing the mural on the

wall that had a Black Moses leading the people to a land that had the words stenciled AS I PROMISED over it.

I closed my eyes and took in a deep breath. Exhaling, I slowly said, "Solomon, Law and I found Picasso dead in his downtown penthouse apartment a few hours ago. He was murdered." I walked over to the chair where he slumped down in and put my hand on his shoulder.

Solomon closed his eyes, put his elbows on the table, and interlocked his hands as if he were about to pray. In a dry monotone, he asked, "What happened?"

Law and I started from the beginning. We told him all we knew. As I started to explain the part about the tapes, I glanced at my watch and noticed the time.

"I'm sorry I have to go pick up Rhythm from the airport." I looked at my watch. "Her flight lands in about twenty minutes."

"You want me to go with you?" Solomon asked.

"No, I better go alone."

As Marvin Gaye crooned his hit, "What's Goin' On?" I wondered the same damn thing.

I was waiting outside my car at the baggage claim area, when I saw her.

"Queen."

"King," she said as we embraced.

"What's going on?" she asked as soon as we got into the car.

I was in a no-parking zone. Chicago's finest were beckoning me to move. For the first time in a long while, I didn't know what to do.

Should I sit here and tell her and get a ticket and probably get into a big argument with some happy-ticket-writing cop? Or should I just drive off and ignore Rhythm's question?

"Baby, let's get out of here before Officer Dolittle does something like write me a ticket. After we get to Solomon's house, we'll talk, okay?" I shifted the car into drive.

She looked over at me and shook her head. "Oh no. You tell me to drop everything, rush to the airport, catch the next flight out to Chicago, and you don't even give me a reason or a chance to ask why. And now, suddenly I have to wait."

I put the car back in park and gently took her hand. I looked into her eyes. "Baby, please trust me on this one. Now is not the place, nor the time."

The ride was relatively quiet to Solomon's house.

The moon's light coming through the den's double patio glass doors was the only light we had as we sat on the multi-colored, earth-toned Persian rug in the middle of the sunken den.

I took Rhythm's hand. "Queen, I have something to tell you."

"He's gone, isn't he?" Rhythm said more as a statement than a question.

I nodded. "Yes, baby, he's gone."

She turned her head to one side. "I knew it. I don't know how, but I knew."

I reached out.

She closed her eyes and inhaled.

I took her hands in mine.

When she opened her eyes, I was looking into them.

"I started crying for Pablo when his mother was taken away from him as a child. I cried even harder when you were taken away from him and sent to prison. I couldn't stop crying when his mother died in prison and was already in the ground buried by the state of New York, before Pablo was even notified," she said.

I didn't feel the need to bother the single tear that slowly started to run down the side of my face.

"King, I cried all the tears that I care to cry. I want to smile again. And I will, once we finish what we started. Pablo was one man who saw the light at the end of his life. But he did see the light, and that's what mattered."

She closed her eyes and took a deep breath. "His dream was for Black folks to see what he saw. We have to get rid of the darkness so people can see the light. We have to eliminate the darkness for Pablo's death to mean something. It doesn't matter if James did this to my brother or not; he has to be destroyed. And I'm not talking about through the judicial system." She squeezed my hand with an incredible amount of tenderness and strength.

ACT 58
The Funeral
Moses

Independence Day had just passed. It was Friday, July 6, 1984. Police were attempting to direct traffic into the church parking lot. Ushers were parking cars, so as to utilize all the space there was on the New Dimensions church grounds.

The church was filled a half-hour before the funeral began. It looked like a gang convention inside and outside the church. The sound system was set up outside the church in a tent with a projector screen, so people who couldn't get inside could still see and hear the final passage of one of Chicago's own adopted sons.

As I walked past the open bronze casket in the front of the church, I looked at my boy's face for the last time. I couldn't remember ever seeing Picasso look so peaceful.

Rhythm didn't leave my side as I took my place at the altar. I adjusted the microphone and cleared my throat before I began.

"Hello, everyone, my name is Moses One Free. I want to thank all of you for your love and support. My brother, Reverend Solomon King, and my fiancée, Aja Rhythm

Azure, sister of Pablo Picasso Nkrumah, have asked me to say a few words." I wiped the tears from my face.

"Picasso, as we all called the brother who we're laying to rest today, was a no-limit, ride-or-die extreme soldier in God's army."

Rhythm squeezed my hand.

"Maybe not the type of soldier that we've come to respect and accept, but a true soldier he was. Picasso was a Disciple, not much different than Paul of old. Picasso was a man who believed in change. He was a man who believed in unity. He was a man who believed in God. Everyone who knew him knew this."

I started getting real emotional. I didn't want to break down, so I paused to get myself together. The last thing Rhythm wanted was to turn her brother's funeral into a pity party.

"Take your time, little brotha. It's all right," Solomon shouted from behind me.

A minute later I raised my head and continued. "Yeah, he was a drug dealer. He was a womanizer. He was a lot of things, but most importantly, he loved him some Black people. He did what he did for the ultimate upliftment of all third world people. Being the offspring of a Cuban mother and Senegalese father, he faced his share of racism. It was this racism that fueled his fire to change the way society viewed race.

"Well, you might ask, How can a drug dealer and a womanizer love the people that he was destroying? And I'll tell you that he did what he did because he believed someone was gon' sell the poison to our people. So he decided he would, then donate hundreds of thousands, maybe even millions, to scholarship funds, inner-city schools, hospitals and, yes, the church."

I turned and looked at my queen, who stood by my side. She smiled.

"Not many people knew these things. Picasso didn't want recognition; as a matter of fact, most times his contributions were made anonymously. He felt that it was his duty to give back some of what he was taking."

"You're doing good, King," Rhythm whispered.

"I'm not saying what Picasso did was right, but I'm saying he acted. He didn't wait on any condition to act. Picasso wasn't a talker, wasn't a reactor, as most of us are.

"The brother was revolutionary and very instrumental in striking a severe blow to the government system of injustice. And even in his death he is still chipping away at this system of oppression.

"Right now, I want to play a special tape for you. I want you to hear bits and pieces of the last hour of Pablo's life. I want you to hear how and why he died."

Picasso's voice came to life over the intercom and the loudspeakers.

Only Rhythm, Law, Solomon, and I knew about the tape. It was Rhythm's idea to take the tape and let the church hear it before turning it and all the others over to the media.

"No, they didn't," someone shouted.

"We gotta fight," another shouted.

The congregation began to chant, "Revolution, revolution, revolution."

The funeral was getting out of control. People started rising from their seats. The church was in an uproar before the tape played out.

Rhythm and I moved out of the way, as Solomon approached the podium.

He said, "Family, please, please . . ."

The church audience began to sit back in their seats.

"We ain't gon' stand for this, Reverend," someone shouted.

"I don't want you to. We preach, we teach, we march, and we complain. We talk about injustice. We criticize politicians. We complain about the man. We lend lip service to much of everything and anything that we dislike. But we don't do anything other than complain. We talk about what we gon' do, but what do we do? Nothing. It's past due that we do something."

Solomon looked back at me.

"My brother made an excellent point when he said that Pablo acted instead of reacted. As a people we have to stop waiting for an injustice to be done to us before we act. We have to act to prevent injustices."

"Well, what we gon' do right now, this minute?" someone asked.

"What you gon' do, Reverend?" another shouted.

"We're going to show our power as a family. And I am joining my brother and changing my last name to One Free, as a show of solidarity and family. I invite everyone to do the same. I invite everyone to re-link themselves to the Black family by name recognition."

I could hardly believe what I was hearing. Solomon was on fire, and there wasn't a fire engine in sight.

"I don't know much about politics and the ways of government, but I do know about people. I know about right, and I know about wrong, and the way our government is being run is not right." He banged his fist down on the podium.

"That's why I'm not going to let Satan run for governor unopposed. I am going to run for governor of the state of Illinois, and with your and God's help we will defeat Satan James in the November election."

The New Dimensions family exploded with applause.

"Hold on now. We have four months to the day before the gubernatorial election. After hearing this tape and others like it, after seeing the legal injustices that are practiced every day, I know we have to act now to reverse the cycle. I'm not running as a Republican or Democrat; I'm running as a soldier in God's Army, independent of any political party."

The church erupted again.

A minute later, after he restored some order to the church, he continued, "I'm sure nothing like this in history has been successfully attempted at such a late stage in the race. But I believe that if God be for me, then—" He turned the microphone to the congregation.

"No one can stand against me," they shouted.

"If we win—no, when we win, it will show the nation the power of the vote and the power of unity. I need everyone's help. I need everyone to vote, and I need everyone to get everyone else—"

Solomon's mouth hung open as he and everyone else looked to the back of the church to see what was going on.

ACT 59
Miracle on July 6
Moses

I was just as shocked as everyone else inside the church, when the doors suddenly swung open. I hadn't seen or heard from my best friend T-Hunt since I'd been released, and now he was wearing blue jeans and a black God's Army T-shirt, holding some papers in his hand as he walked forward.

A young brother dressed the same way followed him. And then another, and then another, and so on.

I rose up and started to move towards them. I stopped when I saw what I thought was happening.

Solomon extended his hand out to me, as if saying, "Hold on."

T-Hunt stopped in front of Picasso's casket. He looked in. He looked up and placed his fist over his heart and shot a closed-fist salute in the air and shouted, "I am Tharellious One Free."

Next, T-Hunt knelt to the ground and neatly placed the papers he carried in his free hand in front of Picasso's coffin.

The brotha behind T-Hunt walked up to the casket. "I am

Kimal One Free." Then he too put papers on top of T-Hunt's, before moving on.

After the third brother started to make his way out of the church and a fourth stood at Picasso's casket, Rhythm rose with tears in her eyes and started clapping.

The choir looked at her. I looked at her. The whole church looked at her. I started clapping next as the endless procession of young Black men made their way to Picasso's casket.

The choir rose and started clapping, and in no time the entire church erupted with applause.

I grabbed my queen's hand, leaned over and whispered in her ear, "Picasso lived for this. Through his death he's given new life to our people."

She nodded.

The procession of Disciples and Gangsta Gods lasted for over three hours, and for three hours the church was on its feet.

The next day, Solomon told me that we had close to eleven thousand name-change forms to process.

I was surprised. But I was happy. I had no idea that Solomon had decided to run for governor. I was behind him one hundred percent, despite the Black population of Illinois being only seventeen percent, and not even a third of this seventeen voted.

The sprinkling of White folks who attended Picasso's funeral was hope enough that change was in the air. And change was what people, Black, White, Red, and Brown, wanted and needed.

In the ensuing weeks, because of the courage, the strength, and the unity of these gang members from all around the city, the name-change revolution began.

We had to hire a staff of twenty. Law had to give them a crash course on the name-change process, so they could take care of the close to seventy thousand forms we received in less than sixty days.

The church became the campaign headquarters for Solomon's bid for governor and a name-change processing center. I don't know how he did it, but Solomon managed to get on the ballot.

After Reshonda Reid of Nightline News listened to the tapes and had them authenticated, she had Solomon and Rhythm on the popular nighttime news program the week after the funeral.

Not only Blacks, but White folks too were screaming for James' blood after the broadcast.

The media went into a feeding frenzy. Solomon was interviewed by news and talk shows all over the country.

When asked about his thoughts to the FBI director's response to the accusations made about Part Two, he quoted Malcolm X, saying, "It's akin to chickens coming home to roost."

The director of the FBI issued a statement denying any knowledge about a subversive government-sanctioned organization called Part Two.

When questioned as to why and how James came up with such an elaborate story, the director shrugged his shoulders and explained to the press that James was a former top-ranking agent who'd always had delusions of grandeur.

The director was very slithery as he snaked his way through the barrage of questions from the press.

James was arrested in the following weeks at his home in Lincoln Park. "No comment," was his lone response as he was taken to the squad car amidst several teams of hungry reporters.

Super Tuesday in Illinois had come and gone. My brother Reverend Solomon One Free was elected governor by a landslide. It was amazing. Never in the history of the world had a democratic election been held in a province, city, or state where over fifty thousand people with the same last name as the candidate had registered to vote.

The world called it a miracle; I called it a new day.

ACT 60
United States Justice System
Moses

Although it was a conflict of interest for Rhythm to be in any way associated with prosecuting Richard James, she did manage to strike a deal granting T-Hunt immunity from prosecution.

The government offered T-Hunt protection for him and his son. Of course, he declined. He knew that no one could and would protect him like our One Free family.

Funny thing was, T-Hunt had never even met James, but it didn't matter. After listening to all the tapes, T-Hunt and Rhythm invented an elaborate story of extortion and blackmail.

Testifying against a stranger wasn't any different than the feds coercing all these young brothers facing hella time behind bars to testify on other brothers who they'd never even met. The law called it perjury; I called it poetic justice.

Funny how the case didn't go to trial until after the prosecution lost their two star witnesses: the same two men who shot my brother years ago; the same two men that Law and Picasso had caught up to; the same two men who told Law and Picasso everything about Part Two and James' involvement with the FBI.

It had taken three years to finally put Richard James on trial.

It was the summer of '88. Rhythm and I followed the two-month trial to the end. We watched as a confident former government official and his legal team made mincemeat of the prosecution.

T-Hunt looked good as he trashed James on the stand. His testimony was the highlight of the trial. Unfortunately, it wasn't good enough.

T-Hunt received his immunity, and James was acquitted at the end of the day. Although the nation and the world had heard, or heard of, the tapes, the courts ruled them inadmissible.

How a man who killed as many people as some serial killers, and a man who almost tricked the people into electing him governor could get off as he did, was just an example of the type of justice that could be expected in this country. As I'd said before, it was up to us, the common people, to force change.

ACT 61
Lifelong Bonds
Rhythm

Ayear after the trial, Moses and I had a beautiful small double wedding with Solomon and Sunflower on the banks of Lake Victoria in Kenya, Africa.

I'm sure Sunflower was surprised, when she returned nine months after going to Peru to care for her sick mother, to find that she was engaged to a governor. I didn't know how she was able to stay sane, away so long without access to a phone.

Moses and Solomon were so proud of Momma King, who stood in front of the four of us, presiding over the ceremony.

I'm sorry. I meant the Reverend Momma King, as she had already corrected me. None of us knew that she was going to school, so it was a complete surprise to everyone when we received invitations to her college graduation a few months before James' trial began.

While my brother-in-law, the governor, had honeymooned in Portugal, Moses and I honeymooned in the beautiful exotic Canary Islands off the coast of the Mediterranean.

Thanks to Law, his attorneys, and the real estate consultant and land development firm him and Moses contracted,

the Ida B. Wells project housing was now the Ida B. Wells upscale, government-subsidized, low-income apart-ment homes.
That's right, upscale project housing.

The grounds boasted two swimming pools with two club-
houses. Each of them was equipped with a state-of-the-art fit-
ness facility and aerobics studio. There were eight tennis
courts and two full-court basketball courts on the colorful
manicured landscaped grounds.

In the center of the complex there was the twenty-thou-
sand-square-foot Pablo Picasso Nkrumah Community Help
Center and the Georgia Smith Memorial Daycare. The center provided childcare for working mothers who couldn't afford it. It catered to the youth in the community who
needed a healthy outlet to express themselves through art,
education, sports, and games. It helped adults who wanted
to get their high school equivalency certificates. The center
also offered cultural classes and workshops to empower
young men and women with an employer mindset, instead
of an employee one.

The Community Help Center was made possible through the
works of the governor. Rev spearheaded a bill that was pushed
through Congress, which allowed mothers to receive vouchers
that provided them free daycare and after-school care, as long as
they worked full-time or went to school full-time.

At first, the bill was almost thrown out before it had a
chance to make it before Congress, but the one hundred
thousand names signed on the book-like petition forced
Congress to act, and act fast.

New construction was going up all over the South Side.
Over eighty percent of the projects were spearheaded and
headed up by the One Free family.

At one time it had been a vision. Now it was a reality. I
could easily foresee a city, a country, a nation without any de-
plorable, vermin-infested, cramped-up project housing developments. I could easily foresee a One Free world.

ACT 62
Rhythm's Last Act

"Even in death I will haunt your nightmares and slaughter your dreams," the tape-recorded voice said.

Richard James looked around just in time to see the chloroform-soaked rag as it went over his nose.

Several hours passed. A white Ford Expedition pulled up to an old abandoned warehouse.

Richard James woke up bound and tied to a beige recliner. He looked around the dark, trashed, damp, abandoned warehouse. "Where am I?" he shouted to the figure emerging from the darkness.

"In hell."

"You're that bitch?"

"No—that would be your mother."

"What the fuck do you want?"

"Your attention."

"You'll get a lot more than my attention if you don't untie me." He struggled to get free.

"Even in death I will haunt your nightmares and slaughter your dreams," the tape played.

"Remember that?" Rhythm held the recorder in front of his face.

"Huh?"

"Let me refresh your memory—" She pulled out a pearl-handled hunting knife that belonged to her brother.

"What are you doing?" he asked in a panic.

In one smooth stroke of the wrist, she cut his white button-down shirt down the middle.

He squealed until he passed out from the pain as she carved the letters P-I-C-A-S-S-O L-I-V-E-S down his chest with the knife.

After she cleaned and bandaged his chest, she put smelling salts to his nose.

He coughed.

"Have some water." She held his nose, tilted his head back, and poured water down his throat.

After gulping the water down, he spat in her face.

She used her shirt to wipe her face.

She studied his face. "I don't see the fire you are trying to put out, so I'll start one, since you want to spray me." She took out her lighter and put it to his face.

He shook his head and squirmed.

"I don't care where I light it." She flicked the lighter, grabbed a lock of his hair, and burnt him on the ear.

"Ahhhhhhhhhhhhhhhhhhhhhhhhhhhhhhhhhhhhhh! You sick Black bitch!"

"Spit on me again; I'll burn your little Oscar Mayer Weiner off."

She pressed the play button on the recorder next to him. "Even in death, I will haunt your nightmares and slaughter your dreams."

Forced to sit in his own urine and feces, he was sweating and jittery in the nauseating stench. James nodded in and out of this world to one that only heroin addicts were privy to. He'd lost all sense of time. All he cared about was the medicine that the girl was feeding him through his veins.

The beige, ripped-up, broken recliner he was tied to was the only piece of furniture in the large, dark, damp, stale-smelling room. He looked around in the drab darkness into a void of nothingness. He thought he heard things scurrying around the room.

Another day had passed. *Finally relief,* he thought. His throat was dry, and his veins were hungry. His heart sped up, as he thought he heard her footsteps.

A few nods of his head and his savior—no, his nemesis was in his face. She put on rubber gloves and fed him some water from a gallon-sized milk container. Next, she pulled up his damp sleeve and tied a dirty rubber tube around his forearm. Then she took out the needle and plunged it into a bulging vein in his forearm.

All the tension in his body suddenly melted away. He threw his head back, and his mouth hung open. Day had turned to night, and night to day. He no longer had the strength to scream or struggle. He didn't care about anything but his shot, as he shivered and coughed.

Over and over, the tape-recorded message played. It was driving him crazy. "Even in death I will haunt your nightmares and slaughter your dreams."

"Ahhhhhhh," he screamed, when he wasn't in a drug-induced haze.

"Hello." Rhythm entered the room with a metal object in one hand and his salvation in the other.

His eyes bulged, as she got closer.

"Come on, come on, come on," he said, ignoring the metal object in her other hand.

She put the metal object down on the dirty, mildewed carpeted floor and pulled out some rubber gloves from her jacket pocket and put them on. Next, she reached in her other pocket and pulled out the familiar satchel she'd been bringing to him the few times she'd been to see him.

He turned his head up and hungrily accepted the water as she slowly poured it down his throat.

Next, she pulled out a spoon, poured a little water on it, and then sprinkled white powder on it. She then heated it with a lighter. Once the powder and liquid became one, she sopped the spoon with a ball of cotton and sucked the liquid up with the syringe she carried in her other hand.

He closed his eyes, smiled, and exhaled, when she pulled up his damp sleeve, tied the rubber tubing around his arm, and injected the warm liquid into his veins.

Without a word, she picked up the metal object from the carpet and unloaded three well-aimed shots in each of his knees.

"Even in death I will haunt your nightmares and slaughter your dreams," was the last thing Richard James heard before he fainted.

She grabbed the recorder and was ready to leave the abandoned warehouse located right outside of Indianapolis. "I'll call 911 from a pay phone. Let's just hope they find this place. After all, it probably doesn't exist, since it was never the headquarters for the illegal government-sanctioned offset of Cointelpro that you testified never existed."

Epilogue
The Fat Lady Has Sung

We'd just gotten off of the plane and were at the baggage claim area of Chicago's O'Hare airport, when two men approached us.

"Mr. and Mrs. Moses One Free?"

"Yes, can I help you?" I asked.

"I'm Special Agent John Ross, and this is my partner Special Agent Mike Camp."

They brandished their FBI IDs.

"We are investigating a kidnapping and shooting that happened a week ago in Lafayette, Indiana."

"Okay, what does that have to do with us?" I asked.

"Could you please follow us downtown?" Special Agent John Ross said.

"Why? Am I under arrest?"

"No, we just have some questions for you and your wife," he said.

Three hours later, Rhythm and I walked out of the Federal building in downtown Chicago.

It seems that Richard James was kidnapped and held

hostage for five days, surviving on nothing but water and a steady dose of heroin, before someone shot him several times in his knees. Unfortunately, both of his legs had to be amputated.

The agents told us that someone James claims was Pablo Nkrumah's sister kidnapped, tortured, and shot him.

After Rhythm's alibi checked out, we were released. I mean, there was no way she could have done what they said, if she was in Aruba on vacation with me.

On the way home from the Federal building, I stopped at a pay phone outside of a local 7-Eleven.

"Hello," a feminine voice answered.

"James, this is Moses."

"Gotdammit, how many times I got to tell you?—It's Juicy," he said.

"Look, I just wanna thank you for everything."

"Shit, anytime I can go on an all-expense-paid trip to Aruba with a fine-ass man and dress up like the boss bitch that I am, you can call Juicy anytime."

"You are a sick man," I said. "Rhythm and I are going to get you some help."

"You need to get stubby, the no-legged White man laying up in the hospital, some help."

"Only God can help him now. But, seriously, if there is anything I can ever do for you, give me a call."

"Okay. You know I will, and Moses . . .?"

"Yeah?"

"You got a fine woman. You take care of her, you hear me?"

"Yeah, I hear you, and trust me, I will." I squeezed my queen's hand.

"Hold on. Don't hang up this damn phone yet; I ain't finished talkin'. You still there?"

"Yeah. What's up, James?"

"Call me James again, and I'll be up to Chicago with that damn book Rhythm got all those ideas from."

"Did you burn the—"

"Yes! I don't want nothing to do with no book called 500 Ways to Cripple a Bitch."

"A person, fool."

"Well, bitch sounds better—I should have named the damn book."

"Bye, James."

"Juicy!"